TRAIL OF THE CURSED COBRAS

BARRY NUGENT

BATTEN PRESS

FOR MUM

CONTENTS

CHAPTER 1

Can't Save the World Without a Protractor

Bobby grabbed the collection of slim orange- and green-coloured books from his bed, stuffing them into his battered navy-blue satchel. He wanted a new satchel, but Dad always said you did not throw away a perfectly good something just because it was old. The fact Dad had put down his newspaper – the Jamaican Gleaner – in order to tell Bobby meant this was serious advice.

Bobby Gibson, focus!

'Sorry Mum, what's next?' whispered Bobby.

Ruler? Protractor? Remember you have Mrs Felstead today.

His bottom lip drooped at the prospect. It was gonna be double trouble today because he also had Mrs Felstead for Social Studies. He still wasn't sure what Social Studies actually was and he reckoned Mrs Felstead was in the same boat. Neither one of them would ever admit it though.

Bobby leapt from his double bed, which was always an adventure. Rather than throw out the old mattress, his dad had stuck a new one on top of it. They must have had the highest double bed in London, and it was the most fun to play on as well. He and his brother Errol, who he shared the bed with, would come up here every Saturday after watching the wrestling and have their own match. The large bed served as the ring. Bobby was always Kendo Nagasaki, of course. He didn't have a mask or anything like the samurai wrestler, but he could imagine wearing one. Bobby could imagine anything; Mum told him it was his superpower. Sometimes Bobby imagined his dad tearing off his shirt like Hulk Hogan and joining them in a massive battle royale, but he never did.

Boy don't make me ask you again.

Bobby muttered an apology, shoved a hand under the bed and drew out his protractor and ruler. He grinned as he stuffed the items into his satchel. It was the start of a new year, which meant he'd get to see his friends again. That was the only reason he even went to school.

'Dunno why we have to have all these stupid lessons,' he said aloud.

Stop talking foolishness boy. You think they are going to let some boy with no O Levels draw comics for Marvel?

Bobby groaned. Mum was right, she was always right

'Bobby!' bellowed Auntie Carol from downstairs.

'Coming Auntie!' shouted Bobby.

He grabbed his school blazer from the wardrobe, tied it around his waist and ran out of the room.

'Don't you run boy!'

Bobby instantly slowed.

'You best not be jumping down dem stairs either!'

But Bobby was already in the air, his thin arms outstretched. He grabbed the small wooden ledge jutting out across the stairs above him, swung out over the stairs and let go. He landed on his feet, bending his knees in a Spider-Man crouch to absorb the impact. The thick patterned carpet helped to swallow the noise.

Bobby grinned to himself. He turned into the narrow passage leading to the kitchen. Two dark shapes moved on the other side of the kitchen door. Distorted by the wavy pattern of the green

Perspex window they looked kind of eerie, like creatures trapped in arctic ice. The glorious smell of bacon lured him inside.

Auntie Carol was stood in front of the cooker as Bobby entered. She was humming the theme to one of the soaps she was obsessed with, accompanied by the sizzling sound of bacon. Bobby tried not to laugh when he noticed Auntie Carol's curly black wig was crooked. He had first spotted the wig in her room, one evening years ago, perched atop a creepy white polystyrene head. It had freaked him out. He imagined it floating into his bedroom while he slept, whispering in his ear, feeding him nightmares. Bobby thought something so scary would make for a great monster in one of his Dungeons and Dragons campaigns. He'd even created the stats for it.

Without turning from the frying pan, Auntie Carol aimed her wooden spoon at the kitchen table.

Bobby sat down opposite Errol, who was demolishing a massive bowl of Weetabix. Bobby tried not to gag. He did not know how his brother could eat that mush. Errol would no doubt say something about it being good for his running or one of the hundred other sporty things he did better than Bobby. Aside from the deep brown of their skin, the two brothers couldn't be more different. Errol was tall, broad-chested and athletic, with a jaw that was all right angles. Bobby was shorter and 'far too mawga' according to Auntie Carol – something he took every opportunity to rectify.

'Bacon ready yet Auntie?' asked Bobby, rubbing his hands.

She always fried her bacon extra crispy. Not like the limp fatty rubbish they did at school.

Auntie Carol stepped up to the table and smacked Bobby hard on the back of the hand with the wooden spoon.

'Me dun tell you already bout jumping down dem stairs,' she said, scowling. Bobby rubbed his sore hand, eyes wide with innocence.

'I didn't, Auntie!'

The moment he moved his fingers away, Auntie Carol slapped the spoon on him again, in the very same spot.

This time Bobby let out a yelp of pain.

'And dat fi lying!' Auntie Carol muttered, giving him a hard look.

'Shame,' chuckled Errol.

Auntie Carol spun pointing the spoon at Errol. 'Anyone chatting to you boy?'

Errol's chuckle quickly turned into a pretend cough, returning his attention to his Weetabix. Satisfied, Auntie Carol moved back to the frying pan.

'How does she always know?' Bobby whispered, rubbing his sore hand.

Errol tapped the side of his head. 'I'm telling you she must be psychic. Bet she bends spoons too.'

The sound of frying increased as Auntie Carol lifted the red lid to remove the bacon. She shook the basket several times then emptied the crispy bacon onto a plate covered with a piece of kitchen towel. She folded the kitchen towel over the top, patting it with her hand to soak up the oil.

Perfect, thought Bobby.

Auntie Carol came over and slid all of the bacon onto Bobby's plate.

'Four pieces!' chirped Bobby, his eyes wide with disbelief. 'Thanks Auntie!'

Things were hard for them, even with both Dad and Auntie Carol working. He knew he was lucky to get one piece of bacon, let alone four. Perhaps things were turning around for them. He reached out to grab a slice, but Auntie Carol snatched the plate away.

'No bacon fi liars!'

She set the plate down in front of Errol, who eyed it as though this was all some elaborate trap.

'Eat it fore it gets cold Errol,' urged Auntie Carol. She held Bobby's shoulders, making sure he watched.

Errol slid a piece into his mouth, apologetically. For the next few minutes Bobby was forced to listen as the best part of his breakfast disappeared down his brother's throat. For his breakfast, Bobby ended up getting a bowl of thick, tasteless porridge. It was manky. Errol paused to look up at Bobby.

'Where's your rich girlfriend, anyway?' asked Errol. 'She's normally here by now, giving me grief.'

'Ada's just a mate and she ain't rich,' said Bobby.

'I don't see us going off to Nigeria for the summer,' Errol replied.

'We don't have family there to stay with do we? Ada does.'

'Still weird that your best mate is a girl,' mumbled Errol.

'Not as weird as you being a school perfect,' Bobby retorted.

'She's here more than I am,' said Errol, ignoring Bobby's dig.

'I ain't the one asking her to stay for dinner all for the time!' Bobby flicked an accusing glance at Auntie Carol as she sat down.

'Hoping dat little girl's manners rubs off on the two of you,' said Auntie Carol. 'She's better than dat other one. What's him name? TJ? CJ?…'

'It's DJ, Auntie,' said Bobby, forcing another spoonful of porridge into his mouth.

'DJ', repeated Auntie Carol. 'Nothing but trouble dat boy; me see it inna him eyes.'

That little girl is more trouble than a hundred DJ's.

Mum was right. If Auntie Carol knew the trouble on the school trip to Norfolk had started with Ada, she would never let her within hundred miles of the house.

Once breakfast was over, Bobby and Errol dumped their plates and bowls into the washing up bowl. Bobby drained the oil from the frying pan into a little cup, as Auntie liked to use it for gravy stock. He dumped the frying pan into the bowl, enjoying the sizzle it made as it slid into the water. The smell of bacon mixed with the lemony washing up liquid was heady.

See what happens when you lie Bobby?

'Oh, give a rest Mum,' he muttered.

'I beg your pardon?' asked Auntie Carol, about two seconds away from dispensing something painful.

'Just saying I need a rest Auntie,' Bobby replied quickly.

More lying Bobby?

'Boy, stop talking foolishness and come out of me way.'

Auntie bustled between Bobby and his brother to make a start on the washing up. It was the one time of the day they got out of doing chores. School always came first. That had always been Mum's number one rule, and Auntie Carol was more than happy to enforce it.

Going to be hard enough in this world, without you being stupid too.

Bobby wished she was here, wished she were more than just a voice in his head.

'Bobby. Get your head out of the clouds!'

Auntie stared at him, her hands gloved in fluffy white soap suds.

'Ain't no answers up there, just the ones the Lord gives. You don't go looking for them.'

Auntie leaned in to do up Bobby's top button and straighten his tie.

'And make sure you nuh late home, you hear me?'

'Yes Auntie,' said Bobby staking a step back.

Auntie Carol swept him into an enormous hug. Bobby looked back at his brother, pointed to door and mouthed 'Save yourself'.

Errol grinned his thanks and slung his sports bag over his shoulder before slipping out of the kitchen. There were days when Bobby wondered if Ninjas were secretly training his brother. It would certainly explain how he was in the top teams for Football, Rugby, Cricket and Athletics. And how he so rarely got caught by Auntie or dad.

Auntie Carol jumped at the sound of the front door slamming shut. 'Me no care if him a school prefect, that boy needs to find him manners.'

She released Bobby at last, who gasped, grateful he could breathe again. She was staring hard at him now, with a fierce love. Tears began rolling down her plump cheeks.

'Auntie?'

There was no answer, only more tears with the occasional shake of the head. It broke Bobby's heart to see her upset. He snatched a large roll of kitchen towel from the table, tore off a couple of pieces and waved them in front of Auntie Carol.

Auntie Carol wiped her face, exposing red and puffy eyes.

'I'm alright Bobby… you just,' she swallowed a few times before she spoke again. 'You look like your mum so much… You got dem same eyes, dat same troublesome look.'

Bobby never thought he looked like his mum, unlike Auntie Carol, who was basically a slightly thinner version of mum.

'Sorry about lying earlier,' said Bobby as Auntie Carol took a piece of kitchen towel. 'I did jump down the stairs.'

'Go on now,' sniffed Auntie Carol, planting another sloppy kiss on his cheek.

'And me want none of dat Norfolk business this year, you hear? If me or your father haffi come to dat school again …'

'None of that trouble, Auntie – got it! Bye!'

Bobby grabbed his satchel and ran for the front door before Auntie's lecture could hit its stride. He opened the first door then closed it behind him. He was now stood in the cosy little space between the two doors. He loved it. Some days he would spend hours sat on the floor here, reading, where no one would find him. He undid his top button once more and breathed in deeply.

Auntie Carol was nice but she was not Mum. This was when he noticed it most: leaving the house.

Where are you off to Bobby?

'No,' he muttered back to the voice in his head. 'I'm not playing today. You're not her. You can't be her.'

Bobby please…just…just tell me. I need to hear you say it.

The voice sounded so much like Mum but she sounded so sad.

'Okay, ask me again,' said Bobby.

Where are you off to Bobby?

Bobby bit back his tears.

'I'm off to save the world, Mum.'

But Bobby couldn't save anything. His world ended the day Mum died.

2

A Funny Thing Happened on the Way to the Graveyard

Ada Amaya sprinted down the high street. The mystery of why her alarm clock had failed to go off remained unsolved, but that would have to wait. She was going to be late for her first day back at school. It was the last thing she needed after what happened in Norfolk last year.

It had been Mum's bellowing from downstairs that had finally dragged Ada from a cosy dream about their trip to Nigeria. Ada never tired of the place. It warmed her heart to be in the place where her parents had lived before coming to England. She always went armed with stories of her adventures in London, whilst learning about the lives of her relatives. She would talk, way past bedtime, until her mum packed her off to bed.

Ada was so caught up in her thoughts that she failed to see the two old ladies chatting in the middle of the pavement. She barrelled through them, sending one of their shopping bags tumbling across the pavement.

'Stupid girl,' one of the women hissed. Her companion hobbled after several tins which were making good their escape down the high street.

Ada stopped and marched back.

The woman who had insulted her wore a thick, grey overcoat and resembled a giant rat. She looked as though she were about to speak but Ada got in first.

'One! This conversation is going to cost me approximately two minutes, which means I'll need to run at least twenty percent faster to catch the bus, so thanks for that—'

'Who do you think—?'

'Two!' snapped Ada, holding up two fingers. 'My mum owns a bookshop, which means I get to read all kinds of books, which is how I know what you two are doing is called 'obstructing the public highway'. It's illegal, and if you get caught you will be fined and *that* means no more Jaffa Cakes.'

'You're just a child; what do you know about anything?' asked Ratty. The packet of Jaffa Cakes which had caught Ada's eye were poking out of the shopping bag. Ada loved Jaffa Cakes.

'I know your name is Marge, and that you work at Finley's Supermarket,' said Ada.

'How did you—'

Ada pointed at the small silver badge pinned to Ratty's top. Marge scowled, buttoning her overcoat to cover her uniform.

'Hardly a strain on my observational skills but it never hurts to get in some practise,' said Ada.

'You're a very rude little girl,' Marge snapped.

'How much ruder would it be if I went into Finley's after school and told your manager that you and your friend over there have been stealing from his shop?'

'What are you talking about, you stupid girl?'

Ada felt a hot rush of anger. She took a breath, pushing the emotion back down. She needed to be calm, just like Dad would have been.

'Finley's doesn't open until nine,' Ada stated, her voice even. 'You two were in early stacking the shelves, and when no one was looking you helped yourself to a few treats. The fact that you were quite happy to stand here gossiping with stolen goods in your bags indicates that you've been stealing stuff for some time now, confident you could get away with it.'

'How did she—?'

'Shut *up*, Cynthia,' barked Marge, snatching the bag from the other woman.

'And now we know who's the master and who's the apprentice,' observed Ada.

Marge dropped the shopping bags and grabbed Ada's arm. 'Why, you little—'

Ada started screaming. She hated being dramatic, but the move never failed. Her screams drew the attention of several passers-by, as expected.

'Oi!' someone shouted.

'Leave that girl alone!' someone else yelled, stalking over.

Marge released Ada, patted her head like she was the family dog then backed away.

'Just having a bit of fun love, nothing to worry about,' Marge shouted, adding a wide smile for good measure.

Ada wondered how often Marge smiled because the expression looked quite painful.

Ada rubbed her arm and flexed her fingers. 'You two better hope this nonsense doesn't make me late for school, or the first stop on my way this afternoon will be Finley's.'

Ada dipped her hand into the shopping bag quickly and pulled out the packet of Jaffa Cakes.

'And this…? This is for calling me stupid.'

Ada ran off before Marge or Cynthia could react. She turned a corner after a little bit and paused for breath, chuckling to herself. Time for a quick reward. She popped a Jaffa Cake into her mouth. A delightful mixture of chocolate, orange flavoured jam and sponge danced across her tongue. She suddenly remembered a short cut some of the fourth-year girls had been banging on about last year. There was a path next to the Post Office which led into the graveyard and brought you out by the bus stop. That was pretty close by.

Ada ate another Jaffa Cake for good luck whilst crossing the road and headed over the graveyard. What the girls had failed to describe was just how dark, dirty and menacing the alleyway looked. Ada's more sensible side told her she'd be better off being late. Instead she sucked in a breath and headed in; she had seen way scarier stuff than this in Norfolk.

Ada stuffed the remaining cakes into her blazer pockets then tossed the box into a nearby bin. Her well-earned prize wouldn't last five minutes if Bobby or DJ knew she had them.

The path was slick with soggy leaves carpeting the cracked, unseen pavement. Trees lined both sides of the path, their gnarled branches stretching over it blocking all but the most stubborn slivers of daylight. Empty beer cans and rubbish lay everywhere. Ada slipped and almost fell flat on her face, just catching herself against the wall.

A prickle of fear slithered up her spine, unbidden. There was no warmth here, just the trees and the horrible whispering sound the wind made as it ripped through their branches.

Short cut draw blood.

It was an old Jamaican saying, and one Bobby's mum often used. It meant danger. She should go back.

Ada suddenly felt herself yanked back by the rucksack. She screamed in terror. Without thinking, she stuffed her hands into her pockets, pulling out a Jaffa cake with one hand and a pen with the other. She flicked the lid off the pen, holding it like a dagger, then she spun hurling the Jaffa cake into her attacker's face. It was a man with a thick bushy beard, dressed in a white shirt and torn brown trousers, both of which were spattered with dirt. As the man blinked in shock at the chocolatey assault, Ada stabbed his hand with the pen. The man yelped in pain.

'It's…you!' the man panted, looking shocked.

'Stay away, Beardy!' snapped Ada, taking in the bloody gash across the man's forehead and the heavy breathing. He'd been attacked by someone else. Before…

The bearded man lashed out, knocking away her pen. He grabbed her wrist and pushed a small wooden box into her hand. The moment Ada's fingers closed around the box, it felt like they had been plunged it into an ice-cold bath. He held his hands over hers for a moment then let go, palms in the air and backed away. She stared at the odd little box, entranced by its complexity. Tiny pieces of glass were embedded into the surface, along with an assortment of strange symbols. Ada had never seen anything like it.

'What is this?' she asked, the question filled with wonder.

The man's eyes met Ada's. There was something… familiar about the stranger, bundled with the certainty he was not going to hurt her.

'Don't…I don't have much time.' The man's voice was edged with panic, his breathing still ragged. 'There are tapes in my office at school… ten to two… The cuckoo will tell you what to do.'

His head snapped around and he dropped into a crouch, ready to fight or flee. Footsteps, echoing off the walls. But Ada couldn't see anybody!

'Find the tapes Ada,' whispered the bearded man. 'And keep the key safe! He will destroy us all if he gets his hands on it.'

She had no time to fire off any questions. A tall figure robed in dark purple burst from the trees with arms outstretched. The newcomer, who was now blocking the way Ada had come, pointed a blacked gloved finger at the box she held. 'So the ESD are conspiring with children now are they, Agent Ash? How the mighty have fallen.'

His voice sent chills down Ada's spine, leaving her grateful she couldn't see his face amid the folds of his hood.

The bearded man turned to face the terrifying newcomer. 'It's not too late Langley. We can still stop this madness.'

'Why would I stop?' the hooded man asked. 'What I am doing will benefit everyone. It is my destiny. I will not be diverted by you or the E.S.D. Not when I am this close to breaking through.'

The hooded man began to weave gestures in the air. Ada gasped. Something was happening in the wake of his movements. The air around him seemed to shimmer.

'Would you like to see some magic, little girl?' asked Langley, his hands spinning faster until the shimmering effect covered his whole body, rendering him almost transparent. She could see *through* him to the darkened path behind him.

'Run!' ordered the bearded man.

But terror was in no mood to let Ada go anywhere. She stood motionless with one hand clamped over her mouth. Langley was now reciting phrases in a language alien to Ada, growing louder on each repetition. Ada gasped into her hand as a second hooded man *slid* from Langley's translucent body. This second figure looked identical and took up the same chant. He in turn was followed by another hooded figure and another. Langley's body became solid once again and the chanting abruptly stopped. His shimmering copies, two on each side, hovered above the ground like spirits.

'Bring me the box.'

Upon the command, Langley's counterparts flowed toward Ada.

'RUN!' the bearded man bellowed.

Ada took off down the path, stumbling and slipping on the wet leaves in her panic. Behind her she could hear shouting. There was a sound like thunder followed by ear-piercing scream, and then... silence.

Ada stuffed the box into her pocket then sprinted into the graveyard, followed by angry curses from her faceless pursuers.

3

How to Make New
Friends and Enemies

As he sagged, breathless, against the gravestone Tony Davies decided that he hated North London.

'He's over there, come on!' shouted a distant voice.

Tony lay his satchel across his knees, shivering as his clammy school shirt stuck to his back.

'Where are you little piggie?' called out another boy, squeaky with excitement.

Tony fumbled open the catches on his satchel and took out a book. On its cover, emblazoned in thick blue letters, were the words LONDON STREET MAPS. Checking he was still alone, Tony turned to the page with the corner bent over. There was a thick red line, zig-zagging across the page from home to his new school. He stood and turned in a circle, trying to get his bearings. It was only a matter of time before—

'Here you are! Time to squeal...'

Tony tried to run but something caught his foot and he pitched forward, landing face first in a pile of wet leaves. The book of street maps hit the gravestone, bouncing away to the sound of laughter. He scrambled after the book but a pair of hands grabbed his ankles and dragged him back. Tony desperately clawed at the earth, trying to grab onto anything, but all he got was fistfuls of muddy leaves. The cruel laughter grew louder around him.

A foot cracked against Tony's side, rolling him onto his back. Three older boys were stood over him. Two of them were grinning like loons, sweaty from the chase. The third boy, who was shorter than Tony and whose face seemed to consist mainly of forehead, looked furious.

'Pick him up,' Forehead ordered.

The other boys each took one of Tony's arms and pulled him up to his feet. As they did so, Tony's bag fell to the side and a bible slid out, joining the map in the mud.

Forehead stepped closer and kicked it, grunting with amusement. He wafted his school blazer to cool down, revealing several sweat stains across his white shirt.

'I'm going to stink all day now because of you, weirdo,' he snarled.

Tony wanted to tell Forehead that if they hadn't chased him into this poxy graveyard in the first place then none of them would be stinking, but that wouldn't do him any good. Instead of pointing out the obvious, Tony flashed his perfect set of teeth at the boy. According to Dad, a smile could fix any problem.

Forehead smiled back, then punched him in the stomach. Tony sank to his knees coughing.

'Not smiling now are you, Church Boy?' asked Forehead, his right fist still clenched.

Tony was in too much pain to speak, but he tried smiling again.

Forehead sneered down, drew his fist back... and then froze.

'You alright Lee?' asked one the boys holding Tony. 'You look weird.'

'You didn't hear that?' he asked.

The silence following Lee's question was broken by the sound of footsteps, moving fast towards them. Moments later the sounds were swamped by a piercing scream.

Tony and the other boys swung in that direction, worry on their faces.

'Told you we shouldn't have followed him in here Lee,' said the boy to Tony's right, his eyes bulging.

The footsteps were closer now. Lee did not move, though his mates were now backing away.

'Leave him Lee. Come on, let's go,' said one of the boys.

'Not until we get his lunch money,' said Lee, glaring down at Tony. 'Sid will kill us if we let a new kid off without taxing him.'

The strange scream came again, much closer.

Lee pointed at Tony, fear and rage battling for control of his face.

'I'll see you in school, Church Boy,' he hissed at last, kicking Tony's pocket bible into a puddle.

Lee and his cronies took off.

Scooping up the bible, Tony dashed back to one of the larger gravestones. He drew up his legs and wrapped his arms around them.

'This is not happening, this is not happening, this is not—'

A small dark brown hand clamped itself over Tony's mouth.

Swallowing hard, Tony slid his eyes to the right. Crouched beside him was an out of breath schoolgirl whose hair, wrapped in a tight double bun, seemed entirely in keeping with her stern expression.

The girl's eyes narrowed to slits as she regarded Tony. She held a trembling finger to her lips and made a tiny shushing sound.

Tony lifted a hand to push her away but then froze as two hooded figures drifted past either side of the gravestone. His eyes widened in disbelief as he realised he could see straight through the terrifying newcomers. The girl's grip tightened around his mouth as he fought every instinct to scream.

'You cannot hide forever, girl. Give us the box and this all ends.'

The words echoed all around them as though it were the gravestones making the demand. The figures drifted onward, and just as Tony thought it was safe to move, two more hooded figures floated past. He shrank lower, watching them join their companions.

'I'm going to take my hand away,' whispered the girl. 'If you scream those things will find us. Nod if you understand.'

Tony nodded, slipping his bible into his inside jacket pocket. The girl removed her hand, switching her attention to her wristwatch. Tony sat there, gripping his thighs and staring at the hooded figures, who were moving further away.

'Okay Tony, in approximately ninety seconds, I'm going to run. And you're going to follow, understand?'

Tony did not answer, his unblinking eyes still locked on the shimmering spectres floating between the gravestones.

The girl grabbed Tony's head and turned it to face hers.

'I get you're scared but—'

'And you're not?' asked Tony, fervently praying he was not about to wet himself in front of a girl.

'Of course I am!' the girl snapped. 'It is stupidity rather than courage to refuse to recognise danger when it is close upon you.'

'Who talks like that?' asked Tony.

The girl shrugged. 'I should think that much was obvious. Thirty seconds. Get ready.'

Tony didn't know if he could move in thirty minutes, let along thirty seconds. His mind had one thought and it was screaming it at him over and over again: *hide.* Tony was about to say as much to the girl when he saw the spectres turn back towards them. He lifted a quivering hand and pointed.

'Don't bother me with the obvious,' snapped the girl. She pointed. 'We're heading for that wall. Tell me you can climb a wall?'

The girl didn't wait for an answer. She was already up sprinting for the wall.

One of the ghostly figures hissed, and they all reacted, gliding towards the children.

Tony bounded to his feet and took off after the girl. He was tall, his stride wide, which enabled him to close the gap quickly. He glanced over his shoulder And saw one of the hooded figures lift a hand. A crackling arc of green lightning shot from its fingertips right at them. It struck a gravestone behind them, and the resulting explosion catapulted the children through the air. They landed in a tangled heap a little way from the wall. Tony was the first to rise. He grabbed the girl's arm and hoisted her up.

She shook off his hand in irritation and made for the wall.

'Come on!' she shouted, jumping up onto a large statue of an angel. Its immense granite wings stretched toward the top of the wall, and the girl scaled them like a squirrel.

Tony watched her jump from the statue, grab the top of the wall and swing herself over. Tony followed the girl's example, with a little less grace and a lot more uncertainty, but fear drove him on. He slid over the wall, jumped down and ran down the street after the girl.

There was a bright red double-decker bus pulling out from the bus stop, full of kids wearing the same school uniform as him. The children crowding the open platform at the rear of the bus were cheering Tony and the girl on as they drew closer. Tony gritted his teeth and pumped his legs as fast as he could, passing the girl. With his last ounce of energy, he sprang onto the platform and grabbed the pole. He spun and stuck out his one free hand. The girl jumped, caught hold of Tony's forearm and pulled herself onto the bus. She sank back against the stairs leading to the top deck, wheezing and coughing as the crowd went wild.

'Respect,' said a tall boy with an impressive afro.

Tony managed a thumbs up, sucking in as much air as he could. His chest ached terribly. Tony looked around at the sea of unfamiliar young faces until he saw the girl. She had already found herself a seat halfway down the bus. As he watched, she took a small wooden cube from her bag and balanced it on her lap. Next she took out a bright red pencil case and a small brown book sealed with a rubber band.

Tony made his way through the crowd and sagged down beside her. By now the girl had taken the rubber band off her notebook and was scribbling away.

'My name is Ada Amaya,' the girl began, mid scribble. 'And no, I don't know what those creatures were or why they wanted a wooden box some weird tramp gave me.'

Ada held up the notebook. 'I am formulating several theories, though.'

'How did you know I was going to—'

'By the way, thanks for your help back there Tony, but of course I'd expect nothing less, given your father's profession.'

'My father's—'

'He's a vicar, right? Or to be more precise, our vicar?'

'What? How did you know?'

'You have your name sewn into the inside pocket of your blazer, very sensible. I also observed you stuffing a bible into your pocket. It's not like the ones they give out at school; it looked expensive. Given that was the first thing you grabbed, I would surmise it held great personal value, most likely given to you by a loved one. Mum said we were getting a new vicar, so it wasn't a difficult deduction.'

'Wow, that's fantastic!' said Tony.

'There's nothing fantastic about using your eyes,' said Ada, coolly.

Tony crossed his arms, unsure how to reply. She'd rescued him, but Ada didn't seem to welcome his presence. Perhaps he should find somewhere else to sit. He looked around, but there didn't seem to be any more seats free.

'You reckon we should tell someone?' he asked at last.

'Tell them what?' replied Ada. 'That a crazy tramp was abducted by a hooded creature who can make translucent, floating doppelgangers that can shoot green lightning?'

'What tramp? And what's a doppelganger' asked Tony, feeling more confused by the second.

'Unimportant,' said Ada, closing her notebook savagely. 'But I agree that this bears investigation. Who would you tell, then?'

Tony opened his mouth but any answer he had died in his throat.

'Come on, this is your first test,' urged Ada, snapping the rubber band around her notebook.

'The police?' replied Tony.

Ada blew a loud raspberry, causing several eyes to turn in their direction. Tony sank in his seat, embarrassed.

'The police would never believe a story this crazy, especially from a pair of school kids. Not without a lot of proof, which we currently do not have. Try again.'

Tony pointed at the wooden cube on Ada's lap. 'That's proof, right?'

'That's right, Detective Inspector Never-Going-To-Believe-Us. We were chased through the graveyard by hooded spectres, and here's this wooden box to prove it.' Ada rolled her eyes. 'Try again. Do better.'

A few of the girls were looking across at them and giggling. *Great*, thought Tony. They probably thought Ada was his girlfriend. His first day at a new school was shaping up to be his worst day ever.

'Tick-tock, Tony,' said Ada.

'How about telling our parents? Or a teacher?'

'Reasonable suggestions, but neither one will work. Both groups are predisposed to distrust everything we say.'

'Seriously, why are you talking like that?' asked Tony.

'Like what?'

'An adult?'

Ada tapped the pencil against her lips as though pondering the question.

'Ida B. Wells worked as a schoolteacher when she was sixteen and Sor Juana Inés de la Cruz learnt to read when she was three. She also taught herself Latin when she was around my age.'

'So?' asked Tony, simmering with frustration and embarrassment. He had no idea who any of those women were.

Ada jabbed the sharp end of the pencil into the tip of his nose, which made him yelp.

'So I can talk anyway I damn well choose to.'

Tony rubbed his nose and glared at her. 'Okay, clever clogs. What would you do?'

Ada held the cube out in front of her, scrutinising it, turning it around slowly. 'I'm going to tell the one group you failed to mention. I'm going to tell my friends.'

'Yeah, right. Like your mates are going to believe you.'

'Oh these mates will,' said Ada, breaking into a wide smile. 'Weird is kind of our thing.'

Tony thought weird described Ada perfectly, but kept it to himself.

'They'll help me figure out what's going on,' Ada continued.

She tucked the box into her satchel and closed the straps tight.

'What, so it'll be just you and your mates against those things?' Tony asked, bewildered. 'No police, no parents?'

Ada yawned. 'Wouldn't be the first time.' She settled back into her seat and closed her eyes. 'Nudge me when we get to school.'

4

First Day Problems

Bobby fought through the mass of kids packed in around the school gates. Laughter, hugs and play fights were kicking off in all directions. Beyond the foreboding black iron gates, waiting to squash any notion of fun, stood St Icilda's. Anyone looking at St Icilda's from a distance could be forgiven for mistaking the school for several badly put together Lego sets. The school was actually a hodge podge of tired white buildings, their fronts pebble-dashed to give the illusion of character.

However, when he stared up at the gates, all Bobby could remember was the fun and he had got into on the other side of them.

'Wotcha mate.'

Bobby turned. A gangly, blond-haired boy waved as he strode on over.

'Alright DJ. How ya—' Bobby paused when he saw the thick rope wound tightly around DJ's wrists.

'Why are you tied up?'

Because the boy is foolish. Him stupider than your cousin Egbert—you remember him?

Bobby did remember. Cousin Egbert had once tried to boil rice without any water.

'It's practise innit,' said DJ, as though that explained everything.

'Practise?'

'I ain't going to be the world's greatest magician if I don't practise, right?'

'I thought you were packing in all that magic stuff after what happened last year.'

'That was a mere setback,' said DJ flippantly, puffing his chest out.

'Mate, you set your blazer on fire.'

'That trick should have worked,' he snapped. 'It was that flipping posh cow Jackie Bailey's fault, weren't it? I'm going to throw a fit if she's my science partner again. Worst magician's assistant ever.'

'Anyway, The Great and Powerful Djinn is loads better since last year,' said DJ.

'The what?'

'Great and Powerful Djinn. It's my magician's name. Mum hates it, but I think it's cool'.

Before Bobby could express a preference, DJ began wriggling and twisting his arms. At one point the cracking sounds coming from DJ's wrists made Bobby wince.

'You wanna a hand mate?' he asked, biting back a chuckle.

DJ answered with curses and more wriggling. Several kids were now staring, and it didn't take long for the laughter to kick in.

'Mate, let me get some scissors,' said Bobby, as more kids joined in on the laughter.

'No! I'm nearly there,' DJ grunted.

But looking at his friend's sore wrists Bobby doubted it.

'I don't get it. It worked when I did it last night!'

Bobby rolled his eyes.

'It did!' shouted DJ. 'And last week I got out of a locked box with handcuffs on too. Well Mum did help a little in the end.'

Bobby did not bother asking why DJ's mum would lock him in a box. The last time he went to DJ's house, his mum had answered the door dressed as a clown.

'Mate, if a teacher sees you like that you'll be for it.'

DJ's large brown eyes settled on Bobby giving him the once over, like he had only just seen him. 'It's cool. The great Djinn has thought of everything.'

Bobby heard his mum kiss her teeth cynically.

Like me said, the boy is foolish.

DJ shook his arms and the sleeves of his school blazer slid down, covering his tied wrists.

'See? It's elementary, my dear Bobson.'

Bobby sighed. 'I told you to stop calling me that.'

'That's what Ada calls you.'

'How'd you like it I if started calling you Dibney Jennings?' asked Bobby.

'Leave off mate I was only joking,' said DJ. He hated people using his actual name. It was hardly a surprise.

Bobby decided it was better to change the subject. 'New blazer then?'

DJ nodded. 'Mum said she couldn't sew up a hole she could put her fist through.'

Bobby grinned at the memory of their science teacher, Mr Roebrush, jumping up and down on DJ's flaming jacket.

'It's a bit big though ain't it?'

DJ sighed as though Bobby was just the latest in a long line of people who had said the same thing.

'They ran out of my size. The bloke in Robbie's told Mum it'll last me longer.'

Robbie's was the clothing shop that supplied all the uniforms and sports kits for St Icilda's. As Bobby's school uniform was a hand me down from Errol, he never needed to go there. From everything he'd heard, that was a blessing.

'So did Auntie Carol give you the big speech this morning?' asked DJ.

'Yep. No trouble this year, or else.'

DJ nodded. 'Yeah. Dad had a right go at me last night about it. He says there's no way him and Mum are letting me go on a school trip again.'

'Bit harsh,' said Bobby.

DJ leaned in. 'You reckon Ada's ever going to let it go? Norfolk.'

Before Bobby could answer, he was shoved to one side as a big man in a brown overcoat ran past them.

'Blimey. Khara's on one early, ain't he?' said DJ.

Mr Khara was the caretaker and the third scariest adult in the school – after the headmaster and the deputy head.

'Oi!' bellowed Khara. There were two boys who were taking turns kicking a football against the fence – a terrible crime in Mr Khara's book.

One boy caught the ball on the rebound, but as he did so Khara caught him by his jacket collar. The boy slipped out of his grasp and took off after his mate, laughing.

'Come back 'ere, you thugs!' bellowed Khara, shaking a fist. 'When I get hold of you it's the headmaster's office...you hear me?'

But the two boys had been swallowed by the mass of blue and grey uniforms.

'He didn't find them last year,' said Bobby, seeing the two kids break free from the crowd and run off behind the science block.

'Here's comes trouble, with a capital A,' said DJ brightly.

The minute he saw Ada running, Bobby knew something was up. She hated running anywhere.

Ada stopped in front of them, grabbed her knees then erupted into a coughing fit.

'Oi,' said DJ, stepping back. 'Don't you dare chunder on my shoes!'

'You alright?' asked Bobby.

Ada open her mouth but all that came out was a high-pitched wheeze. She settled for shaking her head.

Always drama with this one.

'Where'd you run from? Timbuktu?' asked DJ.

Ada stuck up two fingers in response.

'Maybe you should go see the nurse?' suggested Bobby.

Ada shook her head. 'I'm…alright… Bobson…'

Bobby frowned. It had been too much to hope Ada would have got bored with that stupid nickname over the holidays.

'Big bro incoming,' announced DJ.

Don't him look him nice? Is my boy, that, you know?. With him prefect badge.

Errol marched through a crowd of kids, all of whom were fighting each other to get out of his way. A few of the older girls whistled as Errol went past. Bobby felt like throwing up when he smiled back with that cheesy grin of his. There was a boy walking beside Errol that Bobby didn't recognise. The boy's skin was brown, though a lot lighter than Bobby's, and his afro looked pretty sharp; better than Winston Gregson's, whose afro was the stuff of legend. The boy was grinning from ear to ear. Bobby hated him already.

'What do you want?' asked Bobby, side-eyeing Smiley.

Errol nodded to Ada who was still coughing.

'She alright?'

'She's fine, now what do you want?'

'No need for the tough act in front of your mates,' Errol laughed, raising his hands. 'It's all good.'

Bobby kissed his teeth in response. Errol was breaking their number one rule: they never talked at school. That was in stone, and Errol was the one who set it.

'New boy here says he knows Ada,' said Errol, nudging the still smiling boy forward. 'Go on, they ain't gonna bite you.'

DJ growled and flashed his teeth.

The boy stuck out his hand. 'Hi, I'm Tony. Tony Tadsby.'

Bobby glared at the hand like it was a snake, ready to bite him. He kissed his teeth again and folded his arms.

'Tony?' asked Ada, who had stopped coughing. 'I thought you were going to find out who your form teacher was?'

Tony's smiled faded. He rubbed the back of head, gaze dropping downwards. 'I kinda got lost. This school is massive compared to my last school.'

'Lost is right,' agreed Errol. 'I found him in the back playground.'

DJ whistled. 'Wow, new boy's got a death wish.'

'That's his look-out ain't it?' said Bobby, his voice rising to match his annoyance at Errol. 'Why don't you take him over to some first years or something!'

'Actually I'm in the second year,' said Tony, his wide grin returning.

'Like we give a toss.'

'Don't listen to DJ; he can't spell his own name,' said Ada.

'Yeah, well you fancy Errol!' shouted DJ, pointing at Ada.

'You take that back Dibney Jennings!' Ada hissed, shoving DJ back.

'Enough!' yelled Errol.

Everyone fell silent, including onlookers.

'All I'm asking is for you lot to walk with Tony to his new form room,' said Errol.

'No problem Errol,' said Ada, before Bobby or DJ could say anything.

'I ain't his friend. Why do I have to do it?' Bobby muttered.

'Cause it's the right thing to do Bobby, and it's what Mum would want.'

Your brother's right Bobby, heroes help people.

'I ain't no hero, Mum.'

Yes you are. Remember - pit inna di sky, it all inna yuh y'ye.

'I don't even know what that means?!'

The others were staring at him now. Bobby clammed up. He had been talking aloud to Mum instead of inside his head. Stupid! Stupid!

Errol grabbed Bobby's arm and pulled him away from the others.

'Get off me!' shouted Bobby, trying to break free, but it was no good.

Errol leant closer. Bobby could smell the pomade he used in his hair; he always slapped on way too much of it.

'Is Mum talking to you again?'

Mmm hmm.

'No,' lied Bobby, doing his best not to meet Errol's eyes. 'I was joking.'

'You best not be lying to me.'

'I ain't,' said Bobby, still struggling to pull himself free.

'You remember what Doctor Huxley said?'

Bobby hated Doctor Huxley. He hated his crappy office, his crappy bow ties and the crappy way he sat there chewing on his pen and saying mmm to everything Bobby said. He hated all the stupid questions he would ask. And the way he would sneer. There was nothing wrong in making up stories about talking to his mum, he'd say, so long as he knew they were just that. Stories. Mum was gone and she was never coming back.

Me never like that man. Prodding and poking you like you an animal.

'Bobby? You listening to me?' snapped Errol.

'I'm not hearing Mum, okay? So stop hassling me!'

Bobby did not know how it could *not* be real. After all, hadn't Dad told him about the time Mum had seen a ghost back in Jamaica?

Me see that duppy with me own two eyes. Mr Horton was a lovely man, but he was dead for two weeks before we see him.

Bobby had never seen Mum as a duppy but hearing her voice inside his head felt like proof to him. Still, it turned out to be easier all round if he pretended she was gone now. Out of his head, and out of his life.

Errol let go off Bobby's arm. 'Alright. But no trouble this year, okay Bobby?'

'Yeah cos you never do anything wrong,' muttered Bobby.

'You ever seen me get in trouble?' asked Errol.

The way his brother was always able to talk his way out of trouble was just another thing Bobby envied. Errol walked him back to the others.

'Right you lot make sure new boy gets to his form room, okay?'

Ada turned to Tony. 'What's your form room?'

'2JW,' said Tony.

Bobby swung on his brother. 'Mr Wattling's form? But that's—'

'Oh, right. That's *your* form room,' said Errol, before winking. 'Isn't that lucky?'

'I hate you,' said Bobby.

At that moment the bell sounded, and all the kids started moving through the gate and towards the school buildings.

'Hate you too, little bro. Now go look after your new mate.'

Errol patted Bobby's head and started walking away.

'He's not my mate!' Bobby shouted after him.

Errol just waved and walked on. Bobby faced the new boy, who was still smiling.

'Your brother's a bit cool ain't he?' said Tony.

The only answer Bobby gave was a scowl.

'So how do you know the new boy, Ada?' asked DJ, who had started up with the ropes again.

'We met in the graveyard,' said Ada with a shrug. 'There was an American being chased by hooded ghosts with no faces …'

'They could shoot green lightning from their fingertips,' added Tony, trying to be helpful. 'Least I think it was lightning. Could have been lasers I guess.'

'Didn't we say last year, no more spooky stuff?'

'Wait, you've seen stuff like this before?' asked Tony aghast.

'No. You said it, DJ,' said Ada, ignoring Tony's question. 'And besides, it's not like I went looking for spooky stuff.'

'You were in a bleeding graveyard!' shouted DJ.

'So come on then, you gonna tell us what happened?' asked Bobby.

'Tell you everything on the way Bobson.'

'Why do you call him Bobson?' asked Tony.

'It's his sidekick name innit,' chuckled DJ. Bobby seethed.

'Come on,' said Ada, striding off towards the main school building. 'And stop messing about with those ropes, Dibney.'

'Fine,' DJ sighed. He shook his wrists again and the ropes slid off. Tony's mouth fell open. The knots tying the ropes together were still in place.

'How did you do that?'

'Maybe I'm a wizard,' said DJ, winking. He set off after Ada.

'Or maybe just a prat,' muttered Bobby. The new boy had picked up the ropes and was examining them.

'Seriously how'd he do that?'

'His dad's a magician,' replied Bobby, as he turned on his heel. 'Have a nice life Smiley.'

Bobby did not care what Errol said. This year was going to be tough enough as it was without some grinning weirdo following him around.

Bobby Gibson, don't make me have fe tell you again

Bobby stopped at his mum's words. He sighed, pulling the strap tighter on his satchel.

'Oi! Smiley!' he shouted over his shoulder.

'My name's Tony.'

'Whatever. Come on then, if you're coming.'

'I'm not a baby you know. I can find—'

'Good luck with that, then' said Bobby, stuffing his hands into his pockets and walking away.

Tony fell into step alongside him.

Together they headed through the school gates and were swallowed by an ocean of matching school uniforms.

5

2JW

Ada was grateful her insides were no longer churning like Mum's old washing machine. She made a vow to herself that there would be no more running for the rest of the year.

'So, what happened to you?' asked Bobby.

DJ, who was now walking in front of them, slapped his hands over his ears. 'Nope not listening. Lalalalala not listening.'

As they walked through the corridors, Ada told the others what had happened in the graveyard right up to her escape with Tony.

Bobby said something, but Ada paid no attention. There was an itch at the back of her mind, something she could not put her finger on.

Think Ada, what have you missed? It's in there somewhere.

She tried replaying the events at the graveyard in her mind but the rising noise and bustle of the corridor was too distracting. She promised herself she would find a quiet corner of the playground during break to interrogate her memories.

'Oi, you listening to me?'

The question snapped Ada back to the present. 'Sorry.'

'I said I reckon the beardy bloke's a spy or something,' said Bobby.

'What makes you say that?' asked Ada.

'You said that hooded bloke called him Agent Ash and how he worked something called—'

'The ESD,' put in Tony. 'Sounds like the FBI don't it?'

'The FBI sounds like the FBI, dopey,' snapped Bobby.

'Forget beardy, what about those hooded things who shoot green lighting from their fingers?' mumbled DJ. 'We gonna talk about those?'

'I thought you weren't listening?' asked Ada.

'And I thought we weren't doing this stuff anymore,' said DJ.

'Can I see it?' asked Bobby.

Ada pulled the wooden box from her satchel. She handed it to Bobby, who immediately began turning it over in his hand, studying it closely. 'What's all these weird pictures on it then?'

'I have no idea,' said Ada. 'Yet.'

Bobby held the box up to his ear and started shaking it. Ada snatched the box out of his hand, ignoring his plea to give it back.

Tony piped up from the rear of the group. 'We could just give it to the teachers and let them sort it out.'

DJ walked backwards pushing between Bobby and Ada until he was level with Tony.

'Finally, someone is talking sense,' said DJ, throwing an arm over Tony's shoulder.

'I'm not doing that.,' stated Ada, stuffing the wooden box back into her satchel.

DJ let out a mournful sigh. 'And here it comes. Go on, new boy. Ask her why.'

'Why?' asked Tony.

'Because there's a mystery here, and we never walk away from a good mystery.'

'Smiley's right, Ada. You gotta tell someone about all this.'

Ada blew a raspberry, less than impressed by Bobby's comment. 'And what happened the last time we tried that? Mum packed me off to Nigeria for the summer, DJ was grounded and you got stuck doing every chore Dad and Auntie Carol could find.'

'Norfolk was different,' said Bobby, frowning. 'Those hooded things might have kidnapped that American bloke, you gotta tell someone.'

Ada gave Bobby a half smile. 'I just did, didn't I?'

'Don't be stupid, you know what I mean.'

'Ada Amaya! Do you know what a roadblock is?'

Ada looked behind her and saw a man in a brown suit pushing his way through the crowd to stand in front of her and Bobby.

'I do Mr Wattling,' said Bobby.

'No one was talking to you, Gibson.'.

'Sorry sir.'

'Do you want to tell me what's so important you have to stand in the doorway to my form room gabbing about it?'

'Well sir…' began Ada.

'The question was rhetorical, Ada. Get inside and take your seat.'

'Shame,' chuckled DJ.

Mr Wattling swung round so fast Ada thought his tie would have someone's eye out.

'Dibney Jennings. I might have known,' he said, peering closer. 'You been getting enough sleep lad? Those bags under your eyes look terrible.'

'I'm fine,' said DJ, sharply.

For a second Ada thought she saw something like fear cross DJ's face then it was gone banished by a toothy grin.

'Did you miss me sir?' he asked.

'Like a hole in the head, son. Now shift!'

Mr Wattling looked at Tony. 'I don't know you but I'm guessing you must be young Mr Tadsby?'

Tony nodded.

'Right then you wait here Tony. The rest of you lot get a shift on!'

Ada headed into the classroom. Nothing much had changed in the six weeks they had been away. Ada was glad. A lot of kids hated their form rooms, but not her. She loved the way the ancient wooden desks made a massive crash if you let go of the lids. She loved her seat by the window, which gave her a great view of the playground and the giant horse chestnut tree in the distance. It was in the shade of that tree, last year, that a full-scale conker shell fight had erupted between the first and second year pupils. It had taken six teachers to break it up.

Bobby took his seat which was second closest to the window. Ada was about to sit when someone made a loud farting sound.

'Sir! Sir!' said a small boy, his hand in the air and a grin on his greasy face.

'What is it Tanner?' asked Mr Wattling in a pained voice.

'Ada just let one go sir,' announced Tanner to much amusement.

Ada spun round. 'Really? That's the best you can come up with?'

She gave Bobby a vicious side-eye when she noticed he was giggling.

'I think Liam might be dying from the smell sir,' said Tanner.

At the mention of his name, Liam started coughing and rubbing his eyes.

'I think I should take him to the nurse sir,' continued Tanner.

'I think you should Tanner. It looks serious. In fact I'll even write a note for the nurse.'

Wattling opened one of his desk draws and took out a notepad and pen.

'Tanner. Patterson. Up here now,' said Mr Wattling, all the while scribbling onto the notepad.

The two boys strolled to the front of the class. Tanner looked over his shoulder and sneered at Ada.

Ada crossed her arms and sat back in her chair.

'Here you go lads,' said Mr Wattling, tearing the note out and offering it to them.

Confusion slid over Johnny's smug expression as he read it. 'Sir this says detention for Johnny Tanner and Liam Patterson.'

'Glad to see your reading skills haven't slipped over the holidays, Tanner,' said Mr Wattling.

'But sir...'

'What did I tell you about lying last year, Tanner?' asked Mr Wattling.

Johnny's gaze dropped to his shoes. 'You said you won't stand for lying in class sir.'

'And I won't. So with that lesson learned, I'm sure you and Patterson will have no difficulty staying behind after school today to write me an essay on why lying is wrong.'

'Come off it sir, we were only having a laugh.'

'Do I look like I'm laughing Tanner?' asked Mr Wattling. His stony expression suggested a man who had never laughed once in his life.

'No sir,' replied Johnny in misery.

'Good! Now we've cleared that up, get back to your seats, before I think of something else for you to do.'

Patterson and Tanner slunk back to their seats without a word. A few kids, brave enough to risk Wattling's wrath, were giggling quietly and pointing at the pair. Unfortunately for Bobby, he was the one Wattling spotted.

'Do you want to join them in detention Gibson?'

'No sir,' said Bobby, the threat of detention curing him of the giggles.

'Good. I would think you'd want to stay off my radar after the little stunt you pulled last year.'

Bobby opened his mouth to reply, but Ada shook her head. The last thing any of them needed right now was a Bobby Gibson meltdown.

'Very wise, Gibson,' said Mr Wattling. 'Right, you lot. Get yourselves sorted.'

Mr Wattling stood up, hands behind his back as though he were a general overseeing his troops whilst the kids started packing their books and their stationery into their desks.

Ada liked Mr Wattling. He was not a push over like some of the other teachers, but he was fair. If you wanted to learn he would do anything to help – but if you played him up, he would eat you for—.

'Teachers,' she whispered, cutting off her own thoughts. 'Now, why am I thinking about teachers?'

'Welcome to year two everyone,' began Mr Wattling, slapping his hands together. 'You're all a year older now, which means you have a whole year of boys and girls below who will be looking to you to set an example. I expect each one of you to— Nichola Panilides, get up here now!'

A chubby girl with olive skin, dark curly hair and an angry expression stood up. Poking out from the left corner of her mouth was a thin white stick. Over the left lens of her glasses was a large cream coloured patch.

Nikki Panilides was the toughest pupil in their year. Ada, along with most of the school, had seen Nikki flatten a fourth-year boy outside the sports block last year. No one knew what the boy had said to Nikki. He was expelled soon after, and Nikki never spoke of it. All she got was a week's detention and a letter home to her parents. After that none of the kids in their year – or any other year, for that matter – messed with her.

As Nikki reached the front of the class, Mr Wattling held out a metal dustbin.

'What did I say about sweets in class Nichola?' asked Mr Wattling.

'This is my last one sir,' said Nikki.

'You should have thought of that before walking into my form room,' replied Mr Wattling, shaking the bin impatiently.

Nikki glared at Mr Wattling. If looks could kill, Mr Khara would be sweeping up Mr Wattling's ashes.

'I don't have all day, Miss Panilides.'

Nikki spat out the lollipop. It hit the rim, rattled around the edge then clattered into the bin. Wattling dismissed her and replaced the dustbin.

'As I was saying – this year I expect you all to be shining examples of what it means to be a pupil of this school.'

DJ's hand shot up as just as Nikki sat back down.

'Yes, Dibney?'

'Am I a shining example sir?'

'You are indeed a shining example, Dibney – of stupidity.'

Laughter erupted in the classroom. Kids started banging on their desks and pointing at DJ.

'That's enough, settle down,' said Mr Wattling, trying to hide his own smile. 'Now, before we head down to assembly, I've two announcements to make.'

He waved at Tony, who had been waiting by the door.

'New blood!' shouted, one girl.

'Enough!' bellowed Mr Wattling.

Silence fell and Mr Wattling went on. 'Everyone this is…stand up straight son.'

Tony, who looked like he was going to vomit over Mr Wattling at any second, did his best to straighten up and look presentable.

'This is Tony Tadsby. He will be joining the class this year.'

'Welcome to the nut house!' shouted a blond-haired boy with freckles from the back of the class.

'And Kenny Brokhurst has just earned the third spot in detention alongside Tanner and Patterson. Bravo, Kenny. Anyone want to join them?'

More silence.

'I thought not,' said Wattling, pointing to the chair next to Bobby. 'You can sit there, Tadsby.'

Bobby's hand shot up.

'Yes Gibson?'

'Smiley boy can't sit there sir; that's Archie's seat.'

'He'll sit anywhere I tell him to, Gibson,' said Mr Wattling. He gave Tony a slight nudge. 'Take your seat, Tadsby. Go on.'

With a sheepish look on his face Tony walked over to the desk next to Bobby's, by the window, and sat down. Bobby did not take his eyes off him the whole way. Ada was less bothered about that, and more concerned about Archie.

'Which brings me to my second piece of news, of course,' said Mr Wattling. 'Archie Brown will not be coming back to school this year. He and his parents have moved on to pastures new.'

The news kicked off discussion and questions from the around the room. This was only to be expected, so Mr Wattling let it slide for a minute.

Ada felt something hard prod her arm. She looked left to see Bobby holding a ruler and looking worried.

'You reckon Archie and his folks did a runner then, 'cause of what happened to him in Norfolk?' he whispered.

'What did we say about Norfolk, Bobson?' Ada asked the question as though she were talking to her three-year-old cousin.

'Not to talk about it in front of anyone.'

Ada nodded to Tony who was staring at the pair of them. 'That includes him.'

Tony faced the front. Ada felt a pang of guilt. If it had not been for Tony she would have fallen from the bus while escaping from whatever those things were at the graveyard.

Ada shuddered as she remembered the shadowy hooded figures coming at her, slithering through the gravestones.

Give us the box little girl!

She told herself she was safe in class, but the hairs on the back of her neck were telling a different story.

6

Pupils Assemble

Something hard and knobby hit Tony's head, twice.

'Ow!'

'You deaf lad?' barked a gruff voice.

A hulking, black-bearded teacher who looked to be part bear was now blocking his path. The teacher wore a green polo neck jumper, a grey checked jacket and purple track suit bottoms. Tony wondered if the teacher had been dressed by two different people. Or perhaps he'd broken the last of his mirrors. *Maybe Manbears don't live in houses…?*

'Your parents tell you it's rude to stare lad?' bellowed the teacher, rapping his knuckles again against Tony's head. 'Now, what are those?'

'They're my feet sir!'

Tony's answer earned him two more raps on the head and Tony put his hands up to protect it.

'We have a comedian do we?'

Tony rubbed his head and tried not to gag at the smell of the teacher's aftershave. It reminded him of the camphorated oil Mum would spread on his chest when he had the flu.

'YOU LOT! ASSEMBLY! NOW!' Manbear roared at a group
of kids who were stupid enough to gawp as they went past. The
startled children broke into a collective scuttle down the corridor.

'Now, let's try this again,' said Manbear, pointing at Tony's feet.
'What. Are. Those?'

'My trainers sir.'

'I know they're your trainers, idiot. Where are your shoe shoes?'

'I forgot them sir. I told Mr Wattling and he said—'

'Do I look like I care?'

Tony reckoned all Manbear cared about was crushing the heads
of kids who forgot their trainers.

'No school shoes means lunch time detention for you, lad.'

'Oh, I've got a pair he can borrow, Mr Bennett,' another voice
piped up. It was Bobby, with DJ at his side.

Mr Bennett's hands shot up onto his hips, his jacket flaring out
behind him like a cape. He blasted the boy with a full-on rage
stare, but Bobby just stood there all innocence. DJ looked like was
about to wet himself.

'I should have known he'd be a friend of yours, Gibson,'
snarled Bennett.

'He ain't *my* mate sir,' said Bobby.

'So you're giving him your shoes out of the goodness of your
heart, are you lad?'

'Yes sir.'

Mr Bennett poked Bobby's chest. 'You trying to make a fool
out of me, Gibson?'

'I wouldn't know how sir,' replied Bobby, rubbing his chest.

'Is there a problem here Mr Bennett?' asked Mr Wattling, who
had just come around the corner.

'This toerag has forgotten his school shoes.'

'Yes, Tony has already explained that to me.'

'That may be Mr Wattling, but the rules say—'

'I told Mr Bennett he could borrow my spare shoes sir,' cut in Bobby. 'They're in my locker.'

'I don't recall you saying anything in class when I asked if anyone had any spare shoes,' said Mr Wattling, giving Bobby a hard look.

'Must've slipped my mind sir.'

'Hm. Yes, I'm sure,' said Mr Wattling, raising an eyebrow. 'Very well. You can give Tadsby your spares after assembly. Now then, get a move on before we're all late.'

Tony moved to follow Bobby and DJ, who were already walking away, but Bennett's large hairy hand clamped down on his shoulder.

'Falling in with Gibson and his lot is not the best start for you lad. From now on I'll be watching you.'

Tony swore he could feel the ground shaking with each word. His knees were still trembling as Mr Bennett lifted his hand free. Tony scurried after Bobby and DJ, without looking back.

When they felt far enough away to be safe, Bobby let out a massive sigh. 'Blimey Smiley, you don't do things by half, do you? I thought he was going to lamp you one.'

'Lamp me one?'

'Hit you,' translated Bobby. 'Bennett's the Deputy Head. Meanest git in this place.'

'What's with the tracky bottoms?' asked Tony.

'He's also the games teacher and now you're on his list. Good job, new boy!' said DJ, giving Tony the thumbs up.

Tony fought the urge to paint the school floor with his breakfast as he followed Bobby and DJ down a flight of stairs. Kids were filing nosily into their classrooms. Ada waved up at them from the midst of the crowd. The moment they reached her, DJ filled her in on their encounter with Mr Bennett.

'Auntie Carol would've skinned you alive if you got into trouble on the first day back. What were you thinking?'

'Leave off Ada, you ain't his mum,' said DJ. His jaw dropped as Ada glowered, and he realised what he'd just said.

'Sorry, mate. I didn't think— I mean…'

Bobby shrugged. 'Nah, it's cool mate.'

Tony had no idea what had just happened. He looked from one to the other, but that seemed to be it. So he asked the other question. 'If Mr Bennett is such a nightmare, why did you help me?'

'Felt like it, didn't I?' replied Bobby like that was enough. Tony would have pressed the matter, but they were already walking away.

***

'Boys…' Ada mumbled to herself, watching Tony dash after Bobby and DJ. 'Why did I have to be friends with boys?'

Now the idiot trio were on Mr Bennett's radar, it would be twice as difficult to investigate the mystery.

Give us the box.

Ada spun at the whispered demand, but all she saw were pupils and teachers heading to assembly.

Oh, great. Now I'm *hearing things*, Ada thought as she entered the cavernous assembly hall. The scale of it always awed her. Half of her primary school could have fit in here and still left room for ice cream.

Most of the pupils were seated now, with only a few stragglers circling like bees round a flower, trying to find a seat. As always, the two back rows were filled with the 'cool' children. Of course, as far as the teachers were concerned 'cool' meant 'nightmare', and they were watched like hawks. Most satisfied themselves by kicking the seats in front, but two of the girls were actually fighting. Ada spotted Miss McAlister, the girls' gym teacher, swoop down one row to pull the two girls from their seats. As they were dragged from the hall, the rest of the back row began chanting 'Shame'. A withering look from Mr Bennett silenced them.

'Ada! Ada! Over here!'

Ada saw DJ waving from a spot several rows in front of her, one knee on the chair for balance. There was an empty seat beside him, and on the other of that side sat Bobby. At that moment Mr Creasey, the headmaster, walked out onto the stage followed by the form tutors. Ada hurried to Bobby's row and started to edge her way along to the empty chair.

'Oi! Watch where you're putting those clompers!' snapped Liam Patterson.

Ada made sure she trod on Liam's other foot as she went past before dropping onto her seat.

'What happened to you?' asked Bobby. 'Thought you were right behind us?'

'Probably looking for more hooded spooks to chase her,' said DJ, sliding down into his chair.

Ada leant across Bobby and punched DJ in the arm.

'Ow! What was that for?' he asked, rubbing his arm.

'Being you,' Ada grumped.

'I still think you should tell your mum what happened,' muttered Tony. 'Get her to call the police or something.'

'Police have better things to do than talk to kids,' she sighed. 'Or at least that's what they'll tell us.'

In irritation, DJ flicked the ear of the boy in front of him.

'So what are we gonna do then?' asked Tony

The big-eared boy looked around but DJ had already leant back, nodding at Ada as though the two of them were deep in conversation.

Ada rolled her eyes. There were times when DJ's usefulness matched that of a half-eaten cheese sandwich.

'Agent Ash told me there were tapes at school that would explain everything,' explained Ada. 'He said at ten to two the cuckoo will tell you what to do.'

'Well that's a fat load of nothing,' said Bobby. 'We don't know who he is or where his office is, let alone what any of that cuckoo stuff means.'

Ada curled her lip and stared off into space, running through the morning's events again. There was something she was missing. Something…out of focus somehow.

'You're not even listening to me, are you?' asked Bobby.

'Back at the graveyard it felt like I'd met Ash before. He seemed to recognise me, but that makes no sense.'

Ada shook her head as though the action would shake the details free. 'Doesn't matter. It'll come to me, but first we need to—'

'SILENCE!'

Mr Creasey's voice boomed out from the front of the hall. The bustle stopped at once though there were a few stubborn pockets of chatter rustling through the hall.

'The next pupil I hear will see me in detention for the next three weeks,' Creasey growled, stepping up to the lectern. His threat and his glare swept across the hall with silence following in its wake.

'Better,' said Creasey, nodding. He gestured to the people behind him – a woman and a man. 'I will hand over today's special assembly to these fine police officers.'

At the mention of Police, Ada sat bolt upright, along with every other kid. She scrutinised the short, black-haired woman who was now shaking hands with Mr Creasey. *What on earth was she doing here?* The woman took Creasey's place at the lectern.

'Hello children,' she began. 'My name is Detective Inspector Kate Penthrope.'

7

Latecomers

The policewoman opened a small notebook and cleared her throat.

'Now children, we've come here today to talk to you about a very serious matter.'

Well that's a stupid way to start, thought Ada. *You wouldn't be here if it wasn't serious.*

To her knowledge, the only other time the police had been in the school was years ago. A drunk man had climbed over the school fence and was running around the back playground waving a cricket bat. Mr Bennett had rugby tackled the weirdo, then held him down until the police arrived.

'Three days ago, one your teachers went missing.' Penthrope paused to glance at her notebook. 'Mr Rillington.'

The moment she said the name, a hustle of hissed conversations shot around the hall.

Tony tugged at DJ's blazer and asked, 'Who was he, then?'

'A supply teacher, filling in for Mrs Johnson, the history teacher. He was rubbish. Never wanted to answer questions. He always acted like we were wasting his time. As soon as the lesson was done he'd naff off to the library or his poky little office.'

Missing. Teacher. Office. The words slotted into place among the clues in Ada's head. The voice was wrong, but the face—

Ada slapped her forehead. *Some detective you are, Amaya.*

'Find the tapes, Ada.'

He had known her because—

'He taught me! Stupid, stupid, stupid. He never used to have a beard, and I dunno *what* was going on with his accent, but it was him – I'm sure of it!'

Bobby gave her a concerned look. 'What are you on about?'

'The man in the graveyard. Beardy. It was Mr Rillington!'

'You sure?' asked Bobby.

Ada glared at him.

Bobby sighed. 'Course you're sure.'

'I cannot believe I didn't see it before,' said Ada, frowning. 'He was right in front of me, he called me by my name and I just didn't see it.'

'Not easy to remember stuff when you're running for your life,' Bobby pointed out, trying to be kind. Her expression told him he'd failed.

Creasey's thunderous roar demanded silence, and it fell immediately.

'This is no laughing matter children,' continued DI Penthrope. 'The teaching staff are very worried about him. He was last seen walking his dog six days ago.'

Ada slapped a hand over her mouth, unsure if she wanted to hear more.

'We have found the dog but there was no sign of Mr Rillington.'

Ada breathed a sigh of relief. She loved dogs, though there was no way Mum would let her have one.

Penthrope half turned and gestured at Creasey. 'Your headmaster has very kindly given us an office to use for the next few days, so we can talk to the teaching staff. However, if any of you girls or boys have any information about Mr Rillington that may help our investigation, or if you have seen him in the last week, please tell your form tutors and they will bring you to see us.'

Penthrope flipped the pages of her notebook back over, stepped off the podium and went back to stand with her two colleagues.

Creasey took up his spot once more on the podium. 'You heard DI Penthrope, if you need her, she will be in Mrs MacDonald's office. Does anybody have any questions?'

About half of those in assembly hall stuck their hands up.

Creasey gripped the top of the lectern. He leaned forward sternly, holding everyone in his gaze.

'Be warned: any stupid questions will meet with severe consequences.'

Most of the hands dropped back onto their owner's laps, and after the third sensible question Ada stopped listening.

'That's it then,' DJ whispered, sitting back and wearing a self-satisfied grin. 'He's a spy. Hundred percent.'

'You reckon?' asked Bobby.

'It's obvious, innit?' replied DJ. 'One minute he's British Mr Rillington, the crappy supply teacher, and the next he's American Agent Ash, hanging about with shady blokes in robes. Course he's a spy. He's like bleeding James Bond, ain't he?'

'You know James Bond isn't real right?' asked Tony.

'Sure I do. You wanna know something else I know, new boy?'

DJ punched Tony hard in the arm. Tony shot back against his chair, grabbing his arm and crying out.

'I know someone with a dead arm,' grinned DJ.

'Pack it in, you two!' Mrs McAlister shouted from the other side of the row. DJ and Tony mouthed a quiet apology to her before staring daggers at each other.

'The only thing we know for certain is that he's missing; the rest is supposition,' said Ada, as if the dead-arm incident had never happened.

'Supper what now?' asked DJ.

Bobby patted DJ's head. 'She means you're stupid, and we need more clues.' Bobby looked back to Ada. 'Rillington's office then, right?'

'What about his office?' asked Tony.

Ada sighed. She'd had such high hopes for the new boy. 'Look we know Mr Rillington or—'

'James Bond?' offered DJ.

'Agent Ash gave us one solid clue,' said Ada, shooting a displeased look at DJ. 'We know there are tapes in his office that can help us figure out what's going on, and maybe who took him.'

Tony looked over at DI Penthrope, who was now answering a question about how many people she had arrested. 'I still don't get why we can't tell her? I know you said they wouldn't believe us, but they know he's disappeared now. They're already investigating it.'

Ada nodded to DJ and Bobby. 'Boys?'

'We tried that last year in Norfolk, and it went bad. Really bad, like... *epic* bad' explained DJ. 'Like so bad—'

'We don't know if there's anything in Rillington's office,' said Bobby, talking over DJ, who was still laying out just how bad 'epic bad' was. 'So us lot should have a look first.'

Ada beamed like a proud parent. 'Nicely done boys.'

'Right, great,' Tony sat back, folding his arms. 'So instead you're going to what? Break into a missing teacher's office?'

'Of course not,' hissed Ada. Her eyes flicked from side to side, checking they weren't overheard. 'We'll get someone to let us in.'

'The Scrounger?' asked Bobby.

'Should be a piece of cake for her,' replied Ada.

'Who's the Scrounger?' asked Tony.

'Unless you four want to join me in detention keep your mouths closed and your ears open!' Miss McAlister was stood at the end of Ada's row, eyeballing them. 'And I expect better from *you*, Miss Amaya.'

'Sorry Miss.'

'Don't be sorry girl, be better.' With that, Miss McAlister marched towards a boy who was chewing gum. Ada felt sorry for him. Miss McAlister's hated chewers more than anything else.

Ada turned her attention back to the assembly. Creasey allowed a couple more questions then held up his hands.

'Now let us thank Detective Inspector Penthrope and her team for coming in today.'

The headmaster began clapping and the teachers followed. After he directed a few well-placed scowls into the crowd, Creasey was rewarded with the entire hall filling with applause.

I see you little girl but can you see my Faceless? They can smell you. And they are coming...

Ada shivered. It was the weird voice again, echoing in her head. Wait. He could *see* her?

She gazed at the ceiling.

You are cold. Try again little girl.

She turned in her seat, ignoring the boy behind her who was busy making small farting noises.

Still cold. Again, again. Oh this is so much fun.

She turned around and faced forward.

Ooooh hotter, much hotter.

Ada felt sick. Her stomach was doing back flips but she forced herself to look at Creasey and the others on the stage.

You are on fire!

The curtain behind the stage twitched and Ada gasped.

'You alright, Ada?' asked Bobby.

'The curtain just moved; didn't you see it?'

Bobby shook his head. Ada staring at the curtain, willing it to move again.

'She's losing it,' whispered DJ.

'Shut up,' Tony murmured. 'Can't you see she's scared?'

'Who's rattled your cage Smiley?'

'My name's not—'

'Shut it. Both of you,' said Bobby. 'Ada? Ada are you okay?'

Ada blinked again and the curtain still had not moved. 'I'm fine.'

'You sure?'

'I said so, didn't I?' Ada kept her voice low, but the words came out angrier than she'd intended.

'Alright! I only asked,' said Bobby, facing forward and rejoining the applause.

It continued until Penthrope and the other officer left the stage, petering out into silence once more. Mr Creasey held out a hand behind him, and Mr Bennett gave him a large red folder. Creasey lifted his glasses from his chest, where they dangled on a thin gold chain, and put them on.

Ada sighed, crossed her arms and settled back in her chair. Whenever Creasey put his glasses on, it meant they were going to be here for a while.

'Right then.' He began. 'I have a several announcements about room and lesson changes for this year.'

DJ stretched his legs out in front of him and pushed his hands into his pockets. 'Kill me now.'

Ada wanted to oblige, but that strange feeling came over her again. She shuddered. Coldness washed over and through her, sending a shudder down her spine. She touched her forehead and her fingers came away damp with sweat. How she could be cold and hot at the same time?

Give me the Salus Key and this all stops. You can go back to being an ordinary little girl.

The stage curtains snapped back, revealing one of the hooded figures Ada had seen at the graveyard. No one in the hall reacted in the slightest to the creature's appearance.

Or shall I let my Faceless have you?

Ada shut her eyes and shouted. 'It's not real! It's not real! It's not real!'

Mocking laughter was all she heard now.

'Ada! Ada!'

At the sound of Bobby's voice, Ada's eyes snapped open. The shock of what she saw robbed her of movement. She couldn't even scream. A robed figure had appeared in Bobby's place. She could see inside its hood. The creature was without eyes, nose or mouth – it was just a dark swirling mist, crackling with tiny sparks of green and white. It was as though someone had torn a piece of darkness from the night sky and clothed it. The creature tilted its head back and let out a terrifying shriek, sending tendrils of lightning out from the darkness to fork across the room.

Ada's vision went white, as though a thousand cameras had flashed in her face. She blinked and rubbed her eyes. All the pupils had gone. The teachers too. They'd been replaced by hooded figures, hundreds of them. The Faceless were all fixed on her, pinning her in place with fear.

'Give me the key little girl!' The hooded figures demanded as one. 'Give me the key or die!'

Ada screamed and everything went black.

8

The Scrounger

She gonna be alright Bobby. You hear me?

But Bobby was not listening to Mum. All he could think about was Ada screaming in the middle of the assembly and tumbling out of her chair. It was terrifying.

Mr Wattling had reached Ada first, scooping her up and carrying her from the hall, while the other teachers fought to control the chaos. Bobby and DJ had tried to follow but were ordered back to their seats. Once calm was finally restored, Mr Creasey ended assembly and everyone was packed off to their morning lessons. Bobby had not been able to concentrate, as Ada failed to reappear. She was nowhere to be seen in any of the lessons he shared with her. If that wasn't bad enough, the new boy, Tony, sat next to him in all the morning classes. He wasn't Archie. Why was he trying to take his place? As far as Bobby was concerned, Tony did too much of everything: he talked too much, smiled too much, and he did way too much work. On the upside, Mum had pointed out the Flash Gordon sticker book in his bag. Tony couldn't be a complete waste of space if he liked Flash Gordon.

Bobby strode out of the main building at break time. He headed towards the science block.

'This is nuts,' muttered Tony.

'No one asked you to come, Smiley,' said DJ.

Tony stuffed his hands in his pockets, frowned and continued walking.

DJ dropped back until he was walking beside Tony.

'Why are you hanging around, anyway? There's loads of other kids you could be annoying right now.'

Tony rounded on DJ and shoved a finger in his face. 'Ada helped me, alright, so I wanna help her! She's been nice to me.'

DJ eyed Tony up and down. 'You fancy her then, new boy, is that it?'

Outraged, Tony opened his mouth, but Bobby got in first.

'Give it a rest you two. We're sticking to Ada's plan. You can fight over her later, right?'

Tony and DJ huffed but nodded.

Bobby turned and walked up to one of four turrets housing the staircases for the science block. He knocked twice on the glass-fronted door, paused, then knocked three more times.

A light brown hand appeared, accompanied by the jangling of keys. The door opened.

'In. Now,' squeaked a voice.

The three boys slid inside. A girl darted out from the shadows of the corridor to close and lock the door once more. DJ and Bobby had already started to move down the corridor, but Tony stood staring at the tiny girl. She only came up to his shoulder.

'*You're* the scrounger?'

The girl stood on tip toes and clicked her fingers in Tony's face. 'You thick or something? You wanna get us caught? Come on!'

She grabbed his arm and dragged him after the others.

Bobby gave the girl an apologetic shrug. 'Smiley, this is Shamri.'

'Wotcha. I'm Tony.'

'Being new don't mean you have to be a prat,' snapped Shamri, turning to Bobby.

'You got it?' she asked, narrowing her large brown eyes.

Bobby reached inside his satchel.

'Wait!'

Shamri grabbed Bobby's arm and pulled him into a classroom. The others followed behind. Shamri eased the door shut then put a finger to her lips. They crouched on either side of the door and waited. Footsteps moved past the door. A minute later Shamri opened the door again and peered along the corridor, checking both ways.

'Time to go,' she whispered.

She led them out of the classroom, hurried down the stairs and into a dark corridor. Tony reached for the light switch on the corridor wall but Shamri slapped his hand away.

'No big lights!' she ordered.

'I thought we were going to Mr Rillington's office?' asked Tony, rubbing his hand.

'We are.' She flicked on a small penlight. 'He got the assistant caretaker's office when he joined. Dunno why. No one's been in there for years.'

'Years?' asked Tony.

'My dad says this part of the building was here before the school. There's some law or something says that they have to keep it.'

'How would your dad know that?' asked Tony.

'Cause Khara's her dad, dummy,' said DJ. 'How do you think she can get us in here?'

'Dad's got loads of spare keys, so I just borrow them when I need to.'

Shamri continued through the dimly lit corridor, her tiny penlight projecting ominous shadows across the walls. 'Gotta say, Bobby, I didn't think you'd be getting in trouble this early in the year. Not after Norfolk. Respect!'

'Wasn't my idea Shamri,' said Bobby, trying to ignore Mum's disappointed groan.

'Never said it was.' She stopped by a thick wooden door and pulled the huge ring of keys out of her pocket. 'They offered this room to my dad but he said no way.'

She tried a couple of keys, but they did not work. She scratched her head and began going through the keys again.

'How come?' asked Bobby.

'Said this room always gave him the creeps. Like something was in there watching him.'

DJ sighed and glared at Bobby. 'You had to ask, didn't you?'

Shamri tried another key and *Yessss-ed!* in triumph. She opened the door a crack. Bobby started forward but Shamri put a hand against his chest.

'You forgetting something, Gibson?'

Bobby took a comic out from his satchel and handed it to her. She flashed a wide grin.

'Latest issue?'

'Yep.'

'Sweet!' Shamri swung the door open and stepped to the side. 'Right, you got ten minutes then we need to go. I'll keep an eye out from the stop of the stairs.'

'Cool. DJ – you keep a look out from the bottom of the stairs. You see anything whistle. Smiley – you're with me.'

DJ saluted and said 'Right you are captain!' in his best pirate voice.

Shamri handed the keys to Bobby. 'Make sure you lock up.'

With that, she and DJ set off in the opposite direction.

Bobby walked into the room, immediately wishing he had not. The air smelt like rotten eggs, mixed with baked beans.

I hate baked beans, he thought to himself.

The large round rug stuck to Bobby's feet. At each step, it made a weird slurping sound and sent up a plume of dust. Rillington clearly hadn't been one for cleaning. Large cobwebs filled the corners of the room, corners that Bobby had no intention of going into. He could not believe anyone would want to be in here for over ten seconds, let alone use it as an office.

'What a dump!' Tony grimaced and stepped over an old bike with no wheels that was lying on the floor.

The only items in the room not covered in dust were the large oak desk and a high-backed wooden chair on the other side of the room. Papers and books were scattered across the desk. Several of the books had leather covers and looked ancient.

'Have a look around,' said Bobby. 'I'll take the desk.'

'Why do you get the desk?'

'Because I've done this before and you haven't.'

'What? Break into scary old rooms in the school basement?'

Bobby was already at the desk. 'No. It was a dungeon.'

'And you lot think I'm the weirdo?'

'Just—'

Tony threw his hands up in defeat. 'I know, I know. Look around. We want a cuckoo, right?'

Tony moved to a corner piled with assorted items and started searching through them. Bobby tried the desk drawers but they were all locked. He picked up a few papers but all were written in code he could not read. He lifted the one leather bound book not covered in dust.

'The Faceless Scholars, visionaries or madmen?' he read aloud.

Tony, who was holding a rubber duck in one hand, asked. 'What was that?'

'A clue...I think,' said Bobby, already skimming through the book.

'Six minutes,' came DJ's hushed voice from the corridor.

'The tapes aren't here,' said Tony. He was bored and frustrated, and the smell was clearly bugging him. He kept wafting his hand in front of his nose.

Bobby put the book down and leaned back in the chair. 'They've got to be. Keep looking.'

'Why? There's nothing here but dirt and spiders.'

Bobby sat up in the chair, eyes wide. 'Spiders? Where?'

Tony gestured to the corner he had been searching.

'Right. We're out of here,' said Bobby.

'But you said—'

'That's before I was in room with a thousand spiders.'

'More like four,' said Tony, a hint of scorn in his voice.

'Whatever, Smiley. We need to go!'

'Hang on. Look up there,' said Tony, pointing above the door.

Bobby squinted up into the gloom. What was that? It kind of looked like a model of an old-fashioned house.

'It's a cuckoo clock!' said Tony, grabbing a heavy box and dragging it over to use as a step.

'Brilliant.' Bobby snapped his fingers. 'The tapes must be in there. What time did he say, again?'

'Two,' said Tony moving the big hand around gently.

'No, that's wrong,' said Bobby. 'It's the small hand for hours.'

Tony turned to reply and lost his footing. He let out a yell and fell backwards, landing hard on his back.

'Oi, keep it down in there,' whispered DJ. 'You want to bring the whole school in there or what?'

Bobby ran over to Tony, who was already on his feet trying to brush the dust off his uniform.

'Mum's gonna kill me. This is new. Look at it!'

'Nah you look like one of us now.'

Tony up at the clock once more, and gasped.

'What the hell is that?'

He pointed a trembling finger, and Bobby went over to investigate. Embedded in the centre of the clock was a shard of metal, oiled and shiny against the dusty background. The wood to either side of it was cracked. Bobby touched it and swore gently.

'It's a dart,' he whispered. 'Geez. This is a trap. Like… a proper trap.'

'You sure?'

'I play Dungeons and Dragons twice a week—course I'm sure,' said Bobby. He looked back at Tony, hands on hips. 'Good job you fell, otherwise…' Bobby made a gargling sound while drawing an invisible line across his neck with his thumb.

Tony gulped. 'So what now?'

We all leave?

Bobby ignored them both. He stepped gingerly onto the box and focused on the clock. It seemed to have reset itself to midnight again. He took a small brown case from his satchel, opened it up and drew out a pair of silver-rimmed glasses.

'You wear glasses?' asked Tony, shocked.

'I wear 'em for reading. It's not like I'm blind or anything' Bobby snapped. He placed a finger against the larger clock hand. 'You got the time wrong. It's *ten* to two, so maybe we start with the ten not the two.'

'Maybe? Maybe?'

Bobby moved the hand round to X, the roman numeral for ten. held his breath and closed his eyes. Nothing. Bobby breathed out.

'At ten to two, the cuckoo will show you what to do,' whispered Tony.

'Shut it will you!'

Tony fell silent but inside his mind Bobby's mum continued to whisper the words. He reached up again, unable to stop his hands from shaking.

At ten to two the cuckoo will show you what to do.

Even though the room was cool, he felt sweat beading his forehead.

At ten to two the cuckoo will show you what to do.

'Not now mum,' snapped Bobby.

Boy you best take some of that bass out of your voice, you hear?

'Sorry mum.'

'Did you just call me mum?' asked Tony.

'Shut it Smiley!'

Satisfied no one else had anything to say, Bobby touched the smaller clock hand and moved it around to the symbol for 2. Bobby was never so glad they had to do Latin in the first year.

There was a pause followed by a loud click. The cuckoo clock swung open, revealing a large alcove behind it.

'Sweet,' whispered Bobby.

Me always said you were the clever one of the family.

Bobby wrinkled his fingers like he was crumbling bread. He gazed into the darkened hole and swallowed his fear.

'Please don't have spiders inside,' he whispered, reaching inside. *Me can't look.*

Bobby's hand touched something hard and rectangular. He gripped one end of it and pulled it out.

'It's a tape recorder,' he said, and passed it over to Tony. 'Empty, though. Hang on…'

Bobby reached inside again walking his fingers around the space. There was nothing. That couldn't be right. He stood on tiptoes and pushed his hand in deeper, groaning with effort and spider fear. At last, his patience and courage were rewarded.

'Feels like there's a load of tapes back here. Give me a leg-up.'

Tony gave him a boost, and Bobby grabbed one out, a handful at a time. Once they had them all, the boys moved over to the desk. Tony immediately began sifting through the tapes. 'Looks like they're all numbered,' he explained, waving the tape in his hand. 'This is the most recent one.'

Bobby looked at his watch. Two minutes left. 'Let's have a listen.'

Tony set the cassette recorder on the desk, slid in a tape, rewound it to the beginning then pressed the large white play button.

'ESD Log file. Week forty. Agent Ash reporting…I'm convinced Langley followed me back from Syria. I've managed to a secure a position as a substitute teacher at this school in the hopes of throwing him off my trail, while I continue my search.' The voice was American. Male. Rillington, he supposed. Agent Ash.

'The trip to Syria was a complete success. The Faceless Scholars covered their tracks well but I now have the Salus Key in my possession. Now all I need to do is find the—'

The brief silence was followed by footsteps.

Ash swore. There was a bustle, a clattering and then the sounds cut off. Bobby and Tony listened for a few more seconds but there was nothing. Bobby stopped the tape.

'You reckon it was Langley?' asked Tony 'You think he found Agent Ash?'

'How should I know?' Bobby went to hit the rewind button but a high-pitched whistle made him freeze.

'Someone's coming!' said Bobby.

9

Toilet Tantrums

'Crap! Crap!' shouted Tony, pressing the eject button.

'No, not like that,' said Bobby, who was scooping up armfuls of the tapes.

The lid flipped open and, before Bobby could stop him, Tony wrenched the tape from it. Part of the brown strip was caught and the tape started unspooling. Tony yanked it hard and the tape snapped.

DJ appeared in the doorway. 'We need to go. Now!'

'We need to put all this back,' said Tony. 'What if they…?'

DJ grabbed Tony's arm and started dragging him from the room. Tony's arm flailed, catching Bobby full in the face. Bobby shrieked, dropping the tapes as his hand came up to his mouth.

'Leave 'em mate!' ordered DJ.

A disappointed Bobby, his mouth still stinging from Tony's accidental blow, ran back into the corridor. DJ pulled the door shut and locked it.

They headed back the way they came but found Shamri running towards them, waving her hand in the other direction. When she reached them her words came in short blasts.

'My dad's coming… he's got…two blokes with him.'

The footsteps were closer now; discovery was one right turn away.

'We can't go back,' said Shamri. 'It's a dead end.'

'What about those?' asked Tony pointing at two sets of old lockers which sat on opposite sides of the corridor.

'Go!' Bobby hissed.

He ran for the lockers, and the others followed.

'Mr Rillington's office is just round here,' they heard Khara say.

Bobby and Tony dived behind the set of lockers on the right-hand side, while DJ and Shamri huddled behind the ones on the left. Tony squeezed as far in as possible while Bobby peered out from the corner.

He saw three men coming towards them. Shamri's dad was in front, followed by two unfamiliar men.

As they neared the office, Bobby was able to get a better look at them.

One man wore gold rimmed glasses, with a neat black bread. He also had dreadlocks, which flowed to between his shoulders. They were pulled together at his shoulders, and tied with three thick white bands. The second man was blond-haired, he had flushed red cheeks and deep brown eyes.

Mr Dreadlocks' head snapped round, his dark eyes narrowing in their direction. Had he heard something?

Bobby ducked back behind the locker, his breath catching in a stifled gasp.

There was a quiet terror about the men that scared Bobby to his bones.

'You jumping at shadows now, Orlando?' came a voice that reminded Bobby of those posh kids from Prosfield, a nearby private school.

'Thought I heard something,' came a booming American voice. Mr Dreadlocks.

Bobby swallowed hard as a tall shadow fell across the space between the lockers. He crouched lower.

You see what me tell you? Shoulda left sooner.

Bobby ignored Mum. His heart was thumping so loud now, he was sure the two men would hear it.

The shadow was close enough for Bobby to reach out and touch it.

'Seriously, Orlando. There's nothing down there. Rats, probably.'

'Rats?' The boom was gone from Mr Dreadlocks' voice.

'Giant ones. Like in Peru, remember?'

'This is a school, not the Aztec jungle.'

'Precisely, dear Gans,' said Blondie. 'Which means it's nothing. Come on, we don't have time to waste.'

'Can we make this quick? I'll be for it if anyone catches me bringing you two down here.' That was Mr Khara's voice. Bobby had never heard him so anxious.

'Yes, yes,' said Blondie. 'And you will be rewarded for your service. But as we said – this is a matter of grave importance. For *both* our countries. You're just going to have to take the risk.'

'Perhaps I should check with the—'

'No, Mr Khara. You shouldn't. Agent Orlando and I will be gone soon enough. I want to spend as little time in this dreadful school as possible. I don't know how Ash could stand it.'

Their shadows drifted back, out of sight. The next sound Bobby heard was the sound of keys rattling followed by the creak of a door being opened.

'How long do we have, Mr Khara?' asked Agent Orlando.

'First break is almost over,' replied Khara. 'You should have two hours before the children go to lunch.'

'Excellent.'

Bobby risked another glance out from the locker.

All three men had headed inside the office. Now was their chance.

Bobby nodded to Shamri, who gave him a thumbs up.

'What are you doing?' snapped Tony.

'Leaving.'

Bobby grabbed his arm, pulling Tony back into the corridor to join DJ and Shamri. Tony yanked his arm away with a scowl, then crouched down, copying the others. They scuttled along the corridor like four turtles. Bobby heard muffled voices when they passed Rillington's door and paused. He wondered if he reached a hand in he could grab a few of the tapes before ...

Don't even think about it, Bobby Gibson.

Mum was right: they had been lucky so far. Best not to push it. Reluctantly, Bobby moved on until they were clear of the corridor and up the stairs. DJ and Shamri were already sprinting away. Bobby took off after them, with Tony pounding behind him.

Shamri led them back outside.

'Can't believe I dropped those tapes,' said Bobby, glumly.

All he had to show for their time in Rillington's office was broken tape and a split lip.

'Well that was fun,' said Shamri. 'Do you know who those blokes were with Dad?'

Bobby shook his head. 'No. But I'm gonna find out.'

The next lesson was Social Studies, which always felt four times as slow as every other lesson. The only entertainment came when DJ got told off for falling asleep. There was no way any of them would be able to concentrate though, not until they got the chance to listen to the tape.

***

'Earth to Bobson. Come in, Bobson. Over!'

DJ had an upturned plastic cup in his hand. He had made a hole in it, with a pencil.

'You will listen to me, Bobby Gibson!' he boomed, in his best Vader voice. 'It is useless to resist. Don't let yourself be destroyed as Obi-Wan did.'

'Leave off, DJ! I ain't in the mood.'

'Mate, you've barely said a word in hours.'

DJ put the cup beside his plate and started stirring gravy into his mashed potato until it became a thick brown sludge. Bobby didn't know how DJ could eat muck like that.

A fork crossed in front of him, and DJ speared one of his chips before he could react.

'Did you and the new boy really set off a trap in Rillington's office?' asked DJ, as he dipped the stolen chip in his sludge.

Bobby finished his mouthful of chips, which took him longer than usual due to his still painful lip. 'Yeah but I left all those tapes in there. Ada's going to kill me.'

DJ tapped the back of his fork against the cassette tape, its snapped brown tape splayed across the table.

'At least you got this one,' he said. 'Not that I wanted you to find anything, particularly. I was hoping for a quiet life this year.'

'You sure your sister can fix it?'

'Yeah, but it'll cost me big time,' said DJ glumly.

Bobby stared at the school cafeteria entrance as he popped some more chips into his mouth.

'Ada's tougher than all of us, mate. She'll be okay,' said DJ. 'We should be worrying about those scary blokes in Rillington's office. Or should we be calling him Ash?'

DJ burbled on about whether Ash was his real name or a code name, but Bobby tuned him out. He had run to the cafeteria hoping to find Ada waiting, but she was nowhere to be seen. He was starting to get worried about her. She might be proper ill. Had she been sent home after assembly? Or to the hospital?

Over in the lunch queue DJ saw Tony arguing with two bigger lads. 'Not really your new best mate's day is it?' he said, pointing over with his fork.

'He's not my best anything,' Bobby snapped, coming back to himself. 'Our only clue is lying in pieces 'cos of him.'

Him also the reason you found that clue in the first place.

Bobby saw one of the big lads push Tony backwards into several other kids. Before Tony could do anything, the two boys were dragging him over to the exit. The two teachers in the room were too busy talking to see what was going on.

Go help him, Bobby.

'Come off it mum,' murmured Bobby.

Boy don't make me tell you twice.

'I don't even know him.'

You remember the story of the good Samaritan?

Of course he did.

Today that's who you are. Now g'wan.

Bobby groaned, dropped his fork and stood up.

'Where you going?' asked DJ.

'To get my head kicked in, probably,' Bobby answered.

'You know that's Lee Stowts right?' asked DJ.

Bobby slid his tray of chips over to his friend. 'No use both of us getting in trouble. Just keep an eye on my chips for me, yeah?'

'Aye-aye Cap'n Bobby, sir!'

Bobby walked out before he could change his mind. The corridor was empty, but Bobby heard sounds coming from the boy's toilets. He pushed the door open and went in. Little Lee Stowts and his mate were stood either side of Tony. They'd backed him up against the sinks.

Lee slapped Tony hard on the cheek. 'Come on, Church Boy, start jumping.'

'What for?' asked Tony, rubbing his sore cheek.

'Cause you said you ain't got no money. Now jump!'

Tony jumped, and the unmistakable chink of coins came from his trousers.

Lee held out his hand. 'Give it.'

Tony tried to get past, but Lee and his friend grabbed his arms and shoved him back.

'Maybe you didn't hear me, Church Boy? You made me late in the graveyard this morning; I'm in detention 'cos of you, so you're going to pay up. Do it without a fight, and maybe your head stays out of the bog.'

Bobby stuck his chest out and conjured up the meanest look he could manage. Looking tough was half the battle, according to Errol.

'Let him up, Lee,' he ordered.

Lee and his mate rounded on Bobby.

'What you going to do about it, Gibson?' Lee sneered. 'Run to your brother?'

'Come off it Lee, it's his first day. You got the rest of the year to give him grief.'

'I'm starting now. Unless you wanna start something? You starting something, Gibson?'

'I'm stopping something.'

Lee pushed Tony to his mate, who wrapped a beefy arm around his neck. The fiery pipsqueak marched up to Bobby, cracking his knuckles. 'You and whose army, Gibson?'

One of the toilet cubicles opened with a loud creak and Nikki Panilides walked out. Bobby and Lee's mate both gawped at her, neither one knowing quite what to say.

Lee shrank back a little. 'What you doing in here, Nikki? This is the boy's lavs.'

'Any of you lot got a lollipop?' Nikki asked. 'I've run out.'

The boys exchanged looks and one by one they each shook their heads.

'Shame,' said Nikki, and she moved to stand beside Bobby.

'What you doing, Nikki? This ain't got nothing to do with you,' Lee said, looking nervous.

'Being an army, ain't I.'

He wasn't going to let it go. Bobby could see it in his face. Lee couldn't have it get out that he had been scared off by a girl, even if it was Nikki Panilides.

Bobby sighed and raised his fists. This was not going to go well.

The main door swung open forcefully, and Mr Bennett strode in, ready for war.

'And what's going on in here?' he demanded.

Lee's mate released Tony immediately and stepped to the side.

'Nothing sir,' said Lee. 'Just talking.'

Bennett's beady eyes took in the scene before him. 'Doesn't look like nothing to me lad. Why is that boy coughing?'

'We were just having a laugh sir, weren't we?'

Tony said nothing. All he could do was rub his throat and try to catch his breath.

Bennett moved in close to Lee's mate. 'I won't have liars on my football team son, so unless you want to be stuck on the sidelines for the rest of the year, you'd better tell me what's been going on.'

'I didn't want to do it sir, I swear! Lee made me. He said the new kid owed him money.'

'You grass, Andy!'

'That's enough out of you Stowts,' growled Mr Bennett. 'Right. You two, wait outside for me.'

'But sir—'

'OUTSIDE! NOW!'

Lee and Andy darted out, their heads down.

'It's Tadsby, isn't it?' asked Mr Bennett. His voice was quieter once more, but still filled with acid. 'The boy who couldn't remember his school shoes.'

'Yes sir.'

'Making quite the name for yourself today, aren't you lad?'

'Yes sir. Sorry sir.'

Bennett swung on Nikki. 'And I'm sure you've got a very good reason for being in the boy's toilet, girl?'

Bobby saw Nikki clench her fists but she managed to keep the anger from her voice.

'It sounded like someone was being sick in here, sir. My mum's a nurse so I came in to see if I could help.'

'Yes, well. Girls have no place in the boys toilet, am I understood?'

Nikki nodded, looking at the ground.

'We'll say no more about it, then. Get back to lunch, the three of you.'

And with that, Bennett was gone.

Nikki went over to the sink and washed her hands.

'Too easy,' she mumbled to herself.

Bobby and Tony stood staring at her. Tony edged over to Bobby.

'What's she really doing in the boy's toilet?' he whispered. 'And why's she got that patch over her glasses?'

'I look like a flipping mind reader to you?'

'Opticians said it's to sort out my lazy eye or something.' said Nikki, without looking up from the sink. 'You sure none of you have got a lollipop?'

'Think DJ might.'

'Nice one. Let's go.'

Nikki led them out of the toilet. Tony fell into step with Bobby as they headed back to the canteen.

'You better stick with us from now on,' said Bobby. 'Lee ain't going to let that go.'

'Thanks. I will. And sorry again about the tape.'

'Yeah, yeah. Stop banging on about it.'

'You reckon Lee will get suspended or something?'

'Nah. Lee's dad's on the school board. He'll get a telling off, maybe get sent home, but he'll be back. Sid's the one to watch out for. Lee's big sister goes out with him.'

'Who's Sid?'

'Sid Horrun. Fifth year. He's the biggest bully in this place, after Bennett. He pretty much runs the school. He has people like Lee taking money off lower year kids, like us and giving it to him. Lee tried to do me last year then found out my brother was Errol.'

When they got back to their table, Bobby found Ada had returned. She was eating her lunch and talking to DJ. Bobby could not stop the stupid grin spreading across his face when he saw her. 'Ada! I thought they'd sent you home. You alright?'

Ada nodded. 'I was more worried about you two.'

'You took your time,' said DJ. 'You get lost or something?' He glanced over at Nikki, who was staring at him.

'Um. Wotcha Nikki.'

'Bobby says you got a spare lollipop.'

'I was saving it till after my rice pudding,' said DJ, sullenly.

'If it weren't for Nikki we'd be dead, so let her have it, yeah?'

'Fine!' DJ grumped, his good humour soured. He drew a lollipop from his pocket and tossed it to Nikki. She unwrapped it swiftly and popped in her mouth with a satisfied smile, then she then sat at the next-door table.

Bobby put his hand on DJ's shoulder. 'You told Bennett, didn't you? Sent him after us.'

'Only after I made him,' said Ada. 'Mr Big Mouth there was too busy eating to do anything.'

Bobby looked over at his plate. All that remained was a mound of mushy peas and a solitary chip.

'Sorry mate. You did say to eat the chips, right?'

'*Watch*. I said *watch* my chips.'

DJ smiled. 'I thought you wouldn't be able to eat anything after Lee battered you. Looks like you got lucky.'

Bobby sighed and shook his head. Ada was quietly eating her lunch, ignoring all the eyes on her.

Bobby sat beside her and gave her a nudge. 'So, what happened?'

'Nurse said there's nothing wrong with me. Made me feel like a right idiot.' replied Ada. 'She told me to stop imagining things and worrying everyone.'

'What a cow!' said DJ.

'Imagining things? What did you see? What happened to you?' asked Bobby, with real concern.

Ada told them everything, every impossible detail, including the voice in her head. She held Bobby's gaze at that part. It was something they shared now. Bobby shivered when she described the faceless hooded figures filling the hall.

'Like the ones who chased us in the graveyard?' asked Tony, looking worried.

Ada nodded. 'He called them his Faceless.'

'You remember anything else?' asked Bobby.

Ada's brow furrowed. 'No, which is infuriating. How about you? Any luck in Rillington's office?'

As all three boys looked her, Ada pointed her fork at Tony's clothes. 'Despite trying to clean your jackets there's still a fair amount of dust on them that wasn't there this morning. I also spotted Shamri reading a brand new comic which had Bobby's address written on the bottom of the cover. Easy enough to deduce you paid her to let you into Rillington's office.' Ada gave them an angry frown then she took out her notebook, opened it and started writing. 'We can discuss why you did this without me later. For now, just tell me everything from the beginning.'

'I nearly got shot in the head by a poison dart,' Tony blurted.

'From…the…beginning,' said Ada, firmly.

When Bobby and Tony finished talking, DJ slid the cassette tape towards Ada. She picked it up and studied it.

'And you have no idea who those men were?' she asked, drawing a sketch of the tape in her notebook.

Bobby shook his head.

'And now they have all the tapes?'

'Yeah, sorry Ada,' said Bobby.

A thoughtful expression settled over Ada's face. 'It seems we have more questions than answers. Who are the Faceless Scholars? I believe this 'Salus Key' is the box Langley gave me but what does it open? And what was on those other tapes?'

'We could have found out if Smiley hadn't smacked me and made me drop 'em,' snapped Bobby.

'I said I was sorry,' said Tony, defensively.

Bobby turned to Ada, ignoring the apology. 'You said Langley called Mr Rillington Agent Ash, right?'

'Correct.'

'Well, one of the men we saw was called Agent Orlando. What if they were working together? We know Ash works for that ESD lot but maybe those blokes do as well?'

Ada nodded. 'A sound hypothesis, Bobson. There is a high probability that they are all connected to this ESD, whatever that means.'

'I wouldn't trust 'em as far as I could throw 'em,' said DJ. 'They looked well dodgy.'

'So how about we go and see that detective lady, yeah?' Tony pleaded. 'We've got a tape to show them as evidence... Right?'

Everyone turned to look at him, stone-faced. Tony continued, undaunted.

'I mean, come on! I've been beaten up, chased through a graveyard. I almost got shot in the head by a poisoned dart today!'

'How do you know it was poisoned?' asked DJ.

'It came out of a hole in the wall - of course it was poisoned! And what if it wasn't? I'd still be dead! Those hooded nutters kidnapped a teacher, and the detective is trying to find him. We know stuff now that could help her.'

'And tell her what? That Ada saw Mr Rillington get grabbed by some see-through monsters who shoot lightning from their fingers? Or maybe we could show them that tape you busted. 'Bobson's right,' said Ada. 'The police are never going to believe my story, no one is. Not unless we get more proof. Fixing that tape would be a start.'

'I believe you.'

Nikki was still sitting alone at the next table over, sucking her lollipop.

'How much of that did you hear?' asked Ada.

'Enough.'

Ada smiled. 'Thanks Nikki but I think we're going to need more than that to go to the police,'

Nikki finished her lollipop with a noisy crunch and tossed the stick onto DJ's lunch tray. 'I saw one of those hooded things you were talking about.'

Ada sat forward. 'What?'

'You know the new estate they're building up near the grave-yard? The Baxter estate?'

'Hang on a sec,' Ada took out her notebook, opened it and started writing. 'Yes I know the estate. What about it?'

'Two days ago a couple of older lads at my uncle's snooker hall dared me to go there. They said some of the workmen had quit 'cos of seeing some weird stuff. They reckoned its haunted.'

'Go on.'.

'When I got up there I saw one of those hooded things and an-other bloke chanting or something on the roof,' Nikki pointed at Ada's open notebook. 'One of 'em was holding that.'

Ada turned the book around. The others gasped. The page Nikki was pointing at had a detailed sketch of the Salus Key.

'What happened next?' asked Ada.

'The hooded bloke started banging on about how he's found it, and then they just...disappeared, like. It was well creepy, so I legged it.'

'Proper disappeared?' said Bobby, fascinated.

'Like a ghost. Gone.'

'A haunted block of flats? Come off it' Tony grumbled.

'We've seen worse,' said DJ, sharing a concerned look with Bobby and Ada.

'That'd be the Norfolk thing you keep going on about right?' asked Tony.

'We need to consult an expert,' said Ada, ignoring Tony. 'I propose we meet at my place after school.'

'No way am I coming to your house to talk monsters again,' said DJ. 'I'm with Tony.'

Nikki shrugged. 'Beats watching Blue Peter. I'll be there.'

'Wait,' said Ada. 'You don't know where I live.'

'Course I do. Your name's painted in bleeding big letters on the shop window,' Nikki hauled her bag onto her shoulders. 'I go past it on the way to school'

'Am I the only one she creeps out?' whispered DJ, once Nikki had left.

'I like her,' said Ada. 'She pays attention.'

'Anyway,' said Tony. 'Cheers for helping out in the toilets but—'

Ada cut him off. 'We're the only ones who know that hooded man and those monsters took Mr Rillington. That means it's up to us to get him back.'

'No it doesn't,' said Tony 'We're just a bunch of kids and you didn't see those blokes. Who knows what would have happened if they caught us. We should just give the box to Mr Wattling and—'

'Come to my house and I'll show you what a bunch of kids can do! Bobby and DJ can bring you.'

'You sure about this Ada?' asked DJ. 'Maybe Smiley's right maybe we should give the box to Wattling.'

Ada stood, grinning in that way that sent twin jolts of excitement and terror down Bobby's spine. Mum's voice cut through his excitement.

Dat girl's too fast fe her own good. She's gonna get you all killed.

'Never! Not now the game is afoot,' Ada announced, gathering her things together.

See.

'What's that mean?' asked Tony, as Ada bustled off.

DJ let out a heavy sigh that matched his gloomy expression. 'It means everything's gonna get a lot scarier.'

10

The Consulting Room

'Can't believe I'm doing this,' mumbled Tony as he followed DJ and Bobby along the busy high street.

'I can't believe we're letting you,' said Bobby. 'Right mate?'

DJ, who was shoving a handful of small red cubes into his mouth from a paper bag, managed an enthusiastic nod. Bobby reached for the bag but DJ snatched it away.

'Hands off mate! You had your chance to buy some in the—' snapped DJ.

Bobby's hand whipped out again, but this time he managed to grab a few Cola Cubes.

'Oi!' shouted DJ, beyond outraged.

Bobby popped one of the cubes into his mouth and started making exaggerating sucking sounds, rolling his eyes in pleasure. He handed one of the sweets to Tony.

'You best sleep with one eye open, mate' warned DJ.

'Yeah, yeah,' said Bobby, grinning.

'Is it much further?' asked Tony.

'You got somewhere else to be, new boy?' asked DJ.

'My name's Tony.'

'Whatever. Didn't you ring your mum to tell her you were going to be late?'

'Yeah, but I told her I was having some food at a friend's house.' Tony rubbed his stomach. 'So she's not doing anything for dinner.'

Bobby offered him his last Cola Cube. 'Make it last then, yeah?'

Tony took the cube and slipped it into his mouth. He sucked his cheeks as the sugary sharpness hit his tongue.

Bobby waved at some older kids across the street.

'Back in a minute,' said Bobby, jogging off.

'Mates of his brother Errol, I reckon,' DJ muttered. 'Errol knows everyone.'

'Wish I had a big brother,' Tony said.

'Yeah, no one messes with Bobby, except Sid sometimes. Errol looks out for him.'

'When we were in Rillington's office I heard Bobby talking to his mum.'

'So?' said DJ, popping in another Cola Cube.

'I thought his mum was dead?'

'Doesn't stop her talking to him. His dad and aunt took him to a head doctor last year to get it sorted. Fat lot of good that did.'

'So he's nuts then?' asked Tony.

DJ grabbed Tony, pulling him up close. 'Say that again, Smiley, you'll be eating my fist instead of my Cola Cubes. Got it?'

Tony nodded vigorously.

'Dunno why I told you in the first place,' muttered DJ. 'You best not say anything to anyone.'

'I won't,' Tony promised. Why was he even here? He wished he was back at home. It was sausages and mash tonight.

Bobby crossed back to join them.

'Come on,' he said, continuing along the street.

They walked on for a little while until Bobby stopped beside a large shop window, across which the words *'Amaya's Books - A Sanctuary for your Imagination'* were painted in large silver letters.

Pressing his nose against the window, Tony saw row upon row of books. People were scattered throughout the shop examining book covers, flipping pages or chatting. There was a section of tables and chairs to one side, full of people with mugs in one hand and books in the other.

'This is where she lives?' asked Tony, his wrinkled nose pressed to the glass.

'Yup. Come on,' said Bobby, pushing the door open.

The silence was the first thing that struck Tony upon entering the bookshop. The only real noise came from the clanking of tea-cups in the seated area. The shop was quieter than even the library in Tony's old town, which never had more than ten people in it at any one time.

'Why are there people drinking tea?' asked Tony, bewildered.

'It was Ada's idea,' explained Bobby. 'People can read the books they buy over a cuppa, plus there's a stack of used books people bring in that anyone can read.'

Tony frowned. 'What for free?'

'Yeah. But most of them end up buying the used books any-way,' DJ said, from behind. 'Book people are weird.'

'Your mum loves books,' pointed out Bobby.

'And she's weird. She did the washing up in roller skates last week.'

Tony followed Bobby and DJ through the shop. Both boys said hello to the staff who were busy stacking bookshelves. They head-ed towards a queue of people waiting to pay. A few of them threw dirty looks in their direction as though they thought they were try-ing to jump to the queue. The boys held up their hands to show they were empty. A woman stood behind the counter. She had dark brown skin, and a cream blouse that shone in the sunlight.

She was in the middle of serving a bald white man in a thick red sweater, who had just dumped a stack of books down.

'You're going to bankrupt me, Mrs Amaya,' said the man, offering a wide smile.

The woman laughed and flashed an even wider smile and a wink as she tapped away on the cash register.

'I'll take that as a compliment, coming from a Bank Manager, Harold. But how many times do I have to tell you? Call me Nneka?'

Mrs Amaya sounded a lot like Ada, but her accent was thicker.

'Sorry Nneka,' said Harold, fishing out a wad of cash. He noticed Tony, DJ and Bobby and his smile vanished. He turned slightly away from them to hide his wallet.

'Don't mind us mate,' said DJ. 'We ain't mugged anyone in days.'

'Dibney!' snapped Mrs Amaya.

DJ grinned. 'Sorry Mrs A.'

'You know these...these children?' Harold spat out the words.

'For my sins, yes,' said Mrs Amaya, with a chuckle. She took the cash from Harold and deposited it in the register. 'Two of them are friends of my daughter. This one, though...'

She slammed the till shut and peered at Tony for several uncomfortable seconds.

'You two been picking up strays?'

'We tried taking him to the vets, but he keeps following us around,' said DJ.

'I see. And does this stray boy have a name?' asked Mrs Amaya as she packed Harold's books for him.

'It's Tony, miss. Tony Tadsby.'

Mrs Amaya handed the bags to Harold then tapped the gold ring on her finger. 'Such flattery! Do I look like a 'miss' to you, eh?'

Tony was halfway through a stuttered apology when Mrs Amaya's belly laugh shattered the tension. He looked around horrified, but very few of the customers even looked up. It was unnerving.

'Not too quick, your stray,' said Mrs Amaya, signalling to another member of staff.

A bright-eyed teenage girl in brown dungarees slipped behind the counter and soon the queue was moving again.

Satisfied her customers were being taken care of, Mrs Amaya waved the boys towards her.

'How was Nigeria Mrs A?' asked DJ as they passed.

'It was lovely thank you, DJ. There is no substitute for spending time with friends and family. Ada was eager to return so she could discover new ways to turn my hair grey.'

Mrs Amaya patted DJ's shoulder with her right hand and snatched two cola cubes with her left while he was distracted.

'Mrs A!' shrieked DJ, clutching his bag to his chest.

Mrs Amaya set the sweets down beside the till for later. 'The use of my storeroom for your private meetings must be paid for, young man. I am grateful for your custom.'

She stepped back and opened the door behind her, revealing a dark corridor. DJ headed through, disappearing into the gloom. Bobby came up next. 'And how are you doing, Bobby?'

'I'm good thanks, Mrs A.'

Mrs Amaya looked down at Bobby with fondness, and a little bit of concern. She placed her hands on Bobby's shoulders and bent her knees until their faces were level.

'My door is always open Bobby,' she said quietly. 'If you need to talk about things. I know what it feels like to lose someone, and so does Ada. If you ever want to—'

'Seriously.' Bobby said quickly, covering his sharp tone with a smile. 'I'm fine Mrs A. But thank you.'

Mrs Amaya straightened up and gave a tight smile. 'Very well. But the offer remains. I trust you won't be letting my daughter get you into any trouble this year?'

'I'll do my best,' said Bobby.

'You know, I always said she had too much of her father in her.'

Mrs Amaya fell silent, her face solemn.

'Mrs A?'

'I'm fine Bobby, I'm fine. You go on,' said Mrs Amaya hurriedly, her eyes growing mistier by the second. 'If you're still here when the shop closes, I'll give you all a lift home.'

'Cheers Mrs A,' said Bobby, heading through the door.

Tony moved to follow then hesitated. He glanced back at the shop door and the bright sky outside.

'Making new friends is never easy,' said Mrs Amaya, rubbing her eyes and smiling at Tony. 'But trust me – those three are worth the trouble.'

Tony wondered if Mrs Amaya would feel the same if she knew even half of what was going on.

'Oi, Smiley! You coming or what?' Bobby's voice echoed down the passageway.

Mrs Amaya waved him though. 'Trouble is calling, Tony. The question is…are you going to answer?'

Tony took a deep breath, thanked Mrs Amaya and stepped through the doorway, where Bobby was waiting. The pair set off down the corridor.

'Ada's folks own this whole place?' asked Tony.

'Ada's mum does,' replied Bobby.

'Wow! How does she afford it?'

'There was an accident where Ada's dad worked. It was the company's fault so they gave Ada's mum some cash. It was enough to buy this place.'

They reacched the end of the corridor, ahead of them was a metal staircase winding down into the gloom.

'Is her dad alright now?'

'Nope, he's dead. Come on.'

Bobby headed down the staircase.

Tony froze, his hand tight around the bannister. Before today he had never met anyone whose Mum or Dad had died, now he had met two.

He started down the staircase after Bobby, deciding he was going to give Mum and Dad the biggest hug they had ever had when he got home.

There was a warm light at the bottom of the staircase and he could hear voices.

'I can't believe you didn't tell us!' DJ's voice echoed from below.

Tony started moving again and heard Ada reply. 'Stop overreacting it's only research.'

'Your research is gonna get us killed!' shrieked DJ. 'I don't believe you didn't tell us!'

Tony reached the bottom of the staircase and stepped into a large open space. In the centre stood Ada, mistress of all she surveyed. Around her were arranged two battered brown sofas and four armchairs, covered in patches. They looked as though they might collapse if you looked at them too hard. Nikki lay across the sofa, her fingers clasped behind her head in blissful relaxation. DJ was sat on the other sofa, looking far from happy.

Ada saw Tony, and her face split into a toothy grin.

'Ah, there you are. Welcome to the consulting room!'

11

The Faceless Scholars

Tony stared at the countless books stacked on wooden shelves, stretching back into the darkness along the left-hand wall. Piles of precariously balanced old and battered books were scattered throughout the room, like tiny towers of knowledge.

'Mum didn't need all this space for the books so she cleared out a space for me to use,' explained Ada.

Tony had a question but it caught up in a sudden bout of sneezing.

DJ waved a hand in front of his nose. 'I know. Smells like bleeding wet cardboard and rotten eggs in here, right?'

'I... think... it's fantastic,' sniffed Tony, zeroing in on the large bowl of crisps perched on a side table.

Ada took in the room as though seeing it in a new light. 'Yes, I suppose it is' She clapped her hands twice in irritation. 'Bobby Gibson that is an ancient artefact, *not* a toy for you to fiddle with every five minutes.'

'Why you having a go at me?' grumbled Bobby. He stuffed the wooden box back into Ada's satchel.

'Because I expect that kind of behaviour from DJ, not you.'

'Rude...,' said DJ. 'Anyway I'm not telling porkies to his mates.'

Ada sighed. 'For the last time not telling you something is not the same as lying.'

'Whatever!' snapped DJ.

Nikki made no attempt to move her legs, so Tony sat down beside the fuming DJ. He scooped up a handful of crisps and stuffed them into his mouth. On the table in front of Tony were several roughly shaped pieces of paper sat beside a large open book. Looking closer, he could see that two of the pages were filled with stories torn out of newspapers. Beside the book was a small pile of more newspaper stories and a half-squeezed tube of glue.

'What's this?' asked Tony, tapping the book

'My Book of Mysteries,' said Ada as though everybody had one.

'The only mystery is why she didn't tell us about it,' muttered DJ as Tony flicked through the book.

'Shut up, DJ. It's not like you tell me everything you do!'

'I'm not going to shut up!' DJ yelled. 'You *promised*, Ada. We all did.'

'Vampires in Tokyo,' said Tony, staring at one of the headlines plastered onto the open page of Ada's book. 'Huh. That's a joke, right?'

Ada marched across the room and snatched the book from him.

'I never joke about mysteries,' she snapped.

Tony shrugged and started picking through the newspaper clippings instead.

'A freak snowstorm in Jamaica; a Yeti spotted in East Germany; thirteen tourists disappear on Easter Island on Friday the thirteenth—why have you got all this?'

'Because she's m—'

'Finish that sentence, Dibney Jennings and you'll be limping home.'

DJ gave an annoyed grunt.

Ada scooped up the clippings and began sliding them into the book.

Bobby sighed. 'DJ's right though, Ada. You should have told us what you were doing.'

'Someone needed to make sure that if anything like Norfolk happened again, we were ready for it.' Ada patted the book. 'This is me making sure we're ready.'

Bobby kissed his teeth and muttered something under his breath. Tony raised a hand.

'What?' snarled Ada.

'Are you ever going to tell me what happened in Norfolk?'

'NO!' the three shrieked.

'Alright, alright. I was just checking.'

Tony glanced at Nikki, who was still blissfully reclined. Anyone'd think she didn't have a sofa at home. Tony half expected her to purr. There were a few awkward moments, filled with crisp crunching and heavy sighs. Ada paced.

'Nikki. You said you said you saw the hooded things at the Baxter Estate, right?' asked Ada.

Nikki's eyes – well the one not hidden behind a plaster – stayed closed, but she managed a slow nod.

'You sure?'

Another nod.

'Good. I'll be right back!' She slammed the book of mysteries back onto the table and sprinted up the spiral staircase.

Tony reached for the book again.

'TOUCH IT AND DIE!'

Ada's bellowed threat swept down the staircase like a hurricane. Tony's hand snapped back.

'She always like that?' asked Tony.

'Sometimes she's worse,' answered Bobby with a smile.

Tony managed another three nervous handfuls of crisps before he heard the rattle of footsteps on the iron staircase. Behind Ada came a white boy, older than Errol, wearing thick tortoiseshell glasses and a look of intense annoyance. He cradled a chunky leather-bound book under his left arm. With a twist of the head, Tony managed to read the words 'History of the Mongolian Empire' on the spine.

'Wotcha Henry,' said DJ, waving.

Tony shrank into his chair as the boy eyed him.

'Oh great, there's more of you now,' said the boy in a flat tone. 'You said you had something important to show me but now I'm here it's already a waste of my time.'

'Same old Henry,' muttered Bobby. Ada moved to block Henry's view of the Book of Mysteries. 'Look we just want to ask you about the Baxter Estate.'

Henry walked further into the room. 'Why?'

'It's for a school project,' said Ada.

Henry eyes fell on DJ and Bobby who treated him to a succession of nods.

'Your mum pays me to stock books you know, not to do your homework.'

'Don't be a muppet all your life Henry,' said DJ.

'I will not be spoken to like that!' snapped Henry, and he turned back towards the staircase.

'Aw, come on, Hen. I'll tell my sister how much you helped us.' DJ called after him. 'You remember my sister, right?'

When Henry faced them again, his cheeks were crimson.

'You've got five minutes.'

Ada went to where her rucksack lay propped against one of the armchairs. Reaching in she drew out the Salus Key.

Henry's eyes widened. 'Where...?'

'We found it at the Baxter estate,' replied Ada.

'No, we—ow!'

'Like Ada said, we found it at the new estate,' said DJ, patting Tony's arm.

Henry walked towards Ada, his hands stretched towards the box. They were trembling.

'I want it back,' Ada cautioned him.

Henry nodded. Taking the box, he carefully rotated it in his hands, examining every part of it.

'Exquisite. It's exquisite.'

'Ex-what?' asked Tony.

Henry didn't answer, instead he twisted a section of the box sharply to the right, which clicked loudly in response. Ada reached for the Salus Key then froze. Henry was now twisting, sliding and pulling at different sections of it.

'Did you lot know it could do that?' asked Nikki, who had shifted into an upright position on the sofa.

Bobby slowly shook his head.

'How…how did you do that?' asked Ada, staring at the Salus Key as though she were seeing it for the first time.

'It's a puzzle box,' replied Henry, his eyes focused on his movements. 'Ones like this were first created back in the 19th century. They usually contained secret compartments. This one is particularly tricky I'm not surprised you didn't realise you could move the pieces.'

There were more clicks as several of the pieces slid into different places.

Ada stepped closer, her eyes wide. Bobby got out of his chair to join her. Even DJ had stopped eating to watch.

'You solve the puzzle to learn the secret.'

Henry started rotating a large misshapen section on the right side of the box. The minute the section moved, several pieces which had already been fixed into place shifted position. Henry swore and started on another section.

A hushed silence fell over the group, broken only by the sounds of Henry working to solve the Salus Key.

'Never seen one as complex as this,' Henry muttered. 'Nothing like the ones we have in the Museum.'

'Museum?' asked Tony.

'Henry works at a big fancy one, up west,' explained Bobby, still staring at the box.

'If by 'up west' you mean the West End then, yes,' said Henry.

'I thought you worked here?'

'Twice a week after college, but I work at the museum on weekends and during the holidays,' said Henry. He changed tactics and started moving individual pieces of the box rather than whole sections.

'Dunno how they put up with you,' Bobby prodded.

'I'm the smart, respectful and cool employee everyone wished they had,' Henry crowed proudly.

Tony saw nothing cool about a someone wearing a red and white polka dot bow tie, but he kept that to himself.

DJ leapt forward, grabbing the box before Henry could stop him.

'Lemme have a go at it. My dad uses stuff like this all the time in his magic shows.'

DJ lifted a tiny piece of the box, slid it up with his thumb then clicked it back down into place. Turning the box over in his hands, he spotted another piece that looked like it might move. He tried pushing it in different directions but it wouldn't budge. He swore and started on another piece, his thumb turning red as he pushed hard to move it.

'Give it here before you break it,' snapped Henry, snatching back the box. 'Some magician you are.'

DJ stomped back to the sofa, without a word. Tony thought he looked genuinely upset by Henry's words. 'What can you tell us about the estate, Henry?' asked Ada.

'I know why people think it's haunted,' he murmured. 'There's history behind that place. Of course, it's all nonsense and superstition.'

'Just tell us,' said Ada.

Henry cursed and flipped the box over. He scratched his chin. 'Hm? Oh. The estate is built on what used to be a meeting place for the Faceless Scholars,' explained Henry.

Tony spat out a mouth full of crisps. He could feel the hairs go up on the back of his neck.

'No need to wet yourself,' said Henry. 'The Faceless Scholars were just a bunch of very rich seventeenth century academics, during the Scientific Renaissance, with way too much time on their hands.'

'But we saw—ow!'

Again, DJ patted Tony's arm, soothing the bruise he'd just left there.

Ada smiled sweetly at Henry. 'Go on.'

Henry gave Tony a confused look, then continued. 'The Faceless Scholars were obsessed with the occult. They travelled the world searching for mythical artefacts.'

'Artefacts?' asked Bobby.

'Objects. In this case, objects believed to have supernatural powers: Pandora's Box, the Spear of Destiny, The Swords of Solomon, the Ark of the Covenant. You name it, the Scholars were looking for it.'

The kids exchanged worried glances – except for Nikki, who was quite possibly asleep.

'Why did the scholars want that stuff in the first place?' asked Bobby.

'Just like any other group of powerful people throughout history, they wanted more power. I suppose they thought magic would give them an edge.'

'How do you know all this stuff about them?' asked Tony.

'Ah! Well, when they first started work on the Baxter Estate, they found an underground cavern stuffed with all kinds of relics. It was in the newspapers,' said Henry. 'Fascinating stuff. The museum wanted to get a delegation down there but—'

'But they're still building the estate. How come it wasn't stopped?' asked Bobby.

'Some new company took over,' replied Henry, sniffily. 'They brought in their own experts to conduct the survey. Kept us out of it. The company has promised to donate some of the pieces to our museum, but it stinks to high heaven.'

'What do you mean?' asked Ada.

'No one can get to the cavern anymore. Who knows what information we might have gleaned that these idiots have missed? And who knows what they've kept for themselves? It's too late now, anyway, because they've filled in the cavern and started to build a dirty great tower block on top of it.'

Tony's stomach gave a loud gargling sound, though he couldn't tell if it was down to hunger or fear. Ancient cults and magic artefacts - it was all a bit creepy for his taste.

'Does the name Langley have anything to do with them?' asked Ada.

'Yes! Yes it does,' replied Henry. He looked both surprised and impressed by this leap. 'You have been doing your homework! There was a Bertram Langley who was quite infamous actually. He was expelled from the order and imprisoned.'

'Why?' asked Ada.

'No one knows why. Secrets of the Order. Langley later escaped and was never heard from again.'

'What happened to the rest of the Scholars?' asked Bobby.

'There was some nonsense about a curse killing them all, but the evidence is circumstantial at best.'

Tony gulped. 'A curse? Like in those old mummy films?

Henry looked annoyed at this. 'Listen If you want a real expert on this stuff, try Lucas Carnaby. He runs an antique shop called Carnaby's Antiques on Turfouth Lane. He knows more about this kind of thing than I ever will. Tried to get a job with him once, but the miserable sod shut the door in my face.'

'Great! We'll go and see him now,' Ada announced. The others seemed less than enthusiastic. The traitors all had homework or chores that they'd suddenly remembered were waiting for them. Ada was fuming.

Henry laughed and shook his head. 'It's no good going now anyway,' he said. 'Carnaby keeps weird hours. His shop's only opens between twelve and three during the week.'

'What kind of businessman opens their shop for three hours a day?' asked Ada.

'The lazy kind?' DJ suggested.

Tony was delighted. 'We'll be in school when the shop's open. Nothing we can do about it.'

'Can we call him, then?' asked Ada. 'Arrange to meet him?'

Tony guessed that she and her mum got on really well. His parents would never have allowed him to use the home phone.

'Carnaby's not going to talk to a bunch of kids over the phone.'

Henry adjusted his glasses then returned his attention to the Salus Key. 'But get this in front of him, and he'll be all ears, I'm sure.'

'Yeah right,' said Bobby. 'The only way we can see him is if we sneak out during a lunch break and no way I'm doing that.'

'Maybe if we're very careful we could do it.'

'Come off it Ada,' said DJ. 'I'm not risking getting suspended or the cane over some old bloke we don't even know will help us.'

Henry looked at Ada over the rims of his glasses. 'I guess I could take this to the museum; see if anyone there can help?' His tone bordered on begging.

Ada snatched the box out of Henry's sweaty hands. 'That's okay. I've got this. Thanks anyway.'

'That should be in a museum!' he snapped.

'So should you, mate,' chuckled Bobby.

Henry opened his mouth but Mrs Amaya's voice bellowed his name down the stairs. He was needed in the shop. Now!

Henry gave the box one last look, then he raced back to the staircase. 'Promise me you'll give that puzzle box to somebody responsible.'

Everyone gave Henry their best 'of course we will' look.

Henry scowled, then stomped his way up the staircase. No one said anything until the door at the end of the corridor slammed shut.

'Great. We still don't know anything much,' mumbled Bobby.

'We know the Faceless Scholars got killed by a curse,' whispered Tony, his head scanning the room as though some mummy was about to jump out from behind a bookcase.

'Pack it in, Smiley. He said that was just a stupid rumour. We don't know anything.'

'That's not true, Bobson,' said Ada, in detective mode once more. 'We now know that the Faceless Scholars still exist in some form. They didn't all die. We can now surmise that this puzzle box is a supernatural artefact and that it is key to their plans – or perhaps it *contains* the key to their plans within. Hm?'

Tony's mouth opened in awe. 'But…how do you know?' asked Tony, still trying to catch up.

'Because it is my business to know—' said Ada.

'What other people do not know,' cut in Nikki, who was now sitting up.

Ada stared at Nikki.

'The Adventure of the Blue Carbuncle, right?' asked Nikki.

Ada nodded.

DJ threw himself backwards into the chair and rolled his eyes dramatically. 'Do me a favour... Not you too.'

'How many Sherlock Holmes books have you read?' asked Ada, thrilled to find another fan.

'I've only got three at the moment but Dad's going to get me some more.'

'If you can show us where you saw that hooded man after school tomorrow I'll show you my entire collection,' offered Ada. 'I've read them all. You can borrow as many as you want.'

'Pfft. I would have taken you anyway. You don't have to bribe me.'

'Why would you help us?' asked Bobby. 'You've barely ever spoken to us before; now you want to go to a spooky estate with us?'

'You weren't doing interesting things before. Well, not before Norfolk, anyway. I want in.'

'That's sorted then,' said Ada, rubbing her hands together. 'Welcome to the investigation.'

Nikki blushed then tried to cover it with a yawn.

'What you up to Ada?' asked Bobby.

'My guess is the tower block where Nikki saw Langley is the same one Henry was talking about, built on the site of the Faceless Scholars' old meeting place,' she mused. 'Perhaps we can find some proof up there to take to the police.'

'We?' snapped DJ, shaking his head. 'Nah, not me. Not this time.'

'The police again?' asked Bobby. 'You're having a laugh ain't you? I'm not going to that lot, no way.'

'A teacher's been kidnapped by a centuries-old group of occultists.' said Ada, exasperated. 'Even I know we need help.'

'Those coppers didn't believe us in Norfolk,' said Bobby, folding his arms. 'Not that I wanted to go see them then either.'

'This time we'll have evidence. This time they will have to believe us,' said Ada.

'Dunno about that but I'm up for the estate,' said Bobby. 'I can tell Auntie Carol that I've stayed late for chess club.'

'Of course *you're* going,' huffed DJ, jumping up. 'You'd follow Ada off a bloody cliff you would!'

Bobby gave him a hard look. What was he getting mad at him for?

'We got to do something mate,' said Bobby. 'What if it was your mum or dad who got snatched?'

DJ's shoulders slumped and he slid back onto the sofa. 'I hate you all, you know that right? Like…proper hate, no messing about.'

'Yeah we know,' said Bobby, the corner of his mouth twitching into a smile.

'Mum's late home most days anyway,' sighed DJ. 'And Dad will believe anything I tell him, the daft sod.'

Ada turned to Tony. 'So what about it, Tony? You up for an adventure?'

Tony stood up, his hand on his stomach, taking in deep lungfuls of air. 'Can you tell me where the toilet is, please? I think I'm going to be sick.'

12

Gathering Data

The entire science class greeted the bell with a collection of groans and frustrated sighs. Most of Bobby's classmates were still measuring and pouring various liquids into glass beakers when home time was announced. Ordinarily, it would have been a relief, but unless you enjoyed running around a football pitch, messing about with science experiment was the most fun you could have in a school day.

Mr Roebrush called out above the din. 'Remember to turn off your Bunsen burners before you leave. I don't want to explain to the Fire Brigade how one of my pupils managed to burn down the school.'

Some of the class started chuckling, while others begun chanting the word Burn.

'Yes, yes, that's enough of that now,' said Roebrush with a dark twinkle in his eye. 'Maybe next year.'

It was a good job everyone liked Mr Roebrush, because it was hard to fear a squeaky-voiced teacher who was shorter than most of his pupils.

Bobby flicked off the gas tap and watched the flickering thin blue flame vanish. He hung his lab coat up and left to wait in the corridor for DJ and Tony, who had managed the unthinkable and made Mr Roebrush angry.

You remember what your auntie told you?

'No more trouble,' Bobby said, smiling to himself. 'Anyway, it's only trouble if we get caught, Mum.'

The sound of Mum kissing her teeth echoed inside Bobby's head. That was the problem with having a dead mum in your head: she never left you alone.

You nah go nowhere.

'I have to go to the estate, Mum. I promised,' he whispered.

Short cut draw blood, boy.

Bobby ignored Mum's warning and peered through one of the glass panels on the classroom door. Mr Roebrush was shouting and making a lot of angry gestures at DJ and Tony. At last, DJ left the classroom, stomping past Bobby.

'He gave me an essay,' DJ muttered as Bobby fell into step beside him. 'It's only the second day back, and I'm already in trouble. Mum's going to do her nut when she finds out!'

'It's not my fault you can't read instructions,' said Tony, who had now caught up.

'I said one pinch, not the whole flipping bag!' shouted DJ.

'You said one *handful*,' pressed Tony, 'and that's what I told Mr Roebrush.'

DJ shoved Bobby out of the way, grabbed Tony by his jacket lapels and rammed him against the wall. 'You did what?'

Tony glared back at DJ, trying to push him off.

Bobby grabbed DJ's arm and pulled him away. 'Stop mucking about, we got places to be.'

'You wait, Smiley, I'm so getting you back for this one!' Without another word, DJ released Tony and stalked away.

Tony began straightening his tie and blazer. 'I dunno why he's having a go at me for – he knows he did it.'

'He's mad because you didn't back up his story,' said Bobby. 'You dropped him right in it. That ain't what mates do.'

'Is that what we are? Mates? Since when?' Tony snapped. 'Ada's been good to me, but the rest of you treat me like dirt. You can't even remember my name!' Tony shoved past him, and strode after DJ, slamming his bag against the lockers in anger.

Thick laughter resounded in the darkness of Bobby's mind.

I like dat boy.

'You like everyone, Mum.'

Me never like that Archie. Me sorry for what happened to him, but me glad him gone.

Bobby said nothing. He hoped his silence would stop Mum from launching into one of her epic rants; they always left him with a sore head. He caught up with Tony and DJ, each pointedly ignoring one another. They walked in silence to the school gates, where Ada and Nikki were waiting. Ada had her arms crossed. She was tapping her right foot. Her eyes narrowed as the boys approached.

'Before you start, it was these two,' Bobby said quickly.

DJ opened his mouth, but Ada beat him to it.

'I don't want to hear it,' said Ada. 'Just tell me your sister fixed the cassette tape.'

DJ shrugged. 'She says genius takes time.'

Bobby chuckled, then immediately regretted it.

'You think this is funny, Bobson?' asked Ada, hands on her hips, eyes set to kill. 'That tape is the only proper clue we have.'

'Wasn't my fault the stupid thing got snapped,' said Bobby, looking at Tony. 'Why don't we go back to Rillington's office? Those blokes would be long gone by now.'

'No point,' said Ada. 'I spoke to Shamri. She already went back to check. All his stuff was gone.'

The bus was crammed full and chaotic. There wasn't space to sit together, so each of them were left holding on to their own anxieties. Bobby was forced to listen to Mum telling him to leave now and go home every single time the bus stopped. Eventually it pulled up in front of an empty, blackened building where the five of them got off. Nikki explained the building had been a pub until it burnt down several years earlier. They followed Nikki for a few more minutes until she stopped at a muddy path. She placed her hands on her hips.

'Behold. One spooky estate.'

Bobby wished he had listened to his mum as he stared at the site in the fading light. The buildings were in different states of completion and most were still covered in scaffolding. They looked like ugly grey and white boxes thrown carelessly together. Parked near the entrance was a digger and three dump trucks. They reminded Bobby of the Tonka trucks he had once craved for Christmas.

'Are we really going to do this?' Tony asked nervously. 'What about the curse stuff Henry told us about?'

No one's forcing you to come, Smiley,' said Bobby. He took courage from Tony's fear somehow, and set off at a stride.

Nikki caught up and pointed out a small hut up ahead, tucked away on the right-hand corner.

'Security guard's office,' she warned, and led them down the hill to a side street which ended at a high wire fence. It seemed to run the full length of the estate. A large sign was set at adult height, bearing the words, '**KEEP OUT by order of Aeternus Incorporated**'. Underneath the words there was a black figure eight symbol, lying on its side. Ada stepped up to the sign, pulled out her notebook and started scribbling away on a blank page.

'What are you doing?' asked Tony.

'Gathering data,' she replied without looking up. 'This must be the new company Henry told us about – the ones building the new tower block.'

Nikki tapped the fence, which was just a little higher than her head. 'This is where I got in last time,' she explained. On the other side of the fence were several wooden pallets which, along with some paving slabs had been stacked against the fence.

Ada was able to get her fingers through the gaps, but they were too small for the flat toes of her shoes to fit in. She could only get a few inches up before she dropped back, defeated. 'How did you get over that on your own?'

Nikki reached under a green sheet of tarpaulin shoved off to the side, and dragged out an orange milk crate.

DJ whistled in respect.

Hopping onto the crate, Nikki grabbed the top of the fence with both hands, swung a leg up, then levered herself over the top. She dropped onto the wooden pallets on the other side, hopped to the ground and gave them a little bow.

Bobby went next. He didn't bother with the crate. Instead, he took a run at the fence, leapt up and swung himself over. He grinned back at the others. 'Come on; it's easy.'

Ada was next over, treading on DJ's cupped hands. She wasn't elegant, but she didn't make a fuss about it either.

Tony stepped up onto the crate and looked through the fence at them. He did not look eager.

Bad enough you get yourself into trouble, you got to drag this poor nice boy along?

'Not now Mum,' Bobby whispered.

You know who him look like? Him look like your cousin Daryl.

Tony took a deep breath through his nostrils, then hoisted himself up onto the fence. He swung one leg over, then the other. There was a ripping sound as he dropped onto the wooden pallets, and he looked horrified. His hand flew to his rear, checking for damage to his trousers.

DJ started giggling.

He made the ripping sound with his mouth again, then laughed even harder.

'Leave it out DJ,' said Bobby. 'You don't have to be a git all your life.'

DJ was last over. He stumbled on the landing, but was caught and steadied by Nikki. She patted him on the shoulder and gave him a nod.

With Nikki taking the lead, they made their way into the deserted estate. Keep Out signs were plastered everywhere. As they walked along, Nikki explained that the builders generally stopped work about four and headed to the local café, where one of her cousins worked. Bobby wished some of the builders were still here. He didn't know what was worst: the silence or the occasional screeching sound the wind made as it swept through the half-finished husks of concrete and metal. There were no lights anywhere and the daylight was fading fast. The ground was muddy and uneven. There were tools and equipment everywhere. The whole thing reminded Bobby of a public safety advert he had seen on TV, warning about the dangers of playing on a working farm. He doubted there was anything more bloody or more terrifying on TV.

Nikki pointed to the smallest of three tower blocks ahead of them. 'There you go. That's the place.'

Scaffolding ran about three quarters of the way up the tower block. Some of the lower floors had windows fitted, but most were black holes or covered by grey tarpaulin.

'You went in there on your own?' asked Bobby, wrestling with the knots in his stomach.

Nikki shrugged. 'It's not that bad when you get inside.'

'Bet you anything it's worse,' DJ whispered.

13

The Immortal

'This way,' said Nikki, disappearing through the gaping doorway.

Ada took a deep breath, then followed. Inside was cold, damp and gloomy. On the left-hand side of the entrance, Ada saw two lifts. Strips of black and yellow tape criss-crossed their doors, preventing entry. Beside them was a glass fronted door.

'We gotta walk up? You're kidding me,' DJ moaned.

Nikki pushed the glass door open, revealing a flight of stone steps. They headed up to the first floor. Nikki told them they needed to keep going up, right to the top, but Ada couldn't resist poking her head through the door. A long dark corridor stretched out before her, each side lined with doors. Most were closed but some were wide open. She saw unfinished light fittings dangling from wires that snaked up into ceiling. Ada was glad the clocks hadn't gone back yet, otherwise it would be pitch black in here by now.

Tony peered up the steps. 'Maybe I should stay here on lookout?'

Bobby winked at DJ.

'Smiley's got guts, I'll give him that,' he said. 'I wouldn't want to stay on my jacks.'

Tony looked confused. 'On my what?'

'On your *own*, country boy,' sighed DJ. 'But he's right. You must be well hard to volunteer, especially with them hooded things running about.'

Tony's head swung left and right, panicked all of a sudden.

DJ clapped a hand on Tony's shoulder. 'Good luck, mate.' He sprinted up the stairs, laughing all the way.

Nikki was busy searching for something in her pocket. Finally she produced a lollipop and offered it to Tony. 'For luck,' she said.

'No! Wait! I've changed my mind. I'm coming,' Tony said. 'Best we stick together, right?'

'Come on, slow coaches!' It was DJ's voice, echoing back down the stairs.

'Wait up!' yelled Bobby, and they followed him up the stairs.

Ada gripped the handrail and started upwards, taking up the rear. Apart from some occasional bickering between DJ and Tony, the five of them marched up the stairs in silence. Flight after flight, sapping their strength and leaving them short of breath. The staircase ended at a grey metal door. The words ROOF ACCESS AUTHORISED PERSONNEL ONLY were painted in large white letters on it.

'No… way… we're… getting through that,' panted Tony, trying to look disappointed. 'We might… as well—'

The ear-splitting sound of metal grinding against concrete drowned Tony's words out. Nikki had kicked away a brick which had stopped the door from closing and now she and Bobby were dragging it open.

'Workmen wedge it open so they can have a smoke outside,' said Nikki.

'How do you know all this?' asked Ada.

'The workmen eat at my cousin's café sometimes, I heard them talking,' explained Nikki, sliding the brick back in between the door and the doorframe. 'Now, you coming or what?'

Suddenly Ada wanted to say no. She wanted to be at home, watching Blue Peter with Mum. That was how a child would feel, though. She was supposed to be a detective. Sherlock Holmes would not be sitting around eating Jaffa cakes and watching telly when there was a mystery to be solved. Ada pushed down her fear and followed Nikki onto the roof. A ferocious blast of cold wind greeted her. She shivered as she fought to zip up her coat. The wind was whipping up a tiny cyclone of rubbish, filled with crushed drink cans, crisp packets, sweet wrappers and cigarette ends.

DJ stomped up to the pile of rubbish and began kicking one of the cans around as though the roof was a football pitch.

'On your head Bobby,' he yelled, sweeping his foot against the can. They all watched as the can sailed over the roof's edge. A few seconds later they heard it clatter onto the street below.

Ada wondered if DJ had been dropped on his head as a baby. She wondered it a lot.

'You wanna get us caught?' shouted Bobby.

'Maybe,' said DJ, glumly, 'then you lot will see what a stupid idea this all was.'

'No one made you come mate,' snapped Bobby.

'Yeah right, bad enough I couldn't open the flipping box. If I had stayed home you lot would have ribbed me 'til the cows came home!'

'Oi! Check it out,' called Nikki, pointing at the floor.

Ada could see something carved into the floor beside Nikki. She hurried over, her earlier fear swallowed by curiosity.

'Finally!' she whispered, kneeling down to examine it closer.

The carving formed a large jagged shape, covered in red lines that criss-crossed to its edges. Inside the shape were two large circles, and within the inner circle were a series of tiny symbols.

'I've seen these before….'

Ada took out the Salus Key and held it near the symbols. Despite the deepening half-light, she could clearly see that some the carved symbols matched those on the puzzle box.

'Curiouser and Curiouser,' said Ada.

Nikki crouched down beside Ada. 'Weird. This wasn't here the last time.'

There was a bright flash of white light, followed by a whirring sound, and it made Ada jump. She looked round to see DJ holding a large clunky camera. A photograph dangling from its bottom slot. DJ pulled it out, waved it the air for a few seconds, then handed it to Bobby.

'Where did you get that?' asked Ada.

DJ snapped off another shot. 'Borrowed it from the science room, didn't I, when Roebrush went to the bog. Clever, right?'

Ada shoved him hard. 'You stole it?'

DJ frowned. 'I ain't no thief. I'm gonna put it back before camera club on Friday.'

Ada slapped her forehead. 'If you had bothered to look at your timetable, you would know that Camera club is tomorrow.'

'Oh,' said DJ.

'Idiot!' Ada threw up her hands in disgust.

'Sorry,' said DJ. 'I just…I thought we would need it, you know?'

'Make sure you get some pictures of the other side, too,' Bobby ordered.

Ada scowled, but Bobby just shrugged.

'Might as well use it,' he told her. 'Me and the new boy can sneak it back in tomorrow.'

'Why you?' asked Ada, suspiciously.

'We've got double Chemistry in there tomorrow, right Smiley?'

Tony did not answer.

Bobby sighed. 'Tony. Tony! You deaf or what?' he yelled.

Still kneeling, Ada swivelled round. One look at Tony's wide eyes told her something was wrong. He raised his right hand and extended a single finger.

Ada followed Tony's finger and then froze. The hooded stranger from the graveyard – Langley – was stood at the far end of the roof, arms outstretched. His black robes were silhouetted against the burnt orange sky.

'I told you I would find you, little girl,' the stranger rasped. 'Although I must admit, I did not expect you to find you here, interfering with my work.'

Ada put her hands behind her back and tried to slip the Salus Key back into her satchel.

'Is that Langley, then?' asked Bobby

The stranger fixed Bobby with a glare. 'What did you say, boy?'

'He said Langley,' Ada repeated. 'That's your name isn't it? Bertram Langley.'

The hooded figure chuckled, 'What a delight. You continue to surprise me, which is a rare thing I can assure you, when you have lived as long as I.'

'Come off it. You're not really him though, are you?' asked Bobby. 'I mean that's crazy right? What are you? Like, his great, great, great grandson or something?'

Langley held out his gloved hand and beckoned to them. 'I am without end, but my patience is not. Give me the box and you all may walk free.'

Ada did not understand the next words out of Langley's mouth but they were spoken with cold menace. The air around them grew even colder as four shadowy shapes tore their way free of Langley's robes. They slithered onto the floor then rose, two on either side of the man. The shadows twisted and contorted until they matched his hooded form, then they all spoke in unison.

'Keep it from me, and you will suffer the consequences…'

'Give him the bloody box,' whispered Tony, stepping back in terror.

Keep the key safe! He will destroy us all if he gets his hands on it.

Ash's warning echoed through Ada's mind. She clenched her trembling hands.

Langley sighed. 'Ah the curse of childhood. Such an abundance of bravery, stupidity and self-delusion. If you had the wit to understand my plan you would joyfully take my hand and help me in my cause.'

'You calling us thick?' Nikki rumbled, squaring up to Langley.

Langley gave the slightest nod. The spectres let out a single terrible scream then flowed across the roof towards the children.

'Leg it!' Bobby shouted.

Tony was already sprinting for the roof exit. The rest of them followed as fast as they could.

Ada slid through the gap, Nikki close behind. The terrifying shrieking echoed behind them as they pounded down the stairs

'They're coming! They're coming!' DJ bellowed from the rear.

It was too dark now for Ada to see much of anything. She could hear her friends' feet hammering down the staircase, the sounds merging with her own thundering heartbeat. The shrieking cries of the shadow creatures bounced off the walls and seemed to surround them. She tripped but managed to grab the handrail to prevent a terrible tumble. Finally they reached the ground floor.

Tony raced toward the glass exit doors, skidding to a halt just before them. Ada moved alongside him. Looking out she saw two more phantoms gliding towards the tower block.

'Oh crap, oh crap, oh crap' DJ swore, sweat dripping from his face.

Ada looked around, looking for options. Her eyes fell on an open door to her left. She raced towards it, shouting for the others to follow.

Ada led them down the corridor, pushed open a door on her left shutting it behind the last of them, plunging them all into darkness. No one spoke as they huddled together in the gloom; the only sound was their ragged breathing. It was not long before Ada heard footsteps coming down the corridor outside.

Bobby slapped a hand over Tony's mouth, stifling his panicked cry. The footsteps grew louder and closer. Ada held her breath and focused her hearing. There was one pair of footsteps coming down the steps. She motioned towards the window on the far side of the room. Bobby nodded then snuck over to it. DJ and Nikki crept alongside him. Ada saw their backs silhouetted against the window, heard their low groans as they pushed, and prayed their pursuers would pass them by. The window gave way just as the door exploded inwards, sending pieces of wood flying in all directions. Langley stepped into the room, a look of triumph on his face. Streams of green lightning circled his arms, flicking out tiny sparks that snapped and hissed.

Tony sprinted to the window and dived through it. Taking his lead, Nikki and DJ made to follow.

'No escape,' said Langley. He aimed a hand, pulsing with crackling green energy, at Nikki's back.

'No!' screamed Ada, stepping in front of Nikki. 'Take it!'

Ada whipped out the Salus Key just as Langley loosed the lightning. The tendril of sizzling energy was drawn to it. The lightning snaked around the box like fingers, trying to find a way inside.

'Mine at last,' Langley hissed.

But as he reached for the Salus Key, the lightning exploded from it as though repelled. The blast tore him screaming from his feet, catapulting him through the wall. Something struck Ada and she landed hard on her back beneath a hailstorm of brick and dust.

Tiny white spots swirled in front of her eyes. It felt like a herd of elephants had decided to go for a jog inside her head. Looking to the left, she saw two Bobby's getting up and dusting themselves off. The ceiling had collapsed on the spot she'd been standing. He'd knocked her out of the way. Ada blinked and rubbed her eyes until her vision returned to normal.

'Thanks,' she croaked. She started coughing on all the plaster dust.

'You alright?' he asked, reaching out a hand.

Ada touched her forehead and winced. She looked at her fingers and saw two of them had blood on them. She stared down at the box in her hand, then up at the smoking ruins.

'How did you do that?' asked Bobby, staring in wonder at the shattered wall.

'I...'

A low chuckle came from the hole and Ada watched, horrified, as two of Langley's hooded creatures slithered through it into the room.

'Come on!' yelled Bobby.

Ada grabbed his hand and stood up, stumbling across to the window. Nikki's two thick arms reached through the window and yanked Ada through, to land beside DJ and Tony. Bobby hopped over the windowsill and they legged it away from the building. No one said a word as they ran from the shrieking shadows, who were now oozing through the window behind them.

They did not stop running until they reached the fence where they had come through. One by one they clambered onto the pallets, dropping to the other side and sprinting off into the night. Eventually Bobby gave the all clear that the Faceless were gone. They all slumped to the pavement filling the air with panting, coughing and groaning. It was a long time after that before anyone moved or spoke.

Finally DJ pushed himself onto his knees, bent forward and stroked the pavement with his cheek, like a cat snuggling into a sofa.

'I can't believe we're not dead.'

An old man with a flat cap, a large shaggy dog padding beside him, stopped to watch DJ, who was now busy kissing the pavement.

DJ raised his head and broke into a toothy grin. 'I mean we should be dead right?'

The man mumbled something ending with the word 'kids' before hurrying on, pulling the dog with him.

14

Adventures in Geography

Bobby lay on his bed, staring up at the swirling patterns of his bedroom ceiling tiles. Whenever he closed his eyes, Langley's terrifying shadow creatures slithered down through the darkness, their hands reaching for him.

He sighed, sat up and pulled his knees into his chest. He had tried talking to Mum about what happened at the estate. Her response had been nothing more than a terse kiss of her teeth. It meant *Me tell you not to go to that place, but she didn't say it. That's how angry she was.* She had not said another word to him after that. Her silence made everything worse. He had never felt so scared and alone—not since the day he lost her.

Auntie Carol's voice crashed through Bobby's fear, ordering him downstairs. He clambered off the bed, and grabbed his school blazer. It was a mess! He patted it a few times, trying to get rid of the worst of it, coughing at the swirling cloud of dust that emerged.

'Bobby! We waiting!'

Bobby threw on the blazer, hoping to conceal the sweat patches on his shirt. 'Coming Auntie!'

He sprinted from the room, tucking in his shirt as he went. He was halfway down the stairs before he spotted the front room door, wide open. Bobby's heart sank. That meant visitors. The worst kind. Bobby would be dragged in to stand there on display, which he hated, and try to look interested, which he was not. Worst of all would be the stupid comments he'd endure.

'Hmm, you get big.'

'You must miss your mum.'

'Me nah see you since you were a baby! You remember me?'

'Boy, you must learn fer stand up straight.'

'Lord, him look just like her.'

And so on. Bobby slunk over to the front room door, bracing himself for the onslaught. Errol was already there, sitting with his arms crossed beside Auntie Carol on one of the cream leather sofas that dominated the room. Errol gave Bobby a 'please save me' look that disappeared behind a toothy grin as soon as Auntie Carol glared at him.

A large hexagonal table squatted in the middle of the front room, on which a bowl of plastic fruit had been carefully positioned as a centrepiece. Two cabinets sat in alcoves on either side of an electric fire, which was rarely ever used. Bobby smiled for the first time since he had got home. He remembered how Mum used to let him sneak in and use the fire for an hour before breakfast. It was their secret. Bobby spent many a happy hour stretched in front of the fire, like the family cat.

'Boy, you best pull up dat bottom lip and come in here,' snapped Auntie Carol.

Bobby entered the room, and his memories and smile both vanished. When he saw who was sitting on the sofa he thought his eyes would pop out of their sockets and go rolling across the floor.

'Boy, say hello to Father Tadsby,' Auntie Carol ordered. 'He's our new vicar.'

A broad shouldered, round faced man in a red woolly jumper and grey trousers put the small cup back on its saucer and smiled genially. He carefully placed them on the table, stood up and held out a hand. Bobby's own hand looked tiny in comparison and he winced at the firmness of the grip. He reckoned this must be what it felt like to trap your fingers in a car door. The round-faced priest grinned broadly and Bobby supposed it must run in the family.

'Pleased to meet you, Mr Gibson,' said Father Tadsby, nodding to his left. 'I believe you've already met my son.'

Tony looked up from the bowl of plastic fruit which he had been staring at, and gave his best grin.

'He tells me he's had an interesting few days thanks to you.'

***

Bobby and Tony sat on the floor of Bobby's bedroom. Tony kept glancing at the door, nervously.

'Mate. They'll be down there for ages,' said Bobby.

Tony looked unconvinced. 'What about your brother?'

'Auntie wants to get Errol into the church choir, so he's stuck there. Dunno why she's bothering. Ada's cat sings better than he does.'

'Your aunt will be lucky if she gets two words in,' said Tony, shifting his gaze from the door. 'Dad doesn't stop once he gets going.'

'What you doing here, Smiley?'

Tony sighed. 'I wish you'd stop calling me that.'

'When pigs fly mate.'

'I knew Dad was going to do the rounds tonight, doing his little meet and greet, and I told him that I knew you.'

'But why did *you* come with him?' asked Bobby.

Tony pulled two crumpled photos from his pocket and placed them in the space between them. 'To show you these.'

Bobby picked them up.

'You came to show me how rubbish DJ is with a camera,' said Bobby, frowning at the blurred images.

'So, where'd you learn to run like that?'

'Like what?'

'Back at the estate, when that thing came after us, you were proper chipping.'

'Proper chipping?' repeated a confused Tony.

'It's means running fast country boy,' translated Bobby. 'You were running really fast.'

'Oh that,' said Tony, making it sound like it was nothing. 'When you're the son of a vicar you have to run fast. I also ran in the athletics team at my last school.'

'Don't tell Errol that or he'll have you on our school team before you can blink.'

'Look, you got an atlas?' asked Tony.

'You what?'

'An atlas,' he repeated. 'You got one or not?'

'Yeah, there's one downstairs. What do you want it for?'

'Get it and I'll show you why I came here.'

'This better be worth it.'

Bobby rose and kicked off his slippers. He padded over to the bedroom door and did a couple of stretches.

Tony pointed at Bobby's bare feet. 'What did you do that for?'

Bobby gave him a sneaky grin. 'Because I need to go full on Ninja for this.' He pushed on the door frame as he opened the door so it wouldn't squeak, then slipped through the gap, leaving a confused Tony behind. Bobby headed back to the stairs. The living room door was open by a crack, allowing a thin shaft of light to slice across the darkened corridor. Bobby crept down the stairs, treading carefully and avoiding the creakers until he reached the final step. He crouched down. Now came the hard part.

With the raised voices of Auntie Carol and Tony's dad in his ears, Bobby darted across the corridor into the dining room. Just as he was congratulating himself, the voices from the living room stopped. Bobby slid behind the door just as Auntie Carol's face appeared alongside it.

He froze, terror flooding his veins. This was bad. Very, very bad. There was nothing Auntie Carol hated more than being embarrassed in front of guests. If she found him in here she would skip angry and go straight to full on rage. Bobby tried to fade into his surroundings, to be the door and the darkness. He squeezed himself back half a step and held his breath.

'Auntie!' Errol called from the other room. 'Bobby's gone upstairs with his mate. I told you.'

Auntie ignored him and took two more steps into the room. Her head turn from left to right, slowly, like a search light illuminating every inch of the dining room.

'Auntie...' came Errol's voice again.

Auntie Carol spun around and marched from the room. Bobby pressed an ear against the wall and waited until he heard her voice jabbering away in the living room again. Satisfied, he slid out from his hiding place and circled the large dining room table until he faced the cabinet on the far wall. On each shelf, spaced equally, were Mum's collection of glass ornaments. Like everything in this room, they were kept dust free and in immaculate condition. It felt more like a museum than a room to be used. The collection contained tiny statues of various animals, roses and several women in flowing dresses. Bobby's favourite ornaments, the Queen's Guard, stood in a row, keeping a watchful eye over the room.

Bobby eased a heavy wooden chair against the cabinet. Stepping onto the chair he reached up to the shelf of serious grown-up books. Bobby slid his index finger slid along the spines stopping at a large red book. The World Atlas. Bobby carefully pulled the book from the shelf and slipped it under his arm. The chair creaked gently as he climbed down, but the murmuring voices droned on undisturbed. He returned the chair, then snuck back upstairs.

'Thought you'd been caught,' said Tony, relief washing over his face as Bobby returned.

He tossed the atlas onto the floor, between Tony's legs, then pulled a stealth pose. 'Not this Ninja.'

Tony rolled his eyes then laid a hand on the book, stroking its cover.

'Wow,' he said in a hushed tone. 'It's gorgeous.'

Tony opened the Atlas. Every turned page brought a new ooh or aah.

Bobby sat down facing Tony. He saw nothing to ooh or aah about.

'You gonna tell me why I risked my neck for this?'

Tony pulled a piece of neatly folded tracing paper and a pencil stub from his trouser pocket.

'What's—?'

Tony shushed Bobby into silence. He clamped the pencil between his teeth like a matchstick and continued to flip excitedly through the pages.

Just as Bobby decided that no, he would not be shushed in his own damned room, Tony slammed the tracing paper onto an open page. He spat the pencil out and began tracing an outline onto the paper.

'What are—?'

Another shush from Tony. He'd be getting a slap if he shushed him one more time.

Tony held up the tracing paper then tapped his pencil against it. 'There. See?'

Bobby saw Tony had drawn a weird yet familiar shape, crisscrossed with lines. There were also some strange symbols that Tony had down onto the map. Bobby frowned.

'The roof,' he said. 'It's the weird carving on the roof. How'd you remember what it looked like?'

'I can just remember stuff I've seen. Like, everything,' said Tony, tapping the drawing again. 'The carving was the lower half of England, from Norwich right down to Penzance.'

Bobby scratched his head. 'Is London in that lot?'

'You do geography at school, right?'

Bobby shrugged. 'Course I do, but come off it – who's any good at Geography?'

'I am. I was in the top group for Geography at my last school,' Tony boasted. 'Dad says Geography is my superpower.'

'Don't say that to anyone at school unless you want a kicking,' advised Bobby. 'Hang on. What are those wavy line things, those symbols and the two circles there?'

'Dunno. But I'll tell you this: when Langley showed up, those wavy lines started glowing up there on the roof,' said Tony.

'What? Serious?' asked Bobby, wondering how he'd missed that.

'Yep. Like a Christmas tree.'

Bobby slumped against the side of his bed. 'Bloody hell! Anyone else see that?'

Tony shrugged and slumped down beside him. 'Langley and those hooded things are just going to keep on coming until he gets the Salus Key aren't, they?'

Bobby nodded.

'Maybe we should—'

'We can't give it to him,' snapped Bobby. 'Agent Ash told Ada that he's gonna destroy us all if he gets the Salus Key.'

'What do we do then?' asked Tony.

'Tomorrow we come up with a plan. Me and Ada are great with plans.'

'What if Langley doesn't wait for tomorrow?' Tony asked. 'What if he sends those things for us tonight while we're asleep?'

The two of them sat there in silence as Tony's question sank in.

'I hate you,' Bobby said, at last.

Tony grinned. Bobby was about to deliver that long overdue slap when the doorbell rang four times in quick succession.

'Why are you smiling?' asked Tony.

'Wait for it...'

There were some raised voices followed by footsteps thundering up the stairs. Auntie Carol bellowed out and the footsteps slowed to a respectful walk. A few seconds after that, DJ came through the door.

'Alright loser!' he said, diving face-first, onto Bobby's bed.

'Wotcha mate,' said Bobby.

DJ rolled onto his back and pulled a packet of crisps from his pocket. He tore it open and shoved a handful into his mouth.

'Do you have to eat those in here?' asked Bobby, trying not to breathe.

DJ shrugged. 'What's wrong with Oxtail crisps?'

'They smell like wet farts!'

'So does your room but you don't see me complaining.'

Flecks of half-munched crisps spattered onto the bed as he spoke.

'Mate!' shouted Bobby.

DJ scooped up the brownish mush, shoved it back into his mouth and mumbled 'Sorted. Chill out.'

DJ's good humour vanished when he noticed Tony. 'What's *he* doing here?'

Bobby explained Tony's discoveries to DJ.

'Pretty cool right?' asked Tony, puffing his chest out proudly.

DJ's hand snapped out behind Tony's left ear, and when it snapped back DJ was holding a cassette tape.

'Nah, this is what I call cool, New Boy.' DJ lobbed the tape over to Bobby.

'This the tape from Rillington's office?'

DJ nodded. Bobby turned the tape over in his hands.

'You're sis fixed it, then?'

'Yeah. And she's never gonna let me forget it. Says I owe her big time.'

Tony rubbed the side of his head. 'How did you do that thing with my ear?'

DJ tapped his nose. 'The great Djinn never reveals his tricks.'

'More like The Great Idiot,' Tony muttered.

'How about I flatten your nose for my next trick?'

'Pack it in you two!' shouted Bobby. 'This could change everything.'

Both boys muttered curses at each other, but they kept their distance.

Bobby knelt and slid his arm under the bed, sweeping it back and forth.

'Come on. I know you're here somewhere…' Bobby pushed his arm further in.

'Got it!' announced Bobby, pulling out a large silver tape recorder.

DJ and Tony sat crossed legged on either side of Bobby as he pushed the tape into the recorder.

Bobby took a deep breath then pushed the Play button.

'BANG!' shrieked DJ, making the other two jump horribly. He collapsed into a fit of laughter, holding his stomach, practically crying. Bobby punched him on the arm, and a scuffle ensued.

'ESD Log file. Week forty. Agent Ash reporting…'

The boys stopped fighting and fell silent.

'I'm convinced Langley followed me back from Syria. However, I've managed to a secure a position as a substitute teacher at this school in the hopes of throwing him off my trail, while I continue my search. I won't let anything stop me now. Not when I'm this close.'

Tony leaned over and pressed the Pause button.

'What did you do that for?' Bobby demanded.

'Sorry,' said Tony, grimacing. 'Where's the loo?'

'Really? You have to go now?'

Tony was jiggling. 'I tried to hold it; I really did.'

'It's the door right by the stairs,' Bobby told him, rolling his eyes.

'Thanks. Don't start till I get back.'

Tony bolted from the room as if he were a puppy let off its leash at last.

'New Boy is seriously weird,' said DJ.

'Said he was in the top group for Geography at his last school,' said Bobby, as though that explained everything.

'Weird and boring,' said DJ. 'Great combo. So, do you reckon that Langley bloke's really been alive all this time?'

'He said he was.'

'I can say I'm heavyweight champion of the world but it don't make it true, mate.'

'Yeah, but you're not pulling monsters out of thin air when you're saying it,' Bobby countered.

DJ opened his mouth to reply but nothing came out save a strangled sigh.

'You alright mate?' asked Bobby.

DJ was rubbing the back of his neck, while looking nervously back to the open bedroom door.

'Look mate you can tell me. What's up?'

When he met his gaze, Bobby could see what Mr Wattling had been going on about. The bags under DJ's eyes looked like they were carrying their own bags.

DJ swallowed hard then folded his arms.

'It's just with all of this stuff going on and after what happened last year…I'm…well…I just think—'

A toilet flushing sounded from down the corridor.

'You know what forget it. Don't worry about it mate. It's cool, I'm cool, you're cool, we're all cool' said DJ, each word racing to beat the next one out of his mouth.

There was something about the way he said 'don't worry about it mate' that made Bobby do the opposite. He was about to ask DJ again when Tony returned. As soon as he sat down he reached for the Play button.

'Oi!' snapped Bobby.

Tony froze.

'You washed your hands?'

'Course I did.'

Tony showed Bobby both sides of his hands, as if that proved anything.

'Fine,' said Bobby at last.

DJ was back munching down on more crisps. Despite the wide smile he gave him, Bobby decided when he got the chance he would ask DJ again about what was going on.

Tony pressed Play and settled back.

'The trip to Syria was a complete success. The Faceless Scholars covered their tracks well but I now have the Salus Key in my possession. Now all I need to do is —'

The brief silence was followed by footsteps.

'We heard this bit before,' said Bobby.

DJ reached out to stop the tape but Tony warned him off. 'Let it run,' he told him.

For a full minute there was nothing and just as Bobby was about to give up they all heard the sound of a door being closed. A few seconds later Ash's relieved laughter burst out through the tape recorders speaker.

'Apologies. It was just the school caretaker locking up for the evening. All of this has me jumping at shadows,' admitted Langley. 'Right where was I...ah yes I've been able to decipher a portion of the text etched onto the Salus Key. It was written in a code created by the Faceless Scholars, using a combination of Akkadian and Sumerian. I've cracked the code but the translated solution makes no sense to me, however my gut tells me once I do understand the trail will lead me to the Apocalypse Chamber.'

There was a short pause followed by the rustling of what sounded like paper.

'The translation reads as follows. 'Steal the Moon to light the beacon. Pay the goddess to open the gate. Step within the moon's crimson shade to seal our fate.' It makes no sense to me at the moment but I'm going to see Carnaby tomorrow. Hopefully, he will be able to—'

Footsteps in the background.

'Don't know if that's Mr Khara coming back but I'm going to sign off now. Will continue report once I've spoken to Carnaby.'

Agent Ash's voice cut out and the recording stopped. Bobby pictured him stuffing the tape recorder up in the alcove behind the clock. All was silent in the bedroom.

Bobby let the tape run on for another minute or so, just in case there was anything else, but there was nothing. He pressed Stop, crossed his arms, and leant back against his bed.

'I reckon it was after that he got grabbed by Langley,' said Bobby.

'Any idea what any of that stuff meant?' asked Tony. 'Stealing the moon and all that.'

'Nope. Looks like those ESD agents got all the real juicy on the other tapes,' replied Bobby.

'Great! Just great!' said DJ. He got up and kicked the tape recorder. 'So we're in just as much of a mess as we were before!'

'Oi! Kick your own stuff unless you want to tell Errol what happened to his tape deck.'

The colour drained from DJ's face.

'Anyway, we know loads more than we did before,' said Bobby, smugly. He imagined the look on Ada's face when she heard the tape.

'We do?' DJ and Tony chorused.

'Agent Ash said he was going to take the Salus Key to Carnaby. That's got to be the same bloke Henry told us about,' Bobby said.

'Yeah, you're right! He did say Carnaby knew about the Faceless Scholars.' Added Tony.

DJ stood and began pacing wild-eyed around the room. 'So the immortal nutcase who tried to kill us wants the box so he can find something called the Apocalypse Chamber. Brilliant. Bloody brilliant.'

Bobby tried to imagine what could be inside something called the Apocalypse Chamber. Every answer he came up with chilled him to the bone.

15

Knight Terrors

The cherished memory was as bright and vivid as ever. Nikki was five, watching Dad wrap tinfoil around the empty cornflakes box.

'Your shield lady Nichola,' said Dad, holding it out for her.

Nikki pushed her arm through the holes Dad had cut into the sides. It was a tight fit but with a little wriggling she managed it.

'How does it feel?' asked Dad. 'It's not too heavy, is it?'

Nikki shook her head and flashed a wide smile. Her dad carefully slid the shield off, widened the holes a touch, then laid it against the small brown teddy bear on Nikki's bed.

'We shall work on your suit of armour next, while Sir Bedevere stands guard on your new shield.'

Nikki poked the bear with her plastic sword. 'He's just a teddy bear, Daddy.'

Dad wrapped her arm around Nikki. He smelt of wood and smoke from the factory where he worked.

'You may think he's a bear, but Bedevere is a knight transformed by the wizard Palitoy to serve as your guide and protector.'

Dad began unrolling the foil, tearing off sheets and laying them flat on the bed. He began wrapping Nikki's arm with one of the sheets.

'Can girls really be knights?' she asked.

'Well, once upon a time there was a woman who defended her castle against invaders. Some people say she saved England by doing it. Literally. Now, she was not a knight on paper but she certainly was in her heart. Her name was Nichola de la Haye.'

Nikki started jumping up and down. 'That's my name too!' she squealed.

'So it is! Now hold still you little mouse.' He began to wrap Nikki's other arm in foil. She wriggled with impatience as he finished.

'Now arms up, lady Nichola.'

Nikki stretched her arms to the ceiling, wincing at the scraping sound the foil made. Dad placed the roll of foil against her tummy.

'Turn please, milady.'

Nikki spun slowly, like a ballet dancer, until her body was encased in foil.

'Now. When you get older, some people will try to tell you what you can and can't be. When that happens you remember old Nichola de la Haye. The only person who gets to decide who you are is you. Got it?'

Nikki did not really understand, but she nodded anyway so her Daddy would smile. She loved it when he smiled.

'I want to be knight when I grow up.'

Dad did not reply at first. He had a roll of Sellotape clamped tightly in his mouth, but he nodded to show he'd heard. He bit off several strips, applying them with expert precision to the foil covering Nikki. He stood then, but he looked very serious. Nikki wondered if she had done something wrong.

'Dad?'

'A knight must always protect others. She must never lie. She must be brave and loyal. Do you swear to live by this code, Nichola?'

Nikki stood there, looking up at him, confused by his words.

Dad winked at her. 'Say 'I Swear,' sweetheart' he whispered.

'I swear, sweetheart,' Nikki announced.

Dad held up the empty tube of foil as though it were a sword. 'Then kneel, milady.'

Nikki knelt, rustling in her armour. Dad towered above her.

'Do you swear to help the weak, no matter who they are?'

'The weak?'

'Like your brother.'

Nikki thought about that for a little while. He was pretty weak.

'Yes Dad I will.'

'Do you swear you will defend your friends, whenever they are in trouble?'

Nikki didn't answer. The tears were already flowing.

'What's wrong milady?'

'I...I...I don't have any friends, Daddy.'

Dad looked so sad at this. Nikki gave him the biggest hug ever.

He whispered into her ear, then. 'One day you will have the greatest friends ever, and they will love you just as much as I do.'

'Will I?'

'Of course. And I want you to protect them, just like I protect you. That's what knights do.'

'Okay.'

Dad cleared his throat.

'In that case...' Dad stood up and tapped the cardboard tube on Nikki's left shoulder. 'I dub thee Sir Nichola.'

Dad swung the tube in a wide arc over Nikki's head, with a whoosh, then tapped it lightly on her right shoulder.

'Arise, Sir Nichola – sworn knight of North London.'

'WHERE'S MY COOKING FOIL?!' Nikki heard Mum thundering up the stairs.

'Time to face your first challenge, Sir knight,' said Dad, holding out the tube.

Nikki gulped, then took the cardboard tube in one hand. She quickly retrieved her shield from Sir Bedevere and turned to face her fate.

***

Ada's felt something warm and furry curl around her right ankle as she stared out of the window. It snapped her out of her happy memories, chuckling as the large ginger cat nibbled her toes.

'Pack it in Arthur,' Nikki snapped, in a hoarse whisper.

Ada knelt down and stroked the cat under his chin. 'It's fine, I'm the one in his space.'

After enjoying several seconds of fuss, Arthur padded over to the cat bed in the corner of the room and began kneading it with his paws.

'Should be okay now,' Nikki said. 'Takes him ages to settle down.'

'Thanks again for letting me sleep over.'

Nikki was sitting on a large double bed in her pyjamas, a small mound of crisps and chocolate bars in front of her. 'It's cool. My folks are always saying I should have more friends over.'

'Do you have a lot of friends over?'

'You're the second,' said Nikki.

'Who was the first?'

'Sharon Witley. She was my best friend in nursery and junior school. I don't wanna talk about it.'

'Sorry I didn't mean to–'

'Don't worry about it.' Nikki gestured to the pile of books next to the snacks. 'You brought Sherlock over. That makes you a much better friend than that two-faced cow ever was.'

Ada chuckled, while eyeing up a large chocolate bar. 'You did say you were missing a few, so now you can get all caught up.'

Nikki picked up a book and turned it over in her hands.

'Hound of the Baskervilles,' said Ada. 'That's one of my faves.'

Nikki read the back covers one after the other as they chatted. 'So how come you love these so much?'

'Mum told me my dad read them to her while she was pregnant with me. Mum says I was practically born with my nose in a book, just like he was when he...'

Ada's voice trailed off.

'When he was what?' asked Nikki.

'When he was alive.' She said it matter-of-factly, but there was a throb to Ada's voice.

Nikki fell silent. She ran a hand back through her curly hair in discomfort.

'It's okay,' said Ada.

Two stupid words which did nothing to stop the tears clouding Ada's vision. Dad was gone and there was nothing okay about that. Nothing! Ada focused on a spot on the floor, her jaw and her chest tightening. She was blinking rapidly, trying to use her eyelids as barriers against the approaching flood.

'I never thanked you, by the way,' said Nikki. 'If it wasn't for you, I would have got fried back at the estate.'

Ada wiped her sleeve across her face.

'Couldn't let a knight get fried on her first proper quest could I?'

'What?'

Ada pointed at the badge that was sewn onto her school satchel. It depicted a silver shield, and in the centre of it was a woman dressed in robes with dragons either side.

'That's Pridwen right? King Arthur's shield?'

'How'd you know that?'

'I'd love to claim that I know everything, but the truth is I had no idea what it was when I first saw it, back at the shop. I described it to Henry later on, and he knew what it was straight away...the clever so-and-so.'

Ada went over and touched the badge. 'You don't sew something like this onto your school bag unless it's really important to you.'

Ada pointed to one of the shelves on Nikki's bookcase. Between all the textbooks were some smaller more beaten-up looking books. Every one of them was about knights and the days of chivalry.

'Was it your mum or dad who used to read you those stories?'

'None of your business,' snapped Nikki, her fists suddenly clenching.

'Oh. Look, Nikki, I'm not like Sharon,' said Ada calmly. 'I'm not going to tell anyone anything about you—not even Bobby and the others.'

'How'd you know?'

'Sharon was your best mate, but it's pretty clear you hate her guts now. What she did had to be epically horrible. Girls wanting to be knights isn't too common so it seemed a reasonable conclusion that she used it against you. I'm sorry she did that. People can be thoughtless and cruel, sometimes.'

The words seemed to suck the fight out of Nikki. Her fists unclenched and the fearsome girl Ada was always in awe of seemed to deflate before her eyes.

'She told everyone at my junior school. Everything. She even took in Sir Bedevere to show them.'

Nikki held up the small, battered, one eyed teddy bear that had been tucked next to her pillow.

'When I got into school I found him sitting on my desk, and everyone was laughing. They didn't stop laughing until I battered Sharon.'

Ada did not need to imagine the scene. She knew what it felt like to have everyone looking at her, whispering about her.

Yeah that's her the one with the dead dad.

She's so weird…look at her. She can't even do her hair properly.

It always used to end the same way for her, running to find a place where she could let go, where she could scream at the pain and injustice.

There was a look of shame on Nikki's face as she stared at the books. 'They called my dad down to the school. He said he understood why I did it, but I needed to be better than Sharon; I needed to be better than all of them. He said that's what true knights do. I know. Stupid, right?'

'Not right. You stood up for Tony, you led us to the estate, you were prepared to take on Langley – that's exactly the kind of stuff your dad would want you to do. You are true knight, Nikki. I'll bet your dad is super-proud.'

Nikki scooped a load of hair over her face as though trying to smother her blushes.

'And *trust* me – wanting to be a knight is no more stupid than a girl who wants to open her own detective agency one day. I'm not going to tell anyone. Promise.'

Nikki smiled then patted the empty space on the bed on the other side of the pile of sweets. 'All this stuff isn't going to eat itself.'

Ada climbed onto the bed and the two of them began devouring the sweets. While Ada worked on troublesome piece of toffee, she asked Nikki where all the sweets had come from.

'My stepdad,' replied Nikki. 'He seems to think all this will make me like him. Works with my brother, but I know what's what.'

'Where's your real dad now?'

Nikki chewed her lip, staring up at the ceiling 'Dunno. I used to see him every Wednesday. We'd sit up here for hours reading and talking, but I ain't seem him in a couple of years.'

Nikki started to scratch her neck. Ada wasn't sure if her new friend even realised she was doing it.

'Mum said he works on an oil rig now, so he can't get back that often.' Her scratching got harder now. 'But when he does come back, I'll get to tell him all about the box and those hooded things. I'll be like 'I'm on a real live quest now, Dad!' He'll love that.'

Ada was pretty sure that, oil rig or not, her dad would have had some time off by now. She kept her theories to herself, though. Nikki either knew it already, or she didn't want to know. It wasn't her business.

At least your dad is still out there somewhere, she thought.

Ada spotted the small puzzle box and pulled it out from the pile of sweet wrappers. Her pained expression peered out at her from the inlaid mirrored pieces.

Nikki tapped the box. 'Do you have any idea what that thing is?'

'A worthy opponent.'

'That bloke Langley called it the Salus Key.'

Ada's eyes narrowed. 'The name of a thing means nothing without context. We need to know its purpose. What Langley intends to do with it.'

Ada grabbed a handful of chocolate buttons, popping two into her mouth. As the chocolatey goodness dissolved on her taste buds, Ada took out her casebook and turned to her notes on The Salus Key.

~~The Wooden box The Puzzle box~~ *The Salus Key*

As I see it the main problem with solving this ~~box puzzle box~~ *key is two-fold.*

Problem 1: The carvings etched on each piece do not form any kind of recognisable image, so I presume we need to spell out a phrase to solve it. I tried copying some of the carvings onto separate pieces of paper so I could move them around to see if that could give me some clue but that did not help. If the carvings represent some form of ancient language, I have no idea how to read them. (Note to self - I need to study more languages)

Problem 2: Were this a traditional puzzle, there would be an image of the completed puzzle as a guide (a picture on the packaging the puzzle came in, say). I have no such frame of reference to work towards with the Salus Key because the creators only want people who already know the solution to unlock it.

Ada was reminded of chess as she closed her notebook. She would move and the Salus Key would counter move. Ada allowed herself a smile. She had yet to meet a chess opponent who was her equal. She went to work on the Salus Key again, this time with a renewed confidence. Her movements were logical, methodical, and precise. She memorised each move so she could keep track of her progress and retreat if needed.

Thirty minutes, one bag of cheese and onion crisps and three chocolate bars later, she shook the cube and roared 'Oh come on!'.

She started rotating pieces at random. Her logic had given way to her greatest weakness: impatience.

'Here let's have a go,' said Nikki, grabbing for the box.

Ada kept her grip on it. 'Just give me a few more minutes.'

Nikki tugged at the box 'You've had loads already. Give us a go!'

Ada shivered, almost dropping the box in the process. It felt like a giant bucket of ice had been emptied over her head. Ada saw a wispy swirl of cold air spiral up from Nikki's mouth when spoke.

'It's here,' Nikki whispered, pointing past Ada.

Ada forced herself to turn. One of the hooded shadow creatures was slithering out from the darkened corner of Nikki's
bedroom.

'HELP!' Ada and Nikki bellowed.

'No one can hear you beyond this room,' rasped the creature.
'It is just us, my little ones.'

Ada scrabbled backwards, until she was pressed against the
headboard. The hooded figure drifted closer and lay a gloved hand
on the end of the bed and, to Ada's horror, the hand became solid.
Wood cracked beneath its grip.

'The clever little girl who thought she could escape the Faceless.'

The creature held out its other hand.

'Your cleverness has earned you and your friend a thousand
subtle shades of pain before you die.'

Nikki lunged for her school blazer, draped over the nearby
chair. From it, she drew a metal ruler and, spinning, she brought
its edge down hard on the creature's fingers. It recoiled, rubbing its
fingers and hissing with laughter.

'You have courage for one so young.'

Nikki held the ruler up in front of her, moonlight skipping
across its surface.

'Ada's my friend. I won't let you hurt her.'

Nikki snatched the puzzle box from Ada and threw it over the
creature's head. It bounced off the back wall and landed on the
floor. 'Go on take it!'

The Faceless turned to look at the key but then slowly turned
back 'I will take the key after I have finished with you!'

As the Faceless came closer, Arthur leapt onto the bed, landing
squarely between them. The cat gave an almighty hiss, his tail, now
double the size thrashed from side to side.

The creature shrank away from the bed, hissing back at Arthur.
Ada snatched the nearest thing to hand - an open packet of crisps -

and hurled it at the creature. To her amazement, every crisp that struck the creature sent an arc of green lightning snaking through its shadowy mass. It threw itself back, arms flailing in panic, trying to brush off the hissing snacks.

Nikki tore open a second packet of crisps, leapt across the bed and started hurling salt and vinegar projectiles at the retreating creature. A bestial howl erupted from the creature and it exploded in a column of light, wind and green smoke. The shockwave threw the two girls and Arthur backwards, their fall cushioned by the mattress and one incredibly thick duvet. Warmth and light flooded back into the bedroom. Arthur jumped off the bed and padded over to the spot where the creature had vanished. He started sniffing the floor as though checking that the monster was truly gone.

Nikki stared into the empty pack of crisps. 'If it melts monsters, what do these things do to our insides?'

Before she knew what she was doing Ada threw her arms around Nikki in a massive hug. Nikki squirmed, a little uncomfortably, then returned it shyly. At last, when they were calm once more, Ada picked up the ruler as though it were the most precious thing in the world. She held it out to Nikki with reverence.

Nikki took the ruler and stared at it. 'My dad gave this to me when I was nine. Every great sword has a name, he said, and one day I could name mine, once I'd earned the right.'

'So what's it called?'

Nikki shook her head. 'Nothing yet.'

She slipped the ruler back into her blazer, then got off the bed and scooped up Arthur.

'Double tuna for you tomorrow, my lord,' she promised him.

'I can't believe we attacked that thing with a ruler and a packet of crisps,' said Ada, rubbing Arthur's chin.

'It was two packets. And Mum's gonna kill me when she sees all this mess,' said Nikki.

'I don't know if you're the bravest girl I've ever met or the stupidest. I mean…'

'Ada.'

'…I know you want to be a knight but that thing came into your bedroom! Right through the wall! It was going to kill us with a thousand subtle shades of pain.'

'Ada.'

'Of course, dying from a thousand shades of pain is ridiculous. We would have been lucky to make it to five. And can pain ever be subtle? I mean—'

'ADA!'

'What?'

'Why is the weird box glowing?'

Ada looked over at the Salus Key. There were strange swirling patterns on its surface now, each one pulsing with silvery light.

Ada walked over to the box, crouched down and stared at it. 'I see it now,' she announced, grinning.

'See what?' asked Nikki, who had moved now beside her.

Ada ignored the question. She picked up the puzzle box and again began to move pieces. This time though, she had a map to follow. Her movements were calculated, measured and precise.

'The patterns are part of a snake,' explained Ada. 'A Cobra I think.'

Nikki leaned in.

'Yes I can it now…why couldn't we see it before?'

Ada moved the box out of the shaft of moonlight and the glow faded from the box, as did the images.

'The moonlight,' said Nikki, in a hushed tone.

Holding the box in both hands, Ada positioned it back into the shaft of light and resumed her work. Soon her fingers became a blur of shifting, moving and rearranging pieces. She felt as though there was a faint voice…

Yes that's right, now turn it there.

…at the back of her mind whispering to her…

No, you must lift that piece, then turn its twin ninety degrees.

…guiding her movements.

Good! Now push there. Well done.

A voice that was not her own.

Finally she paused, her finger on a tiny section. 'I move this piece and I complete the puzzle.'

'You sure you that's a good idea?' asked Nikki.

'Says the girl who fights monsters with crisps.'

Ada took a breath then slowly moved the final piece into place. Now every one of the six sides of the box was entirely smooth. Wrapped around it, the completed image of a swirling cobra, in the shape of a figure eight

Ada turned to Nikki. 'See it's nothing to worry about.'

An intense white light blinded Ada. She felt herself sink through the floor like quicksand, falling into the blinding light. She screamed, but no sound came. Panic took hold of her, and she flailed with her arms and legs. There was no wind, no sensation but the fall. And suddenly the light receded, leaving her in a moderate gloom. Ada was no longer falling, but standing alone before two vast stone doors. Carved into each were the twin cobras intertwined in that sideways figure of eight pattern. She pushed the doors opened, revealing a long dark passageway. Far in the distance, Ada saw a pinprick of flickering light. A fire? Ada tried calling out for Nikki, and was relieved to hear her own voice echoing back to her. Then she felt a stab of fear. Did she want to be heard down here in the dark? She touched the passageway wall. It was clammy, its surface jagged and rocky. The air was rotten.

Ada pinched herself a few times but nothing happened beyond a throbbing pain in her arm.

Ok, so not a dream, she thought.

Well…she wasn't going to learn anything standing here. Ada headed towards the light.

The journey was surprisingly swift for all her hesitancy. It was as though she were being drawn to the light, carried seven steps for every one she took. The passageway widened out into a large chamber. Ada froze at the entrance, trying to take it all in. The only illumination came from ahead; a jagged strip of pulsating light suspended in the centre of the chamber, but it revealed the vastness of its scale.

Facing the light was a robed man, stood on a large hexagon shaped platform with his hands raised. A wide chasm surrounded the platform and separated it from the rest of the chamber. A narrow stone bridge seemed to be the only access point. The man was chanting in a language unknown to Ada.

The chanting grew louder and with each pulse from the light, the chamber seemed to be getting hotter. Ada wondered if the two were connected somehow.

The man was yelling the words now, incomprehensible yet beginning to be edged with doubt. The strip was even brighter now.

The chanting stopped. The man lowered his hands and turned. Ada stumbled back when she saw the man's eyes. They were blank. In the light they appeared to be solid sliver.

'Wha…What have we done?' he asked himself.

The man then screamed the sound shattering the scene before Ada's eyes as though made of glass. The spinning fragments were sucked back into blinding white light.

As the light began to fade Ada heard Nikki's voice calling out but all she could see was a shard of glass, spinning in front of her. It was a little bigger than her hand. Soon more spinning pieces of glass appeared – different sizes and shapes – each containing a moving image. The whirlwind of glass spun faster and faster around Ada, linking together like a jigsaw, arranging themselves into a completely new scene. She found herself within a great hall, the type you might expect to see in a medieval castle. A dozen or

TRAIL OF THE CURSED COBRAS · 157

more robed figures were seated in high-backed chairs around a long wooden table.

The doors at the opposite end of the hall swung open and a man staggered in. The fire, roaring within the ornate fireplace, cast his crooked shadow against the cobbled stone floor and up against the tapestry on the wall behind him. Ada recognised him at once: the man who had been chanting to the tear of light. As the man approached the table he stumbled. Two others sprang from their chairs to catch him. They half led, half dragged him to an empty chair and sat him down with some delicacy. Once seated the man snatched a large goblet, hungrily downing the contents in one go.

'Well, Jasper?'

The man wiped the liquid from his mouth, sighed and shook his head.

'The breach is too powerful now; it cannot be closed.'

The hooded man who was seated at the far end of the table stood.

'I told you all. We should never have continued Bertram's work. Now, in our hubris, we have doomed not only this world but also the countless others we sought to save.'

Jasper slammed the tankard down onto the table. 'Self-recrimination will not serve us now, Francis. If we do not find a way, here and now, everything we hold dear will be laid to waste.'

'But you said it was hopeless.'

'I said we cannot *close* the breach Francis, but perhaps we can contain it.'

'How?' asked a black-bearded man.

'You know how, Cedric.'

'Bertram will never help us and more than that we cannot risk bringing him here.'

'We do not need to bring him here,' said Jasper, refilling his goblet. 'And he will help us or that prison cell will be his tomb.'

Ada felt something shaking her, bodily. The images shook with her until they settled on the image of a wall on one side of the great underground chamber. Dozens upon dozens of small alcoves had been chiseled into wall. It was a spectacular sight. Running alongside the wall was an immense, twisting wooden staircase comprising of several landings.

One of the robed figures, who Ada recognised as the one called Jasper was perched atop the second landing on the staircase, about halfway up the wall. In one hand Jasper held the Salus Key. In front of him were nine nearly identical alcoves, all surrounded by strange writing similar to what Ada had seen on the Salus Key. The quality of light in the chamber had changed. Now it was bathed in a strange crimson hue.

'Please work,' whispered Jasper, pushing the box into the first alcove in the middle row.

The scene faded once more and Nikki's face loomed large above Ada. She was back in the bedroom. Nikki's large hands were clamped to Ada's shoulders, shaking her in panic.

'It's… o...k… I'm… back,' Ada managed to judder out.

Nikki released her and stepped back in relief. 'You were proper out of it. Your eyes rolled back like a zombie or summink. What happened? Was it like in Assembly again?'

Ada rubbed her neck and then realised both her hands were empty. 'Where's the key?'

'I knocked it out of your hand when you fell over.' She pointed to the corner of the room where the box lay, half under the bed. 'When it hit the floor you opened your eyes.'

'Intriguing,' Ada mused. She must write all of this down, she thought, while it's all fresh in her mind. She scrabbled around for her casebook and a pen.

'So you gonna tell me what happened?' asked Nikki.

Ada told her about it as she jotted it all down. It was quite help-ful, actually. Nikki's questions made her really think about the details. She made sure to draw the nine alcoves, shading in the spot where Jasper had placed the key.

'What do you think it means?' asked Nikki.

Ada stared over at the Salus Key and shook her head.

'It means we need help. Big time.'

16

Police Matters

'See em yet?' asked Bobby.

DJ was perched atop his chair, the edge of his hand held to his forehead as though he were scanning the vast ocean for danger. In this case the ocean was whatever lay beyond the classroom door.

'Nothing yet Cap'n Gibson,' DJ replied in his best pirate voice. 'Maybe the sharks got 'em.'

'Jenson! Get Down!'

Mr Wattling stormed into the form room, red with rage.

'Aye-aye Cap'n Wattling,' said DJ, jumping down.

Wattling closed the door. 'One more aye-aye out of you and you'll be swabbing the decks in detention!'

Bobby's eyes remained fixed on the door. 'Where are they?' he whispered.

'Maybe they've bunked off to go see that antiques bloke,' Tony suggested.

'Ada miss school? No flipping way.'

'Gibson!' snapped Mr Wattling. 'Is there anything you want to share with the rest of class? Or would you rather share a detention?'

'No sir,' said Bobby, slumping back into his chair.

'Sorry sir,' added Tony, looking suitably embarrassed.

'Then perhaps I can take the register before the year is out.'

He was just calling the sixth name when Ada and Nikki burst into the classroom.

'Ah, Amaya and Panilides, how nice of you to join us.'

Neither girl answered at first, as both were gasping for air.

'Sor…Sorry we're late…sir,' said Ada. 'We were…'

'I don't want to hear it,' snapped Wattling 'Just stand there and wait while I finish the register.'

Mr Wattling continued, with Ada and Nikki's heavy wheezing in the background.

As soon as the register was complete, Mr Wattling announced they were to head straight to their first lessons. He'd talk to the girls about their tardiness later. Bobby and Tony flew out of their chairs to join Ada and Nikki whilst DJ dawdled along, trying out one of his magic tricks on a couple of their classmates.

Bobby slapped Ada on the shoulder. 'Thought Wattling was going to proper lose it then,' said Bobby. 'How come you two were late?'

Ada rubbed her bloodshot eyes. 'We overslept.'

Tony grinned. 'And we got loads to tell you.'

Bobby shoved him. '*I'll* tell 'em, Smiley.'

'Get lost! I was first. And stop calling me Smiley!'

DJ appeared out of nowhere, throwing his arms around the pair. 'They tell you those weird lines on that roof was a map, yet? Tony traced it to show us. Pretty cool, right? And I fixed the tape and we listened to it, and there's all sorts of stuff on there about the ESD and some Apocalypse Chamber or something. It was awesome.'

'*Thanks*…mate,' snarled Bobby, his thunder well and truly stolen.

Tony's grin grew wider at this. DJ stared at them confused.

'What did I do?'

'Apart from being a prat? Nuffink,' said Bobby.

Ada sighed. 'When you lot have grown up, maybe we'll tell you what happened to *us* last night.'

'Come off it, Ada – nothing's gonna beat what we did,' Bobby boasted.

'Nikki fought off one of the Faceless, with her cat and a ruler, and then we blew it up with a packet of crisps,' said Ada, examining her nails.

'Oh! And Ada made the puzzle box glow when she touched it, and she saw lots of weird stuff, too.' Nikki added.

'But you're right Bobson,' Ada continued, patting his hand, 'that's nowhere near as exciting as tracing a map.'

'Or listening to a tape,' added Nikki, with a smirk.

'Nah,' said Tony, grinning. 'They're winding us up; it's all a joke.'

Nikki punched Tony in the arm.

'Ow! What'd you do that for?'

'Call me a liar again and I'll do the other one,' said Nikki, eyeing Tony's other arm.

As they filed out for their first lessons, before they went their separate ways, Bobby made everyone agree to meet outside the science block at first break to continue their discussion.

Bobby found it even more challenging to stay awake in the morning lessons than in an assembly. Tony, on the other hand, was so excited by the prospect of Double Geography that he had practically sprinted to his seat.

Bobby could not remember seeing anyone put up their hand so much during one lesson. At first Miss Connelly had been all smiles, applauding Tony's answers, but Bobby watched as the light behind her eyes began to fade.

'Does anyone *else* have an answer?' she groaned at one point. 'Come on, now. Someone must have an idea,' she pleaded. 'It doesn't have to be right. Anyone?'

'I know miss, I know!' barked Tony.

'I think the new boy's broken, Miss Connelly,' said one girl, sitting behind Bobby.

The class erupted into laughter.

Bobby sighed, banging his forehead against the desk. He began to count down the seconds to the end of the class.

The next lesson was History with Mr Dixonville, who was dressed in the same rubbish green suit he had worn last year. Everyone reckoned Dixonville had a wardrobe full of green suits at his house. Either that, or he never cleaned it. Bobby always held his nose as he passed, just in case.

Once he'd set the work for the lesson Dixonville patrolled the room, making sure everyone was working and doing so in silence. Even the most hardened of troublemakers knew that no one messed around in Mr Dixonville's class. The rumour was that he had been a prison guard before he became a teacher.

As soon as the bell for break sounded, Bobby and Tony went to find the others. Ada, DJ and Nikki were sitting outside the science block on a patch of grass that ran the length of the building.

You best not get that uniform messed up, boy.

Bobby smiled to himself. It was good to have Mum back.

Me can't always be here to watch you. Especially when you is up to no good.

Bobby tossed his satchel onto the grass and sat on it.

Good boy.

'Clue check,' said Ada, clapping her hands. 'We have a puzzle box that has unique reflective qualities in moonlight, and my vision. Now—'

'Don't forget about the poem,' said Bobby.

'You mean the poem you're only telling me about now?' asked Ada, taking out her casebook. 'Tell me it again.'

'Steal the moon to light the beacon. Pay the goddess to open the gate. Step within the moon's crimson shade to seal our fate,' said Tony.

'Well that makes no sense,' said Nikki.

Ada made Tony repeat the poem while she jotted it down in her casebook. Once she was satisfied she continued.

'So, as I was about the to say, Bertram Langley believes the box is something called the Salus Key, which can help him find this Apocalypse Chamber.'

'Oh! Oh! Oh!' shouted DJ, his arm shooting up.

Ada slammed him with her shoulder. 'Put your arm down, dummy. We're not in class,'

'I forgot to say – I know what Salus means!'

'You mean that Henry knows? He told me he dropped off some college work for your sister,' said Ada. 'How are they...getting on?'

'Do you want to know or what?' asked DJ, disgusted at the thought of any romance between his sister and Henry. 'Salus is the roman goddess of safety.'

'Goddess! just like in the poem Agent Ash translated,' said Ada, grinning. 'Pay the goddess to open the gate.'

DJ shook his head. 'What's it mean?'

'No idea,' said Ada. 'Yet.'

'You know, we really should tell our parents,' said Tony.

Bobby thought at least one of his parents knew.

That's not funny boy.

'If I tell Mum and Dad what we've been up to, Dad will make me disappear,' said DJ sullenly. 'And he'll say it was a magic trick gone wrong.'

'They wouldn't believe us anyway,' said Ada.

'What about the headmaster?' suggested Tony, who was clearly uncomfortable with the idea that everything was up to them to solve.

Everyone stared hard at Tony then the laughter started, lots of it.

'New boy's a joker,' chuckled DJ, wiping his eyes. 'Like Creasey's gonna give a toss.'

Tony swore, sending an award-winning glower in DJ's direction.

'We need to go and see that Carnaby bloke Henry told us about,' said Bobby.

Ada scratched her chin thoughtfully. 'Bobson's right. We know now Ash was going to see him, so this is the next logical course of action.'

'Logical?' Tony jumped to his feet, his hand slashing the air in a diagonal motion. 'No way! No flipping way! We only just made it out of that estate. Now Ada and Nikki got attacked – in Ada's own bedroom. He knows where she lives! Why am I the only one who thinks this has gone too far. We need to go to the police.'

'Anyone got a lollipop?' asked Nikki, as if she had not heard any of the conversation.

'*Not* helping Nikki,' said Bobby. 'And no one's going to the police Smiley, you got that?'

'Henry said Carnaby's shop is only open during school time, so how we going to do that one, genius?' snarked Tony.

'Tony's right. I think we talk to DI Penthrope first. See if she can help,' Ada said.

A thin line formed between Bobby's eyebrows as he glared at Ada. 'Like she's gonna believe anything we tell her.'

'It's worth a try. And anyway you're out voted Bobson.'

'We didn't—'

Ada's hand shot up, cutting off Bobby's complaint. 'All those in favour of going to the police, raise your hands.'

Tony and DJ's hands joined Ada's.

Mi hand is up too.

'I hate you all,' muttered Bobby, then added a whispered 'Not you, Mum.'

Ada set off for the main school building. 'Come on then; we can catch her before the next lesson.'

***

'Slow down, slow down,' said DI Penthrope, rubbing her forehead. 'You did say The End of the World, right?'

Ada, Tony and DJ kept talking over each other, fighting to be the one to tell the story.

'ENOUGH!'

Penthrope's fist crashed against her desk, scattering paper everywhere. She took a deep breath, lifted her head and pointed her pen at Bobby.

'You. Mr Quiet. You want to say anything?'

Yuh remember what mi tell yuh. Be polite, none of that lip.

Bobby shook his head. 'Not to you I don't, Pi—'

Boy!

Bobby covered the last word with cough. He started again, shaken by Mum's fury. 'No. I ain't got nothing to say.'

'Wise boy,' said Penthrope, turning her pen to Tony. 'Right, You and you alone tell me what happened.'

Tony looked at Ada.

'Don't look at her, look at me,' ordered Penthrope. 'Now. Tell me what you saw and what it has to do with our missing Mr Rillington?'

'Go on,' whispered Ada. 'Tell her.'

Tony stepped up to the desk, opened his mouth and no words came out. The other officer who was stood beside Penthrope came around the desk. He crouched in front of Tony, giving him a wide smile half hidden by a brushy brown moustache.

'Your name's Tony right?' he asked, adjusting a pair of glasses that were so thick Bobby wondered if they gave him x-ray vision.

Tony nodded.

'My name is Detective Sergeant Hoplin. It's my job to protect you and your friends, do you understand?'

'Yes.'

'Good. Now I promise you're safe here Tony. You can say anything you want in this room, okay?'

'Okay.'

'Do think you can tell us what happened?'

More nodding. Calmer this time.

Hoplin stood. 'Go on then, son.'

As Tony talked, the grin on Hoplin's face widened while Penthrope's face was growing redder with each new element of Tony's tale. Eventually she snapped.

'So let me get this straight. You're saying Mr Rillington was spirited away by a hooded ghost? And that's because he's a spy, working undercover as a substitute teacher because he wants to find something called the Apocalypse Chamber? That about cover it?'

'Yes,' said Tony.

'He sounds like a very busy man,' said Hoplin.

Penthrope sighed. 'I told you we wouldn't need a teacher for this Hoplin.'

She aimed her pen at Tony.

'Do you know what wasting police time means? Or trespassing for that matter?'

Ada raised her hand. 'I do, miss.'

'Then you'll also know how much trouble you lot are about to be in.'

Ada scowled.

'Nothing to say? Here let me help you.' Penthrope held up a finger. 'One: I don't believe a word of your story, which means you're wasting police time.'

Penthrope lifted another finger. 'Two. If I were to believe *any* part of your story, it would be the five of you breaking into a building site. That's trespassing, for which at the very least I would be talking to all of your parents.'

Nikki huffed, Tony made a gagging sound, while Ada and Bobby's eyes stayed rooted on the Detective Inspector's stern face. DJ stared out of the window, whistling the opening bars to 'Eye of the Tiger', entirely oblivious.

'What DI Penthrope is trying to say,' said DS Hoplin, in a more friendly tone, 'is that she knows you came here because you wanted to help us find Mr Rillington, but that perhaps your imaginations got carried away with you.'

Penthrope turned to DS Hoplin, her face still beetroot red. 'I told the commissioner this whole idea was nonsense. Setting up an investigation in a school for God's sake. Then sending over someone I've never worked with before for a bog-standard missing persons case.'

'The commissioner felt you could benefit from an outside perspective and...'

'That we need to work more closely with the community I remember the speech. I'm just saying I could have done with my old DS and not some fella I don't know...no offence Hoplin.'

'None taken,' said Hoplin with a shrug. 'I go where I'm told ma'am.'

'Yes well if the commissioner had known we would be babysitting a pack of liars.'

'We're not liars!' snapped Ada. 'We have a tap—'

'We only wanted to help,' said Bobby, cutting off Ada. 'We heard one of the upper years talking about the estate and seeing something weird...'

'...And you wanted to be the heroes of the school by telling us, right?' asked Hoplin, smoothly.

Bobby wrung his hands. He had been in trouble enough times to know how to act sorry.

'Yes, sir. Sorry sir.'

'And you never actually went to the estate did you?'

'No. sir. My auntie would have skinned me alive if I did that.'

'My Auntie Doris is the same,' laughed Hoplin. He slapped one of his hands on Bobby's shoulder. 'Don't worry about it. It was a great story – best I've heard in a while.'

'Then we're not in trouble?' Bobby asked.

'Of course you are!' stormed Penthrope.

'Even you were a kid once Ma'am,' said Hoplin, looking over his shoulder at Penthrope. 'You telling me you never told the odd fib?'

Penthrope slumped back in her seat, her anger ebbing away.

'So how about this?' continued Hoplin. 'We won't say anything to your parents or teachers if you stop with all this nonsense and we'll call it even. Deal?'

Hoplin held out a hand towards Bobby, who looked at it for a long moment before finally shaking it. 'Oh, and don't be going near that estate that you say you never went to in the first place, eh?' Hoplin tapped his nose. 'Building sites can be dangerous places.'

'Yes sir,' said Bobby.

'If I ever see you lot in here again, you won't like how that little chat ends,' promised Penthrope, pointing to the door. 'Now get out, whilst I'm still feeling generous!'

Hoplin gave them a wink as they left, told them to stay out of trouble, then closed the door.

'Told ya they wouldn't listen,' said Bobby.

He leant against the wall trying not to meet Ada's furious glare.

'Why didn't you let me tell Penthrope about the tape?' she demanded.

'You saw how it was in there. That lot were never gonna believe kids like us. Penthrope would have said we recorded the stuff on the tape off the telly or something. Besides on the tape Agent Ash sounds nothing like Mr Rillington does he? Not with that American accent of his.'

'That is true,' admitted Ada.

'Still could have been worth a try,' said Tony. 'We didn't even get to tell 'em about Orlando and Gans.'

Bobby nodded back at the closed door.

'Go then Smiley. You tell them coppers how we broke into a teacher's office and nicked that tape, you see what happens to you. I've got a better idea.'

'Oh yeah and what's that?' asked Tony, not moving.

'We're going to break out of school to go see that Carnaby bloke.'

17

The Great Lunchtime Escape

The horse chestnut stood on the biggest section of grass in the whole school. It stretched the length of the lower years' playground, past the bulk of the school, all the way down to the back playground, where the upper years hung out. Sat beneath the thick branches of the towering tree Ada was racking her brains, trying to understand how someone as intelligent as she had been talked into this crazy plan.

'You absolutely sure this is the only way?' she asked.

'You think I *want* to see that headcase?' asked Bobby. 'But we need to see Carnaby, and Sid's the only one who can help us sneak out. Trust me, I got us covered. Just stick with me when we get up there.'

Trust was not Ada's issue. It was the fact that Bobby's 'plans' tended to be made up as he went along, often relying on a huge dollop of luck. It was a terrible strategy.

'I still think we could pop a card through Carnaby's letter box on the way home from school,' suggested Tony.

DJ cuffed him round the head.

Tony shoved him back. 'Oi! Pack it in!'

DJ held up his left hand and pretended to write upon it as though he were holding a pen. 'Dear Mr Carnaby, we've got this puzzle box that some immortal headcase wants back so he can complete his evil plans. Please can you help us? Signed the biggest loser going, Smiley Tadpole.'

'Git,' said Tony, rubbing the back of his head. 'I dunno why you're bothered, anyway. You're not even coming with us.'

'I can't be everywhere, can I? Ada wants me in the library doing research. What's a boy to do?'

'So what are you doing here then?'

DJ crouched and began scooping up conker shells, stuffing them into his pockets. 'I'm backing up my mates, ain't I? Where's Nikki, anyway?'

'She said to go without her,' explained Bobby, dropping back. 'Dunno why but she said once we sort things out with Sid she's back in.'

'So, we're talking to that nutter without our secret weapon?' said DJ, throwing up his hands. 'Flipping marvellous.'

Tony pointed at the conker shells. 'What you going to go with those?'

DJ hurled one of the green conker shells at Tony, who yelped as the spiked shell struck his hand.

'That answer your question, Smiley?'

Ada nudged Bobby. 'This plan of yours better be good, Bobson.'

'Best plan ever,' he said with a wink.

Ada saw two girls and three boys stalking towards them from the back playground. They looked like they meant business. She shushed the others into silence.

The kids were a mix of different years, shapes, sizes and colours. Their one unifying trait was they all looked meaner than next door's pitbull. Ada knew who all of them were by sight, having spent her first year at school taking extensive notes on the more unsavoury pupils. It paid to know your enemy.

Ada spotted the Ofune sisters, whose favourite pastime was doling out cruelty. Their speciality was stuffing heads down toilets then pulling the chain. Next to the sisters strode Mikey Cojure. The hulking skinhead oozed a brutish menace. Mikey was Sid's second in command and his head enforcer, roles which he undertook with violent enthusiasm. When he was not punching in faces under Sid's orders, he tended to punch metal lockers, or doors. He even punched a brick wall once, but the wall was undamaged. The fact that both he and Sid had been made prefects made Ada's blood boil. Like they needed any more power! Prefects were supposed to be shining examples of how pupils should behave at St Icilda's, not belligerent thugs.

At the centre of the villainous crowd, laughing and joking with his minions, walked a tall, muscular, blond-haired boy. The immaculate condition of his school uniform was matched by his perfectly permed blond hair. He looked angelic, except round the eyes. Every school has a villain and within the walls of St Icilda's that was Sid Horrun. Ada remembered the section in her casebook which summed up the boy.

'Sidney Ignatius Horrun lacks any basic empathy towards his fellow pupils. He has a fierce intellect and an innate animal cunning which, coupled with his good looks, enable his criminal endeavours to remain undetected by the faculty. Sid Horrun would be a dangerous adversary. Any direct contact with him or his lieutenants should be completely avoided unless absolutely necessary.'

Ada had uncovered Sid's vast criminal network during her first year, and the depth and breadth of it left her aghast. These crimes included – but were not limited to – stealing lunch money, forcing smarter kids to do homework for anyone willing to pay Sid, stealing and copying exam papers, and falsifying school records. All the while maintaining his reputation as the headmaster's favourite prefect. It was disgusting.

'Well, well, well,' said Mikey, his gold prefect badge glinting. 'If it isn't the little nutter and his monster club.'

A burst of chuckles rang out from Sid's cronies as they surrounded Ada and the others, cutting off any escape. Sid hung back, just as Ada expected.

Letting your lieutenants do the dirty work for you, like any good general, thought Ada. *Impressive.*

'You got ten seconds to tell me what you want with Sid, nutter,' said Mikey. 'I know your brother's thick as a plank but even he should have told you this place is off limits.'

Bobby looked past Mikey. 'Sid? You—'

Mikey gave Bobby a light slap on the cheek. 'Oi! You talk to me, Gibson.'

Come on Bobby, thought Ada. *You can do this.*

'Dead mum got your tongue?' asked Daria Ofune, chuckling. 'She still talking to you? Does mummy read you bedtime stories in your mind?'

'Little nutter thinks no one knows,' sneered another of Sid's mates. 'But everyone knows. Everyone knows he's sick in the head.'

Ada saw Bobby's eyes glisten. His fists were clenched. Whatever Bobby's plan was, the mention of his mum was making him forget it.

'You come here for a fight then, nutter? Is that it?' asked Mikey, jabbing Bobby in the chest. 'You trying to step into big brother's shoes?'

DJ and Tony took a step back but Ada stayed put. She had known Bobby since Nursery. All those years spent getting in and out of trouble together had taught her one thing: Bobby Gibson could talk his way out of *anything*.

'Stick to the plan Bobson,' she whispered

Bobby blinked as though coming out of a trance.

Mikey cracked his knuckles, his gleaming white teeth beaming at the prospect of violence. Bobby looked past Mikey at Sid, then did something that surprised everyone. He smiled. Not a small, timid smile, but a I'm-King-of-the-World kind of grin.

'You owe me a favour, Sid,' Bobby called loudly. 'I'm here to collect.'

Favour, thought Ada. *What flipping favour?*

She shot a questioning look back at DJ, who just shrugged, mystified.

Mikey grabbed Bobby; his fist ready to get to work. 'Sid doesn't owe you anything, you little s—'

'Leave him,' said Sid.

Mikey released Bobby then moved to one side, glaring.

Sid stepped into the space, spat at the ground by Bobby's feet, then eyed him up. Bobby met Sid's gaze with his own steely look.

'Third day into the year and you want to pull in a favour? The only favour I've ever given *anyone* in this dump?' asked Sid.

Bobby nodded and Sid laughed.

Out of the corner of her eye, Ada noticed dozens of kids crammed against the lower years' playground fence, watching and hoping they had a front row seat to seeing someone get a kicking.

I hope you know what you're doing Bobson.

'You've got nerve, I'll give you that. Alright tough nut, what do you want?'

'To get out of school at lunchtime.'

Ada had expected Sid to laugh at Bobby's request but instead the older boy looked...impressed.

'Yeah I can do that.'

'Really?' piped up Tony from behind.

'Who's the smiling muppet?' asked Sid.

'He's new,' explained Bobby.

'If Kermit says one more word he'll have the stuffing knocked out of him. Now you meet me back here dead on one o'clock, you got it?'

'Got it,' said Bobby.

Sid clicked his fingers, swung round and swaggered away, the others following. As soon as they were out of ear shot, Ada pushed Bobby so hard he tripped and landed flat on his back.

'What did you do that for?'

'Sid Horrun owes you a favour? Sid Horrun! And you didn't think it was worth telling me before?' asked Ada, her temper rising.

Bobby sat up, swatting away several conker shells that had embedded themselves in his blazer. 'I told you I had a plan didn't I? Besides Sid telling me he owes me, and me actually getting him to pay up...' Bobby blew the air out of his cheeks. '...that's two different things, ain't it?'

Ada kicked a pile of leaves into Bobby's face and stalked off, ignoring the spluttering behind her.

***

It's okay to be scared, Nikki. A true knight can only triumph by staring down their own fear.

Nikki was pretty sure that Dad didn't have a gang of surly looking fourth and fifth years in mind when he had given her that advice. In the distance she saw the horse chestnut tree where Ada and others were due to meet Sid again so he could keep his promise to get them out of school. Nikki had told Ada that this time she would meet her and the others there. Nikki saw no need in making her trouble theirs. She had known once she set foot in the back playground, her very own dragon would be waiting.

The crowd of fourth and fifth years parted, taking the colour from Nikki's face with them. The Dragon strode forward. It was tall, with flaming red hair, but instead of blasting fire from its mouth it was blowing a pink bubble gum. When the dragon stopped just a few feet from Nikki, the bubble burst.

'You got some front coming round 'ere, I'll give you that,' said the Dragon. It made some clackity-clack chewing noises as it looked down its nose at her.

The dragon hefted a hockey stick across its broad shoulders. Nikki wondered if Jenny Atkins, ever used her stick to play actual hockey or whether it was purely for beating up younger kids.

'I'm just going to meet my friends.'

Jenny slid the hockey stick from her shoulders and let it swing to and fro.

'Nah, you ain't going nowhere, Panilides,' she sneered. 'Karl still ain't right after what you did to him last year, you cow.'

Suddenly a short girl with braces darted forward, snatching Nikki's satchel strap. Nikki tugged back and the satchel flew open. Nikki's battered old teddy bear tumbled to the ground. With a single swipe of her hockey stick, Jenny had swept the bear up into the air and caught it.

'Ah, look at the little *baby*. Look at her little tear bear,' she cooed, shaking the bear and displaying it triumphantly.

Some of the other girls joined in with insults of their own and mocking laughter. Nikki had heard them all before. They hurt a little less each time, but she couldn't deny it – they did still hurt. She took a deep breath and thought about what Dad used to tell her.

A true knight does not speak of their deeds; their deeds speak for themselves.

Jenny leant against her hockey stick while tossing Sir Bedivere up into the air and catching him one-handed. Nikki gripped the strap of her satchel tightly.

A true knight knows when to stand their ground.

'Tell you what, teddy bear girl,' said Jenny, 'you get on your knees, say you're sorry for what you did to Karl and…give me your lunch money, and maybe I'll leave you with a few tee—'

Nikki swung her satchel in wide arc, sweeping away Jenny's legs and sending her hockey stick spinning into the air. She crashed sideways straight into two girls, who hit the deck with her like ninepins. Nikki took off through gap, seizing Sir Bedivere on the way.

And they know when to give it.

***

Sid was waiting for Bobby and the others when they reached the top of the hill, but only Mikey was with him this time.

'You're late, Gibson,' Sid griped.

'Only by like a minute,' said Tony. 'It's still lunchtime.'

'Anyone talking to you, Pan Face?'

Sid turned and started walking down the grassy slope.

'Come on losers,' he called over his shoulder.

Ada whispered to Bobby. 'What about Nikki? We should wait for her.'

'She knows what we're up to, maybe she got cold feet,' suggested Bobby. He hoped he was wrong. He had no idea what they would discover at Carnaby's shop, but having Nikki there would make him feel better.

'You coming or what?' Sid asked.

Bobby reluctantly followed, Ada and Tony close behind. As they entered the back playground, Bobby felt like a cowboy in a western, walking into the saloon. Loads of older kids stopped what they were doing to stare at the newcomers. In one of the far corners, a large group of kids stood shouting and jeering. Bobby felt sorry for whoever was in the middle of all that, but he had his own problems. A few kids were moving towards them now, followed by a few more and a few more, like metal filings drawn to a magnet. None of them looked like they wanted to be friends.

'We're going to die,' muttered Tony.

'Shut up,' snapped Ada. 'We'll be fine. Right, Bobby?'

But Bobby was beginning to agree with Tony.

'They're with me,' Sid said evenly, his voice just loud enough to be heard.

Mikey cracked his knuckles. Instantly the kids melted away, back to their previous activities.

'Make an example of three of 'em after school,' said Sid, without breaking his stride. 'No broken bones, but remind them who runs this dump.'

Mikey nodded.

Bobby felt sorry for them. They had gone back to playing football, oblivious of the two-fisted missile heading their way.

Sid led them to the far corner of the playground fence where it was stopped by the wall of the garage, next to the school. Two big sixth-formers were stood there, leant up against the fence. Bobby noticed that they were wearing prefect badges. Were there any prefects in this school, besides his brother, who weren't working for Sid?

'Wotcha Sid,' said the taller of the boys. 'What you need?'

'Three to go out, Adam.'

'It's…four.'

Everyone turned to see a breathless Nikki rocking up. Her tie had come loose and her clothes were dishevelled as though she had been wrestling. She moved to stand beside Ada, who looked her up and down.

'What happened to you?'

'I had… a dragon… to slay,' gasped Nikki.

Sid's eyes narrowed. 'How'd you get through the back playground?'

'I… walked.'

'You think you're funny, cyclops?' snapped Sid.

'I have… my moments.'

Nikki kept looking behind her. Following her gaze Bobby saw a group of girls, led by a tall redhead with a hockey stick. They were a bit of a distance away, looking right at her. He knew they would not come any closer, though. No one interrupted Sid when he was doing business. Judging by the smile Nikki was giving them, she knew it too.

Mickey moved in front of Nikki, towering over her. Nikki shifted her attention to him, her expression unchanged. 'I know you,' growled Mikey. 'You're the one who beat up Karl Atkins, right?'

Nikki nodded.

'I ain't no fourth year, you get me?'

'Loud and clear.'

'Don't think I won't smack a girl.'

'Brave boy.'

No more words passed between them. All Bobby could hear was the sound of Nikki's lollipop. It was like watching David and Goliath face off, but in this case David was a twelve-year-old Greek girl.

'We doing this or what, Sid?'

Adam's question broke the tension, and Mikey eased back.

Sid pointed at Nikki. 'She going with you?'

Bobby nodded.

Sid sighed. 'Fine. We all clear, Adam?'

'Hold up, lemme check.'

Adam lifted his hand. Farther along the fence, a skinny pimply faced boy looked out onto the street, then gave them the thumbs up.

Adam then looked over at the two boys who were stationed at either corner of the sports hall. One boy, who wore a blue turban and was pretending to read a thick textbook, gave a subtle thumbs up. The boy on the other side was kicking a ball around with two mates. Spotting Adam, he snuck a look around at the corner, gave a nod, then returned to his game.

'No teachers or truncheons,' Adam announced. 'We're all set.'

Impressive, Ada thought. All good information for her notebook when she got the chance to update it.

'What's a Truncheon?' asked Tony.

'Truant officers,' said Bobby. 'If they catch us, it's instant suspension.'

'Great,' sighed Tony. 'Flipping great.'

'You sure you lot want to do this?' asked Sid.

Bobby and the others nodded, apart from Nikki who had resumed her stare off with Mikey.

'I do this and we're even, Gibson. You say one word about Norfolk and—'

'I won't.'

Sid grabbed Bobby by his jacket lapels. 'You better not, or you and your mates are dead.'

'I won't, I swear it!'

Sid let him go and said. 'Do it.'

Adam gripped the end of one of the fence bars and twisted it. There was a screech of metal as he lifted the bar clear.

'Get caught and you're on your own,' Sid scowled. 'You grass me up and your own families won't recognise you.'

Bobby didn't answer. He was saving his courage for what he was about to do.

'Come on you lot, let's go,' he said at last.

With that Bobby slipped between the bars. As soon as he was clear, he sprinted across the road, the others hot on his heels.

18

The Shopkeeper

I know it's starting at a new school Tony, but with that smile of yours I know you'll be making many new friends and having fun in no time.

Tony was pretty sure that breaking enough rules to get himself expelled was not what Dad meant by 'having fun'.

Glancing over his shoulder, he saw the two sixth-formers twisting the fence bar back into place.

'Better get a move on, mate,' said Adam, tapping his watch. 'You got forty-five minutes.'

Tony gulped. *I should've gone to the library with DJ.*

Nikki grabbed Tony's arm, pulling him after her. Tony broke free then watched horrified as Nikki raced across the road, angry car horns blaring at her. Tony used the pelican crossing just down the road, then dashed to catch up.

This was the maddest thing he had ever done but he could not stop a slow smile creeping across his face. There was something exciting about all this. Dangerous, sure, but he felt part of something. Included.

'Run now, smile later,' said Nikki.

She headed down a side alley next to the Kebab shop, and Tony followed at a jog. His stomach growled at the scent of sizzling meat and spices wafting out through the open door. No time for lunch today, though. This was their only chance to get some answers.

Bobby and Ada were waiting outside a manky-looking shop. The paint on the frontage was weathered and flaking off. The shop door gave the impression that a good sneeze could blow it in. To the right of the door was a large grubby window, its frame chipped and smothered with dirt. The words _Carnaby' Curios y op_ were written in an arch on the glass.

Tony pressed his nose against the window and peered in. The shop's interior was cloaked in gloom and filled with junk. It reminded Tony of his Uncle Victor's garage, except that was cleaner and had far fewer spider's webs.

'Shouldn't you lot be in school?'

They all turned. Facing them was an old man in a crisp business suit.

Bobby stepped forward. 'We're on special leave, helping to clean this shop. You can check with the school – just ask for Mr Sheen.'

The man muttered something under his breath, but he moved off, satisfied.

'Quick thinking, Bobson,' said Ada.

Bobby bowed.

'We need to get inside. The next person could be a Truncheon,' warned Nikki.

'Alright, keep your patch on,' said Bobby, holding a fist out to Ada. 'Rock, Paper, Scissors? Loser opens the door?'

'We don't have the time, Bobson. Just open the door like a good little sidekick or get out of the way.'

Bobby kissed his teeth, grumbled something about being no-one's sidekick, then began to open the creaking door. A shove from Ada sent him tumbling into the shop.

'Oi!' barked Bobby, aiming an angry scowl at Ada. She rolled her eyes and pushed past him, followed by the others.

The shop seemed much larger now he was inside, adjusting to the gloom. Everywhere Tony looked, the strange and the bizarre stared back. Wooden shelves ran from floor to ceiling, stacked with oddities. A giant statue of a polar bear (wearing a bright pink top hat for some reason) stood in one corner. Bobby oohed and aahed as he wandered along the shelves. He lifted a bronze skull to eye level and peered into its eye sockets.

'This shop is proper!' he said.

Tony brushed some cobwebs from his sleeve. 'It's a dump.'

Bobby swapped the skull for a metal helmet from the shelf above. It looked like a small metal football which had been sliced in half, a brim jutting out from one end.

'Hey, look. Knights had baseball caps!'

Bobby pulled on the helmet and threw a pose, arms wrapped around himself.

'Take that thing off!' Ada snapped.

'Chill out, A,' grinned Bobby, the helmet wobbling. 'Only having a bit of fun.'

Bobby's hand curled around a twisted black cane that sat in an umbrella stand. He studied his new toy with fresh delight. The cane's silver tip had been sharpened to a point so it looked more like a spear than a cane.

'Put that back, Bobson before—'

'WHAT IN HADES NAME DO YOU THINK YOU ARE DOING!?'

The thunderous voice boomed through the shop with such force Tony thought it would bring the entire place crashing down. They all froze at the sight of a hulking, black-bearded, barrel-chested man whose immense shoulders scraped the door frame on both sides as he stomped in. The man wore a crisp white shirt under a bright purple waistcoat which barely contained his gut.

Escaping its shadow was a pair of black and white checked trousers. If he were lying down, you could play chess on them.

'RAPSCALLION!' the man roared, pointing at Bobby. 'PUT THAT BACK!'

'Did he just swear at us?' asked Tony.

Nikki shrugged.

'Those artefacts have not endured centuries of chaos and war to be despoiled by your grubby digits!' the man bellowed. 'You have precisely sixty seconds to return them to their place and remove yourselves from my shop!'

The man's furious gaze never left Bobby's back as he carefully returned the cane and helmet to their spots. The man strode past Bobby, brushing him to one side. He edged the cane left then stepped back, cocking his head to one side. He harrumphed.

'It will have to do.'

'You are Mr Carnaby, I take it?' Ada asked.

'And who else, pray tell, would you expect to find in Carnaby's Curiosities?' He rolled every R like thunder.

'Excellent!' she grinned, extending a hand. 'I'm Ada Amaya and these are my friends, Tony, Nikki, and Bobby. I'm sorry about him. We came to see you today to talk—'

'LISTEN to me, girl!' Carnaby's cheeks quivered with each word. 'I do not have the time nor the inclination to converse with children today. Particularly ones who should be in school rather than ruining my displays.'

As he spoke, Carnaby herded the four of them towards the door, like an overstuffed sheepdog. Tony gulped as he saw the strange collection of symbols tattooed onto Carnaby's hairy forearms, ending in two giant eyes on the back of his hands. The eye on the left hand was open while its counterpart was closed. They were inked in a combination of black and red.

Nikki whistled. 'Cool tats.'

Carnaby responded by driving them out onto the street.

'Begone harpies,' he snapped, and began to swing the door closed.

Ada held the Salus Key up to the door's glass panel.

Carnaby's eyes sparkled in outrage, then surprise as he stared at the puzzle box. He opened the door once more and peered closer.

'The craftsmanship is spectacular,' he said with something like awe. 'Wherever did you find it?'

'Let us back in and I'll tell you,' Ada said.

Carnaby scratched his beard as though weighing up his options.

'Agreed,' he said. 'But not him.'

'Didn't want to go back in your poxy shop anyway,' mumbled Bobby.

Ada pulled the box from the doorway and held it over her open satchel. 'Everyone, Mr Carnaby.'

Carnaby sighed then swung the door open.

'Inside then, before I change my mind.'

Carnaby led them to the rear of the shop, pausing once more by the cane. 'Perhaps I may have been unnecessarily harsh to you, young man, but you see that cane and helmet are amongst my favourite pieces.'

'The cane's Roman, right?' asked Bobby.

Carnaby looked like someone had just gut-punched him. 'You have an eye for history!'

'Nah, I saw one in an Asterix comic once.'

Carnaby gazed proudly at the cane. 'It's called a vitis and has been in my family for generations. When I was a little older than you, my grandfather told me it belonged to a Roman centurion who marched with Julius Caesar. Do you know who that is?'

Bobby nodded.

'More Asterix comics?'

Another nod.

'Humph. Well the vitis was a centurion's symbol of authority, which was also used to discipline unruly men under his command.'

'Very cool,' breathed Bobby, staring at the cane.

'I certainly thought so,' agreed Carnaby with a gleam in his eye. He removed the price tag, tossed the vitis up in the air and caught it once more then, tucking it under his arm like a drill sergeant, he opened the door to the back room.

They followed Carnaby into a large sitting room, packed with trinkets and oddments. Carnaby gestured to the grey two-seater sofa and assorted wooden chairs scattered around the room. As they fought over the sofa Carnaby left the room. Minutes later, he returned – without the vitis, but carrying a tray laden with mugs of tea and a plate of biscuits.

'By way of a humble apology,' he explained, passing around the mugs. 'I don't get many visitors, and I daresay my manners have suffered.'

Tony held his mug of tea in one hand while shovelling biscuits in with the other. Bit by bit, his stomach unclenched. All the others had cups of tea apart from Nikki who simply sucked her lollipop, sat atop a stack of old newspapers. She was watching Carnaby like a hawk.

'Tea and biscuits, the perfect start to any conversation,' said Carnaby.

Ada swiped two chocolate biscuits from the plate before Tony could snaffle them. 'Tea and Jaffa Cakes is a much better start, but these'll do.'

Carnaby settled back into his armchair and crossed his legs.

'Now, I should very much like to know how you came into possession of that spectacular puzzle box—and please, spare no detail.'

Ada told Carnaby everything. She hadn't meant to be so forthright, but once she began, it all came pouring out: her meeting with Agent Ash in the graveyard right through to the vision she saw when she touched the glowing box.

Carnaby drank his tea and listened intently throughout. When Ada had finished, Carnaby shook his head and whistled in admiration.

'Quite the adventure,' he said.

'So, you believe us then?' asked Bobby.

'Let us say I'm willing to give you the benefit of the doubt. For now. Though I have no idea who this Agent Ash is, nor why this ESD would want to talk with me.'

'Oh! You don't know them?' asked Ada, crestfallen.

'I believe I would remember being contacted by a clandestine organisation.' He held out his hand. 'May I see the puzzle box again, please?'

Ada wedged a biscuit halfway in her mouth then handed it over.

The shopkeeper returned to his seat with the box and examined it once more. 'And you are sure he used the term 'Salus' Key.'

Ada nodded.

'Fascinating.' Carnaby turned to Tony. 'Do you still have the rubbing you made?'

'Oh right.' Tony dug through his pocket and pulled out the tracing paper with the map on it.

'And you are certain these markings are identical to the ones you found at the Baxter Estate?' asked Carnaby, raising the image to the light.

'Yes,' said Tony.

Carnaby laid the tracing paper on the table then placed Tony and Bobby's mugs at either corner to hold the paper in place.

'And the puzzle box glowed when it was bathed in moonlight – correct?'

Ada nodded. 'That's when I—'

'Yes, yes the vision. I was listening, my dear.'

Carnaby stalked over to a cluttered desk and began rummaging amongst the various items, knocking several onto the floor. Ada scowled, then mouthed *Why did he ask then?*

'There you are my little beauty,' Carnaby beamed, holding a tiny blue pebble up. 'I knew you were around here somewhere.'

'What's that?' asked Bobby.

'A stone,' Ada said gruffly.

'It is a Moonstone, as a matter of fact,' Carnaby murmured, returning to the table.

Ada rolled her eyes. 'So a stone, then?'

Carnaby held the pebble over the puzzle box. 'This stone is charged with the energy of the New Moon, and – if your recreation of the symbols is corr–...'

Carnaby's words dried up as the puzzle box began to pulse with light, as did the tracing paper. Soon everyone's faces were bathed in its unearthly glow.

'This really *is* the Salus Key,' whispered Carnaby.

19

The Heartbeat of the World

Ada's mouth fell open at the sight of the shimmering network of lines crisscrossing the tracing paper. The biscuit she had just taken a bite from plopped onto the floor.

'How did you do that?' she gasped as the glow faded from both the key and the tracing paper.

'Your experiences with the Salus Key gave me the idea,' said Carnaby, holding up the moonstone once more. 'And this little beauty did the rest.'

Carnaby slipped the stone into a pocket on his waistcoat then pointed at the lines on the paper. 'Whoever made those symbols upon that roof has found a way to tap into the heartbeat of the world.'

'What's that?' Tony and Ada asked together.

Ada shot Tony a look then folded her arms so tight she could almost touch her back.

'Do any of you know what ley lines are?'

They sat there in silent shared confusion.

'Ley lines are the transport system for an energy that has existed since time began. They run the length and breadth of this world, pulsing with preternatural energy.'

'Do you mean supernatural?'

'It exists as part of the world; we simply don't know much about it yet. However, it would be accurate to say that phenomena we think of as being supernatural have ley line energy flowing through them. In fact we all do. Some of us are even able to wield this energy. The study of this is sometimes referred to as the Elemental Sciences.'

Carnaby tapped a point on the paper where several of the lines converged.

'Each place where the lines intersect is called a Nexus. This is where reservoirs of this energy are stored. Some of these nexuses are more powerful than others.'

Carnaby got up and walked over to a drawstring which dangled from a long metal tube that ran the length of the wall.

'What do you think?' whispered Bobby.

'I think he's crackers,' Nikki whispered back.

Ada stayed silent. She did not have enough data on Carnaby to come to any conclusions yet, but she was getting there.

'Afternoon registration is at two remember? We need to be back in school by then,' pointed out Tony.

Carnaby produced a gold fob watch from his waistcoat. He flipped it open, glanced at it, then returned it to his pocket. 'So I have precisely twenty-five minutes to explain how the world really works, so pay attention.'

Carnaby pulled the string and a map of the world unfurled down the length of wall.

Tony gasped 'Cool!' and almost fell out of his chair trying to take the whole thing in. It was vast.

Bobby shook his head. 'You are so sad.'

'Should've just stayed in school,' groaned Nikki.

Carnaby began pointing at places on the map. 'Sumatra, Ecuador, Tibet, California, the Mariana Trench and the Ring of Fire.'

'What's *that*, Mr Carnaby?' asked Tony, thrilled by the evocative name.

'It's a string of volcanos on the edges of the Pacific Ocean.'

Tony made a cooing noise and slid forward on his chair.

'What does any of this have do with the Salus Key?' asked Ada.

'Each of these locations contains an extremely powerful nexus point,' explained Carnaby. 'The symbols you found appear to be part of a ritual to enable someone to locate and track ley lines. It is my belief this person is searching for a nexus here in London.'

'Describe your vision again, Ada, but be brief.'

Ada recounted her story about the men and the strip of energy. Carnaby clapped his hands and grinned, placing his hands on hips in a full-on superhero pose.

'The Faceless Scholars in your vision talked of dooming not just this world but also countless others - are you sure that's what you heard?'

'One hundred percent. Why?' asked Ada.

'Bertram Langley believed that our world was but one of many worlds, all identical in many ways, yet subtly different. As though history played out differently in each. It is a difficult concept, I know—one which I do not expect you to fully—'

'Parallel worlds, right?' asked Bobby.

'Sure. Germany won the second world war in one, America never became independent in another...' Ada continued.

'...And on another one we never landed on the moon, or the Titanic never sank, right?' added Bobby.

Carnaby stared at them in shock. 'How did you—'

'Doctor Who!' shouted Bobby and Ada, who then high fived each other.

'Quite,' said Carnaby, raising an eyebrow. 'In any case, Langley believed he could travel to these parallel worlds if he could breach the barrier between them.'

'Breach it how?' asked Ada.

'Langley theorised the energy from an extremely powerful nexus of ley lines could be used to force an opening in the barrier,' explained Carnaby.

'How come you know all this stuff?' asked Tony.

'Once upon a time the history of the Faceless Scholars was an obsession of mine. I was able to obtain some of the original scientific journals Langley wrote before he joined the Faceless Scholars, where he detailed his multiple world theories,' explained Carnaby. 'Now, many historians believed that, after joining the Faceless Scholars, Langley began to conduct experiments with the supernatural to test his theories. Fearing what he might unleash Langley was imprisoned by the Scholars for many years until his eventual escape. However, during his imprisonment the scholars constructed a labyrinth of interconnecting tunnels and chambers beneath London, seeking to continue Langley's work. The tunnels supposedly followed the path of the ley lines until the Scholars found a nexus.'

'Do you think it was one of those chambers I saw in my vision?' asked Ada.

'Not just any chamber my dear, but the very one within which they breached the barrier between worlds – if your vision is correct.'

'It looked like something went wrong,' said Ada.

'Sadly yes,' agreed Carnaby. 'You see, according to Langley's own research, within the barrier was said to reside the darker elements of what we think of as the supernatural. When the Scholars breached it, a good many terrible things would have escaped. The legend goes that, fearful of the damage the breach could cause, the Scholars found a way to seal the breach. As the years passed one by one the Faceless Scholars all died horrible deaths. The rumour was that a curse had been released when they created the breach, which stalked them down through the years.'

'What did I tell you?' Tony shouted triumphantly. 'I said the curse was real but did anyone listen to me? Noooo.'

Carnaby frowned at the interruption. 'After the deaths of the scholars, the Salus Key was lost. Over the centuries, as the legend of the chamber grew, historians, archaeologists and treasure hunters sought to find it. There was even some evidence that Nazi spies came to England, seeking to raid the chamber for its secrets, but no one ever found it.'

'And now Langley's looking for the chamber so he can use the Salus Key to unseal the breach and go through the barrier,' concluded Ada.

Carnaby blew out a long sigh.

'If Langley is somehow still alive then yes, that would be my conclusion.'

'So what?' asked Bobby. 'Let the weirdo go, I say.'

'According to legend, should the breach ever be reopened, the unstable energies inside would cause the barrier to fall and the world along with it. I mean, why else do you think the Scholars named the location of the breach the Apocalypse Chamber?'

'Oh,' said Bobby.

Ada put down her mug of tea, leaned back in her chair and closed her eyes.

'Is she all right?' asked Carnaby.

Bobby nodded. 'She always does this when she's thinking big.'

Ada's eyes opened and focused on Carnaby. When she spoke, her tone was even but deadly serious. She sounded much older than her twelve years.

'Why are you lying to us, Mr Carnaby?'

Carnaby's features darkened. 'I beg your pardon? How dare you!? You come here begging for my help and in return you call me a liar!'

'Anger does not change the truth, Mr Carnaby. The facts are quite resilient.'

'Ada,' whispered Tony. 'Can you please not make the big bear-man mad?'

'When I asked if you knew Agent Ash, you blinked six times in rapid succession. This told me the question unnerved you. You are also right-handed.'

'What the devil does that have to do with anything?'

'Just before you said you had never met Agent Ash, you looked up and to your right.

'And?'

'And the right is where your imagination is stored. If you had been telling the truth, you would have looked up and to your left, accessing your memory. It's science. Those facts, whilst small, were enough to tell me you were lying about having never met Agent Ash.'

'I will not be interrogated in my own shop by a child!' roared Carnaby. 'I do not know this Agent Ash, and I will not be called a liar.'

Ada released one finger from her steepled hands and aimed it at Carnaby.

'And yet the sweat on your forehead and the way your eyes are darting tell me a different story.'

Ada took another sip. She made sure it was louder than the previous one for added dramatic effect.

In the outraged pause, the shop door opened with a creak. This was an unusual enough occurrence to cut Carnaby's outrage short. Tony ran over and peered through the gap in the door. When he turned back he looked like he had seen a ghost.

'You remember those two blokes we saw outside Ash's office?' he whispered.

Bobby nodded.

Tony hooked a thumb over his shoulder. 'They just walked in.'

Ada raced to the door in time to see two men in dark grey suits moving through the shop.

'What are they doing here?'

'Shopkeeper,?' called one of the men. 'Service!'

Ada and Bobby backed away from the door as Carnaby leapt to his feet. He packed away the map, shoved the tracing paper into Tony's hands and tossed the puzzle box to Ada. All the time his gaze kept shifting back to the door. Without a word, he ushered them to a fire exit at the back of the room. He opened it, revealing the street beyond.

'Bury the key, burn the paper and forget about this,' Carnaby ordered. 'All of it.'

'Why?' asked Ada, who planned to do no such thing.

'Because you were right; I was lying. I was just going along with you to get hold of the Salus Key so I could sell it. I apologise for the deception. Now off you go, back to school – and don't come here again.'

'Still lying,' said Ada, folding her arms. 'We came here for help.'

'I *am* helping you,' said Carnaby. 'You are not ready for any of this. None of you are.'

Carnaby disappeared back inside the shop, the heavy door swinging closed behind him. At the last second, a metal ruler jabbed forward and wedged between the door and the frame, stopping it from fully closing.

Nikki slipped her fingers into the gap and opened the door once more. Ada squeezed her arm.

'Good work Nikki,' she said.

'Wasn't ready to go back to school anyway.'

'I am,' said Tony, looking at his watch. 'And we've only got ten minutes to get back!'

Nikki held the door open while Ada slipped back inside.

'Didn't she hear me,' snapped Tony. 'What she's doing?'

'Being Ada,' said Bobby, pulling Tony back into the shop. Once they were inside Nikki followed them in. She let the door close quietly and slipped the long ruler back into her jacket.

'How you'd fit that in there?' Tony asked.

'Skilfully.'

With Bobby taking the lead, they crept back through the living room and up to the door to the shop. Bobby signalled to Ada and Nikki then pointed to the far-left side of the open door. He grabbed Tony and moved to the right side of the door. Ahead she could see the two men. Carnaby towered over both men but the shopkeeper looked nervous.

'Agent Ash never came to see me, I'm sorry. And no, I don't know anything about a puzzle box. 'We have listened to the tapes Ash made before his disappearance. We know he was close to finding the Salus Key. Do you know what that means?'

Carnaby chuckled. 'It means you've lost your mind, Agent Gans. The Apocalypse Chamber is nothing but a bedtime story to scare frightened children.'

'Did you hear that Agent Orlando? I do believe Carnaby is calling us children.'

Agent Orlando ran a gloved finger across the counter; it came off caked in dust. 'It's sad to see how far the great Lucas Carnaby has fallen, skulking in this hovel like some wretched animal.' He picked up a small clay jar. 'Quite frankly, it's an insult to your reputation, and to ours.'

Carnaby snatched the jar from Agent Gans. 'Fortunately, I don't work for the ESD anymore. Your reputation means less to me than the mud on my shoes.'

Ada's eyes widened at hearing Carnaby's words. She looked across at Bobby who mouthed the words - *you were right*. Tony was tapping his watch and his meaning was clear. *Can we go now?*

Ada held up a finger and mouthed back one minute.

'Carnaby, do you realise what the Apocalypse Chamber is? The danger it represents?' Agent Gans demanded.

'You couldn't care less about the danger,' said Carnaby. 'All you care about is how you can use it for the good old US of A.'

'Have a care, Lucas,' hissed Agent Gans. 'Our respect for you is not without limits.'

'By the way, speaking of children,' said Agent Orlando, 'It seems someone had been in Ash's office before us. I don't suppose you've seen any pupils from——?'

At that moment a loud beeping sounded from the back room. Ada stepped back aghast, to see Tony desperately fiddling with his digital watch. All three men were now staring directly at Ada.

20

Fight! Fight! Fight!

A malevolent smile slithered across Agent Orlando's face. 'There's no need to be afraid, my young friends. We just want to talk to you.'

Agent Orlando's attempt at reassurance had the opposite effect. Tony bolted back the way they had come. Ada and Nikki raced after him. Orlando and Gans leapt forward as Bobby took off. He ran through the back room, heading for the fire exit. Ada held it open, waving him on. Bobby broke out onto the high street, kicking the door shut behind him. He ran to the top of the street and was never so happy to see the drab buildings of St Icilda's in the distance. Something grabbed his shoulder, pulling him back into an alley. He tried to move but the arm held him fast against the wall, just as Orlando and Gans tore past. Bobby broke free and spun, fists clenched. It was Nikki. Ada and Tony were pressed in beside her.

'Check the fence,' said Nikki.

Bobby peered out and his heart sank. Orlando and Gans were nowhere to be seen, but marching along the school fence was a man dressed in a white shirt, black trousers and a black tie, holding a clip board.

'A Truncheon,' muttered Bobby. 'Just what we need.'

The clipboard was a dead giveaway. Truncheons used them for compiling lists of those kids out of school when they shouldn't be.

In the distance the school bell sounded.

'It's the five-minute bell,' said Ada, sounding worried. 'If we don't go now we'll be trapped out here. Adam won't wait.'

Nikki stepped out from their hiding place.

'Go for the fence,' she ordered.

'What are you doing?' shrieked Tony, trying to pull her back.

Nikki spat out an empty lollipop stick. 'My duty.'

She then ran across the road, veering off as soon as she hit the other side. The Truncheon spotted Nikki straight away and gave chase, shouting at her to stop. Nikki ran up the street, cutting a sharp right by the dry cleaners, the Truncheon hot on her heels.

Bobby, seeing Nikki's plan, ran for the fence, the panicked clip clop of Ada's hefty shoes behind him. Tony tore past them as they crossed the road, his school tie flapping like a flag in a hurricane.

Adam was already lifting the bar clear and waving them in. Tony practically dived through the gap. Bobby and Ada tumbled through and the three of them lay there in one exhausted heap.

Adam swore as he twisted the fence bar back into place. 'Bleeding second-years. You nearly dropped us all in it!'

Ada rose, grabbing the bar. 'Nikki's still out there!'

Adam shoved Ada away from the fence. 'That's tough for her then, ain't it? I would have left you all out there if it wasn't for Sid.'

Adam stomped away and the back playground started to empty.

Ada gripped the bars in both hands, her head resting against the fence. She was near to tears. 'I can't believe she did that.'

'Nikki's hardcore. She's probably already back in class.'

Ada sighed, pushing away from the fence. 'I hope you're right, Bobson. I really do.'

Lying again, Boy?

Mum was right. And the thought of Nikki being caught by the Truncheons, or by the sinister Agents Orlando and Gans, made him feel sick.

'I reckon we try the police again after school,' suggested Tony. 'Because this is getting stupid now.'

'Yeah about as stupid as that bloody thing,' snapped Bobby, pointing at Tony's wristwatch.

Tony pushed Bobby. 'I didn't know the alarm was going to go off, did I?'

'It's your flipping watch!' shouted Bobby. 'Bad enough you nearly got yourself killed in Ash's office.'

'Leave him alone Bobby,' said Ada.

'And none of it would have happened if he hadn't dragged us to Ash's office in the first place.'

Tony started to walk away.

'You heard what those ESD blokes said to Carnaby!' Bobby called after him. 'If Langley's trying to find the Apocalypse Chamber we need to—'

'WHAT?' roared Tony, whirling to face Bobby. 'WHAT ARE WE GOING TO DO, GREAT LEADER? Nikki's probably going to get suspended because of your stupid plan and now there's two psychos after us. Cheers, mate!'

'Yeah, well I can—'

'You do what you want mate,' said Tony, tapping his own chest. 'Me? I'm going back to the police after school. I'm done with all this.'

'They won't believe you, Tony,' said Ada, moving into his path. 'We need to—'

'You can shut it as well. I'm done listening to your Sherlock Holmes rubbish,' he snapped.

Bobby stepped in at that, shoving Tony hard.

'Don't talk to her like that!'

A few of the older kids, who were heading towards the sports hall, heard the shouting and stopped to watch.

The older kids began to chant, low at first, but gaining in volume.

Tony pushed Bobby, who stumbled back. He righted himself and stepped in, fists raised.

'FIGHT! FIGHT! FIGHT!' More kids took up the chant now. Everyone within earshot was now running to join the gathering crowd, coming closer, jostling for a good position.

The anger surging in Bobby left him deafened to the chant. All he could see was Tony and a sea of red mist. They circled each other like boxers, waiting for an opening.

'Stop this, the pair of you!' ordered Ada.

Yes, stop this.

She tried to get between Bobby and Tony but she was pulled out by a few of the crowd members. Rule one at St Icilda's was this: unless you were a teacher, no one stopped a fight.

Boy! Boy, you stop this now!

'You've been a flipping nightmare ever since you got here,' snarled Bobby, ignoring Mum. 'Why don't you just sod off back to your old school, Smiley. No one wants you here!'

Bobby shoved Tony again, much harder this time.

He crashed back against the wall of kids who now encircled them, and a big *ooooh* went up from the crowd. The chant was in full force now.

'FIGHT! FIGHT! FIGHT!'

'You gonna let him talk to you like that?' a freckle faced blond boy hissed.

'Yeah, no way he'd talk to *me* like that,' added another.

The kids pushed Tony back into the centre of the ring. Bobby looked Tony up and down. There was fury in his eyes, but Bobby didn't care. Next door's kitten was more frightening.

'Oh so you're a big man now, Vicar's Boy?' sneered Bobby.

'Least I'm not a headcase who talks to his dead mum!' Tony shouted back.

The chant stopped. In the silence Bobby heard Mum's desperate voice calling out.

Him didn't mean it Bobby! Him just scared, just like you. Him—

'Chin him!' someone shouted.

Bobby's right fist cracked against Tony's jaw. He staggered but did not fall. Pain flared in Bobby's jaw as Tony's fist struck him. In the next instant their hands were clawing at each other.

'FIGHT! FIGHT! FIGHT!'

Bobby managed to kick Tony's legs out from under him, but Tony held firm to Bobby's jacket as he fell, bringing him down on top of him. The hard concrete did not stop the punches nor the insults from either boy.

Bobby felt his strength fading. Tony was stronger than he looked and all the while they struggled, Bobby's Mum screamed at him to stop.

'Scarper! It's Bennett!' someone yelled, and the crowd scattered in all directions.

Bobby kicked Tony away and rolled onto his back, breathing hard. The metallic taste of blood coated the inside of his mouth, but he couldn't spit it out. Blurred, and upside-down, he saw a pair of green trainers striding towards him.

'Right then!' shouted Mr Bennett.

Bobby and Tony were pulled shakily onto their feet by two hairy arms. The stern-faced Mr Bennet was now wearing a bright red tracksuit, its sleeves rolled up to the elbow. He pointed at Bobby's shirt.

'That's not gonna tuck itself in, is it Gibson?'

Bobby started shoving his shirt back into his trousers with both hands. 'Sorry sir,'

Mr Bennett swung on Tony. 'You can't seem to go a day without getting a beating it seems.'

'Yes Sir.'

'Did I say you could speak?'

'No sir,' said Tony, wiping his bloody nose. 'Sorry sir…I mean, sorry I'm still speaking, sir.'

'Another brain-box of Britain I see,' observed Mr Bennett, rolling his eyes. 'Right, who started it?'

At this point Ada pushed in between Bobby and Tony.

'No one did, sir,' Ada stated. 'Tony tripped and Bobby was just helping him to get up.'

'From where I was standing, Gibson was doing a lot of 'helping' with his fists.'

'With all the big kids in the way, I'm surprised you saw anything, sir,' said Ada. 'I estimate you were at least twenty feet away when Tony tripped.'

Bennett jabbed a pudgy finger at Ada. 'You trying to be smart girl?'

Ada looked confused. 'Well…yes I am, sir. I mean that's why I come to school, sir: to be smarter. Isn't that right, sir?'

'Well yes… Yes of course…but I mean…'

Bobby almost felt sorry for Bennett. The deputy head stood no chance. It was a knockout in the first round.

'Is what she's saying true, lad?' asked Bennett 'Was Gibson helping you?'

Tony rubbed his bruised cheek, locked eyes with Mr Bennett and nodded glumly.

'Gibson?'

Bobby tried not to smile when he answered. 'Yeah, I was helping him up sir. Stumbled a bit myself.'

'Fortunately for the pair of you, I don't have the time or the inclination to take this any further, so I'm going to let you go. But if I see you messing about again, 'falling over' will be the least of your problems, got it? Now get out of my sight!'

With that, Bennett stalked away.

'That was close,' said Ada. 'Getting yourself in detention is the last thing we need right now. So come on then, shake hands, the both of you. You've got it out of your system.'

Do what she says, Bobby. You were both wrong, and you know it.

'And you're not real so what do you know? You're dead and I just made you up!'

The words were out before Bobby could stop then. At first there was nothing but silence then in his mind he heard mum say three words after which the silence returned.

Alright then Bobby.

Ada just stared at him, not knowing what to say. Bobby aimed his best dirty look at Tony then marched straight past him, knocking his shoulder with his own.

'Don't worry, Tony. He'll calm down.'

'Like I care,' Tony snapped, and stomped away himself.

Bobby walked into his form room for afternoon registration and slumped himself down angrily. Tony came in a little bit afterwards, pieces of toilet paper shoved up one nostril. He swapped seats with someone at the front of the class without even glancing at Bobby. It was the smartest thing the new boy had ever done, Bobby thought.

'Gutted! Can't believe I missed you giving the new boy a kicking,' DJ said.

'He wasn't the only one to get a 'kicking',' said Ada, casting a disapproving gaze at Bobby's split lip.

'He started it,' Bobby muttered. 'Shouldn't have been calling you names, should he?'

'This is what I get for be friends with boys. I swear my hamster has more brains cells than the two of you,' Ada snapped, throwing up her hands. 'Tony was just scared and worried about Nikki, you idiot. We all were!'

DJ told them he had something to show them after school. When Ada asked what that something was, DJ winked and just said 'You'll see.'

Bobby was still thinking about Tony and what he had said about Mum. It made his blood boil. He had told him all that stuff in secret and he had just blurted it all out to everyone, like it was nothing.

Mum. Suddenly Bobby remembered what he had said to her.

'Mum? Mum are you there?' he muttered, desperately 'I'm sorry Mum…Mum?'

He ignored the concerned looks DJ and Ada threw his way. Thanks to Tony, the whole school probably knew he was talking to Mum now. Errol would find out and tell Auntie Carol and Dad. Before the end of the month he'd be back in Doctor Huxley's office, listening to him droning on. He might have to start taking those pills again too.

Bobby would not say a word to Tony for the rest of the afternoon. It was not easy, especially as he had to sit next to him for two of the lessons. Luckily Tony never even looked at him, which made it easier.

'You think she's alright?' asked Ada, when she and Bobby were finally sitting together again in history.

Bobby looked up from the comic strip he was working on whenever the teacher's back was turned.

'You what?'

'Nikki! Do you think she's alright?'

Bobby covered the comic with his book as the teacher drifted past their desk. Once she moved out of range he began shading the picture.

'She's cool,' he whispered. 'Don't worry about her.'

'Don't worry? She was being chased by a Truncheon!'

'We'll go find her after we meet up with DJ.'

'You are a terrible friend, Bobby Gibson.' Ada gestured over to Tony, who was sitting two rows ahead of them. 'You should talk to him, too.'

'If he comes near me again, I'll have him.'

'Look, Bobby, he shouldn't have said what he did, but you have to remember he wasn't in Norfolk. This is all new to him! And you really shouldn't have said that stuff about his dad.'

'Maybe, but 'cause of him I can't hear mum anymore. Why won't she talk to me? I said I was sorry.' asked Bobby, his voice getting louder.

'You know everyone can hear you, right?' said Ada dropping her voice to a whisper.

'Everyone probably knows anyway thanks to that smiley faced git!'

'Bobby and Ada! Up Now!'

Both Bobby and Ada looked up at the same time. With the exception of Tony, the whole class was staring at them. The heavy-set teacher was standing two rows away, arms crossed. The two of them of stood up and apologised.

'One can only assume that the two of you were having a vigorous discussion over the Great Fire of London essay. You do remember, don't you? It's the essay you're both going to write for me by next Friday?'

'But Miss, I thought we were doing the Great Plague?'

'Oh, so you *were* listening earlier, Bobby. That's something I suppose. In any case, the report on the Great Fire of London is your reward for talking in class and being stupid enough to get caught. Sit down.'

Bobby and Ada sat to a whispered chorus of *shame*.

Bobby stuck his elbow on the desk and leant his head against his hand.

When the final bell rang, Tony snatched his satchel and shot out of the classroom.

'Where's he going?' asked Ada.

Bobby watched Tony through the classroom window, running along the corridor.

'Dunno. And I don't care.'

'What if he's going back to the police, like he said?' asked Ada.

Bobby slung his satchel strap over his shoulder. 'Nah, he was just mouthing off. Probably running home in case I smack again.'

'He seemed extremely committed to me,' said Ada. 'I think we should follow him.'

Bobby stuffed his hands into his pockets and strode on. 'Do what you want. I'm going to see DJ.'

Ada sighed, and fell into step beside Bobby.

'You reckon DJ found something in the library?' he asked at last, his anger gradually fading.

'If he hasn't, he's in big trouble,' said Ada. 'I have no time for his nonsense. I've had enough of that today.'

Bobby led Ada through the main school building.

'We meeting him in the usual place?' asked Ada.

Bobby nodded. They had figured out the room last year thanks to Shamri; the last room her dad checked when he was locking up the school. He liked his routines and stuck to them. They would have plenty of time to talk and get out before Mr Khara arrived.

Bobby and Ada headed down a long corridor. Fighting through the tide of kids, they stopped by the last classroom door on the right. Bobby entered to find DJ perched on a desk. Beside him was a stack of thick textbooks.

'Bout time you lot got here,' said DJ. 'I don't want to miss tea; Mum's doing bangers and mash.'

'Any luck in the library?' asked Ada.

DJ patted the books. 'The school librarian gave me these for our history project.'

Ada raised an eyebrow. 'What history project?'

'Oh - excuse me, Mrs Librarian. Me and my mates are chasing this evil immortal bloke and we wanted to know if you had any books on him. Can you show me?'

'Ah. A subterfuge. Bravo, DJ.'

DJ looked past Bobby to the door. 'Where's Smiley? You smack him again? You better not have without me.'

Bobby scowled. 'Do I look like his dad?'

DJ sighed. 'Great, I'm going to have to say all this again when he shows up.'

'I don't think you need to worry about Tony coming back,' said Ada. 'Isn't that right Bobson?'

Bobby didn't answer or meet Ada's withering glare.

'Shame. I was starting to like the weirdo.'

DJ hopped off the desk and took a thick blue book from the pile.

'Come along class, follow Mr Jennings.'

DJ walked up to the teacher's desk, setting the book on top of it. Bobby and Ada moved to either side.

'So, I found this book while the librarian was rabbiting on about Salus and showing me various pictures of her—well of her statues anyway.'

DJ jabbed a finger on the open page and said, 'Who's the brainiest one here, then?'

The chapter was called '*Bertram Langley and the Faceless Scholars: Fact and Fiction,*' but Bobby did not care about the words. His eyes were focused on the full-length painting on the right-hand page and his mouth was agape.

'It can't be,' he murmured.

Ada leant in and studied the page. She took out a pencil and started drawing on the painting.

'Oi! I've got to take that back to the library,' complained DJ, trying to stop her.

Ada slapped DJ's hand away and continued drawing. Once she had finished, she shared a panicked look with Bobby.

'How sure are we that Tony *hasn't* gone to the police?' asked Ada.

'The police?' repeated DJ. 'What about the police?'

'You two get to Tony!' shouted Bobby, vaulting over the desk.

'What about you?' Ada called after him.

But Bobby was already gone.

21

Revelations

Tony leant against the wall beside DI Penthrope's office. His mind kept coming back to Bobby, and he felt his anger rising again.

'Dunno know why *I* should say, sorry,' Tony muttered to himself. 'He was the one who hit me.'

If Dad were here, Tony knew he would have quoted the Bible at him, telling Tony how he should love his enemies. Well Tony had turned the other cheek, and it had met knuckles traveling in the other direction.

It was all their fault, he concluded. If he had never met Ada in that stupid graveyard, none of this would have happened. He might have made some real friends. He couldn't believe they'd just left Nikki behind. Not after the way she'd stepped up. And now she was probably going to get expelled. It wasn't right.

That did the trick. It did not matter if he was scared, he needed to help her. Tony pushed himself off the wall, turned and knocked lightly on the door.

There was no answer, just the muffled sound of people talking.

Tony took a deep breath and knocked again, louder this time.

'Don't worry Nikki,' he whispered to himself. 'I'll save you.'

The door opened. Tony swore the veins on Detective Inspector Penthrope's neck bulged when she saw him.

'YOU!' she bellowed. 'Back with more stories about monsters are we?'

Tony stalked past Penthrope.

'Everything we told you before is true,' said Tony. 'We're in trouble and we need help; that's your job right? You help people?'

'Look,' said Penthrope, taking in a deep breath through her nostrils, trying to find calm. 'This may all seem very real to you, but we're trying to find a real human man who's gone missing. You can't just walk in here with stories about the end of the world. This is serious!'

At that moment Ada and DJ burst into the room, gasping for air.

'Fantastic,' groaned Penthrope. 'More of you.'

Tony turned to face them. 'What are you lot doing here?'

DJ grabbed Tony's arm. 'We need to get out of here, mate.'

'My thoughts exactly,' Penthrope agreed.

Tony tugged his arm free. 'I ain't going anywhere with you lot. We need their help. We need to tell her about the Apocalypse Chamber.'

Ada spoke through her teeth, trying to get across the seriousness of the situation. 'Tony. We need to leave. Right now.'

DS Hoplin emerged from the classroom behind Penthrope. 'Leave? When things are just getting exciting? I know I would love to hear more about this Apocalypse Chamber.'

'Have you taken leave of your senses, Detective Sergeant?' asked Penthrope. 'The time for indulging these children is long past.'

Tony felt Ada wrap her hand around his and pull. He looked at her face. The same terror was mirrored by DJ. What was happening here? When Ada pulled again, Tony relented and let her guide him. Hoplin cocked his head – nothing more – but the door to the corridor slammed shut, as though kicked by an invisible boot.

'How did you know?' asked Hoplin, his eyes locked on Ada.

'I saw you in a book about the Faceless Scholars. You didn't have the moustache or those glasses, but I recognised you.'

Hoplin dropped his glasses on the table. He seemed to grow straighter, taller, more powerful. He gave Ada a wink and an approving smile.

'You continue to be an annoyance, child, despite your upbringing,' Hoplin paused to wipe a line of dust from the windowsill. He took in the shocked faces and rubbed the dust between his fingers. 'I mean, if this grubby institution is what passes for education these days, it's a wonder you can read at all.'

Hoplin's voice sounded different now. Colder. And familiar somehow.

'Time to give me the key, Ada.'

A shiver ran down Tony's spine as he recognised the voice at last. From the graveyard, the Baxter Estate and in his nightmares ever since.

'It's you!' He cried. 'You're Bertram Langley!'

'What's the boy raving about, Hoplin?'

'It is just as you said, Detective Inspector: the time for indulging these children is long past.'

Langley waved a hand in front of Penthrope and her eyes rolled back in their sockets. She stumbled, opened her mouth, then collapsed to the floor.

'The game is over child.'

Ada backed away, gripping the straps of her satchel.

Langley made a fist with his outstretched hand. Strands of green lightning crackled across his knuckles.

'GIVE!'

A low rumble filled the room.

'ME!'

The whole room shook as though at the centre of an earthquake.

'THE KEY!'

As the final words left Langley's mouth, the windows along the far side of the office exploded outwards allowing a fierce wind to come rushing in. The howling gale swept Tony into the air and slammed him against the wall, arms and legs outstretched like a starfish. Tony slid his eyes left and right. Ada and DJ were similarly trapped on either of him, held by an invisible force.

'My blood flows through every part of that key! My birthright beats within its heart.'

Langley walked forward until he was level with the immense wooden desk. He slid his hands along it, taking hold of one corner. Ada suddenly thought back to her vision of the Faceless Scholars, surprised how much of it she could remember.

'He will help us or that prison cell will be his tomb,' she murmured. 'I got it so wrong. The Faceless Scholars never made the Salus Key. It was you. It was always you.'

Langley gripped the desk harder, the wood splintering as his fingernails bit into it.

'Years after they imprisoned me and stole my life's work, they offered me my freedom, but only if I helped them to seal the breach. I refused them at first. I didn't have much of anything down there in the filth, but I still had my pride. They were determined, though. Merciless. They took their time, and in the darkness they broke me.'

As the last words left his lips, Langley hurled the desk across the room. It shattered into pieces against the wall.

'When I finally escaped, I made it my mission to hunt down every one of the Faceless Scholars.' He laughed, then. 'They thought a supernatural curse had been brought down upon them for opening the breach, but it was me. And it was richly deserved.'

Images of Langley's torment and vengeance whirled around Tony's mind, clawing away his last shreds of bravery... *And I'm next*, he thought. 'I generally prefer to remain behind the scenes, but your intervention rather forced my hand. Witnesses can be so inconvenient,' Langley explained.

'But how do you just...become a policeman like that?' asked Ada, still struggling against the power which held her.

'My dear girl, I have lived for centuries, cultivating wealth, contacts and power. I can do whatever I like. This role...' he indicated his uniform, 'was arranged with a single phone call.'

'So now you'll use the Salus Key to open the Apocalypse Chamber, right?' asked Ada.

'Open it?' Langley's looked bemused. 'My dear child, the chamber has been open for days.'

Langley picked up Ada's satchel. 'I should have guessed that idiot Ash would get cold feet after we found the chamber.'

'Agent Ash was helping you?' asked Ada.

Langley slipped a hand into the satchel and pulled out the puzzle box.

'Finally,' he breathed, gazing at the ancient relic. 'I have what is mine.'

Ada flicked her gaze to the door, then to Langley. 'The chamber may be open but the breach is still safely contained, otherwise you would be off running around other worlds by now. You still need the Salus Key to help you break open whatever is containing the breach.'

Langley chuckled, rolling the Salus Key in his hand as though searching for some unseen starting point to the puzzle box.

'An impressive series of deductions young lady but trying to stall until help arrives will not save you.'

Langley began to rearrange the pieces of the Salus Key. He looked like he knew exactly what he was doing. Seeing him at work on it reminded Tony of the top players in his old school chess club. They had practically played out the whole game before they moved their first piece. Langley slid, lifted and rotated the tiny wooden sections, all the while smirking at Ada.

'There is no one coming Ada; no last second saviour for the three of you.'

Langley tapped a finger over a small circular piece of wood, and with a click it flipped up, revealing a small indentation.

'I even have time to show you the real secret of the Salus Key.'

Langley took off his ring, pushed it against the indentation and turned it anti clockwise until it clicked. There was a hiss and Tony gasped as the interior of the box began to pulse with a crimson light.

'You see, the Salus Key was simple to create for those short-sighted idiots. Even when they used it to seal the breach they never understood the full extent of the power they sought, nor the knife-edge upon which they walked. In secret, I used the tools they gave me to build a device which would allow me to cross the breach in safety.'

Langley reached into the box and to Tony's amazement his whole hand descended into the Salus Key, as though it were bigger on the inside. He pulled out a smooth scarlet orb, no bigger than an apple.

Langley's tear filled eyes were wide as his smile as he held the Orb in one hand and the Salus Key in the other. 'All this trouble for so small a —'

At that moment Bobby came flying in, an open saltshaker in each hand. He hurled one straight at Langley scattering salt all over the immortal. The villain screamed, dropping the Salus Key as he tried to swipe the salt from his clothes and skin. The way he acted, he might have been on fire. And like that, the unseen force holding Tony vanished. He dropped to the floor beside DJ and Ada.

'Come on!' Bobby shouted, hurling the remaining saltshaker at Langley's head.

Tony did not need to be told twice. He was up on his feet and running. Ada snatched the Salus Key out of Langley's hands as he writhed on the floor in agony. He tried to grab her ankle, but Ada grabbed a handful of the salt from the floor and tossed it into his face. She scooped up her satchel and fled, Langley's screams echoing after her. As they pelted down the corridor, the classroom door exploded. Langley strode into the hallway, his face blistered and sore, his eyes blazing.

'Time to die!' he screamed, making shapes in the air with his hands.

Tony and the others stopped in their tracks as two of the Faceless rose up through the ground directly in front of them.

Langley started towards them, his hands a blur of magical energy. Small puffs of greyish smoke erupted from his scarred face and reddened eye. The Faceless mirrored his every step, closing the gap all too quickly.

'Nowhere…to run…children,' he croaked.

'ET ABIERUNT!' boomed a deep voice.

With a great WHOOSH, the Faceless were tossed into the air. The kids turned in wonder to see Lucas Carnaby hulking just below the light fittings at the far end of the corridor. The shopkeeper's arms were outstretched, his eyes closed, and he was mouthing words that sounded like Latin to Tony. The tattooed markings on his forearms shimmered with a faint amber glow. When Carnaby opened his eyes, they were solid silver, the sight making Ada gasp. Bowing his head, the shopkeeper crossed his arms.

'There is nothing for you here, shades!" he roared. "I cast you back beyond the veil. Begone!'

The hooded tore into a thousand shreds of shadow, then vanished.

'And now for the puppet master,' said Carnaby, stalking forward with fury. 'LIGA INIMICI MEI!'

Silver bands of light shot out from Carnaby's hands. Tony shivered as the bands of light passed him and into Langley, encircling his body, until his arms were pinned to his sides.

'Now!' ordered Carnaby.

A door behind and to Carnaby's left swung open.

'In here!' Nikki yelled, waving from the doorway.

Langley gritted his teeth and took a step forward. Carnaby howled and was driven to his knees. The immortal laughed and flexed his shoulders as the bands began to fade around him.

'You cannot hold me with parlour tricks!' he mocked. 'The infinite is mine to wield.'

'Hurry,' Carnaby forced through spittle-flecked lips. 'I'm losing him.'

They raced down the hall past Carnaby, toward the room where Nikki was waiting.

Langley screamed in triumph, shattering the last of the bands that held him.

His hand flew up and Carnaby was hurled into the wall with bone-crunching force. Langley raced past the unconscious shopkeeper grabbing for Ada as she reached the doorway.

Tony, his head down, shoulder-barged Ada into the classroom before common sense could stop him and, instead of Ada's arm, Langley found Tony's in his grip. The air around them shimmered, Tony screamed, high and loud, and then he and Langley...vanished. In Ada's mind they burned brightly first, like magnesium in science class. The only sign left of them were wisps of smoke and a nasty smell, not unlike rotten eggs. Sitting on the floor, shaking and crying, Ada clutched at empty air and regrets.

'It should have been me,' she shouted. 'He should have taken me!'

Bobby put an arm around her, but she just sat there, eyes wide.

'I should have given him the stupid box!'

Carnaby staggered into the classroom as the final wisp of smoke floated away.

'A brave lad,' said Carnaby with admiration. Blood trickled from a jagged cut above his right eye. 'But now I need you all to be even braver, and come with me.'

'Come with you where?' asked Bobby.

'Back to my shop. I do not believe Langley will try again today, but at least there I offer you some protection while we talk.'

'Talk about what?' DJ asked.

Carnaby produced a black silk handkerchief and started to dab away the blood from his face.

'Why, the end of the world of course.'

22

The Mars Bar Apocalypse

Bobby wanted to put his fingers in his ears. Everyone was shouting at once, trying to tell Carnaby what had happened. The shopkeeper just stood there, taking it all in, trying to make sense of the noise. Bobby thought that was weird. Most grown-ups would have lost it by now.

At last, Carnaby bought up his hand and everyone fell silent.

'As I have said several times, I believe young Mr Tadsby is in no immediate danger.' Carnaby turned to Ada.

'To recap: you believe Bertram Langley has already opened the Apocalypse Chamber, correct?'

Ada nodded.

'And that Agent Ash helped him do this?'

'That's what he said, yes.'

Carnaby shook his head. 'None of this makes any sense. Ash would never help him. There must be something we're missing here.'

'You sure that salt will keep him out?' asked DJ, nervously. There was a thick line of it spread in front of the shop door. More salt ran along the edges of the windows.

'I'm going to be very embarrassed if it doesn't,' said Carnaby, tapping a finger against his chin.

Ada, as though noticing Nikki for the first time, ran over and hugged her.

'Sorry we didn't come back for you Nikki. We should've done,' said Ada.

'It's okay, I did tell you to go…I just wish I could've helped Tony.'

'You saw those things; what else could we have done?' asked Bobby.

Ada released Nikki then slumped into a chair. 'Something. We should have done something…'

Bobby had seen Ada upset before, plenty of times, but never like this. Sitting there, sunk into the armchair, she reminded him of Auntie Carol at Mum's funeral. She looked small. Powerless. Fragile. It broke his heart. He wished mum was still with him. She always had the right words. She would have known just what to say to make Ada feel better. He'd just have to do the best he could without her.

He sighed, went over and knelt in front of Ada

'Don't worry, we're going to get him back,' said Bobby. 'I promise.'

Carnaby cleared his throat.

'If you're done feeling quite so sorry for yourselves, perhaps we can get back to the man who wants to rip a giant hole in our reality?'

Bobby thumbed over his shoulder at the door. 'Few hours ago you were kicking us onto the street.'

'Lad, I am nearly sixty-eight years old. I don't have the time or the patience to pussyfoot around. If you've got something to say, get to it.'

'How come you're helping us now?'

'It certainly wasn't because of that eye-patch-wearing harpy over there, though her threats were most…inventive.'

Carnaby cast a withering look at Nikki who deflected it with a shrug.

'But I did realise that some people would be rather upset with me if I did nothing whilst London got sucked into hell.'

'You mean the ESD?' hissed Ada. 'Orlando and Gans. You used to work with them, didn't you?'

Carnaby nodded. 'And there isn't a day where I don't regret my connection with those insidious vipers and that organisation.'

'That much was obvious from your conversation,' Ada folded her arms, her expression fierce and unyielding. 'So perhaps now would be the time to tell us something we *don't* know.'

'Follow me,' said Carnaby, and he led the way to the living room at the back of the shop once more. 'In nineteen thirty-nine a supernatural entity attacked a small town in America. The entity was eventually destroyed, but not before it killed a good portion of the townsfolk.'

Carnaby went through to the room they had talked in before.

'After the attack President Roosevelt asked William J Donovan to draft a plan for two intelligence services. One became known as the OSS, which was a predecessor to the CIA. The other organisation was created in secret to investigate and develop defences against the more…supernatural threats.'

'The ESD?'

'Correct, Miss Amaya,' said Carnaby. 'The Elemental Sciences Division spent the next four decades scouring the earth for supernatural artefacts which could be used as weapons.'

DJ mouthed a single word.

'A vulgar but an appropriate summation,' agreed Carnaby.

'So how come you left?' asked Bobby.

He knelt in front of a thick grey rug in the middle of the room. 'That's my business, which means it's none of yours.'

'Alright, Tubby, keep your hair on,' said DJ, wincing as Nikki punched his arm.

'During my time at the ESD, I discovered that most supernatural activity was harmless – nothing that the organisation needed to concern itself with.'

Carnaby rolled back the rug to reveal a door with a brass ring fastened to it.

'Tasty!' said Nikki.

Bobby snorted. He thought the attic in his house, with its entrance above the stairs, was far cooler.

'I also learnt there were some supernatural risks which, if left unchecked, had the potential to cause, what my former colleagues referred to as a WEE. I believe Langley's plan to enter the Apocalypse Chamber and unseal the breach will cause just that.'

Carnaby gripped the brass handle, twisted it then lifted the door, revealing a dusty set of steps. He took an oil lamp from one of the shelves and lit it. As he descended, the dancing flame made his stern and bruised features look twice as scary.

'Mr Carnaby,' called Ada, pausing at the first step. 'What's a WEE?'

'Well, when you go to the bog–'

Bobby cuffed DJ mid-sentence.

Carnaby's voice echoed back from the gloom. 'It stands for World Ending Event.'

'I don't like this,' Bobby murmured.

'You don't like anything, Bobson,' said Ada. 'Now come on.'

At the bottom of the stairs, Bobby found himself standing in a large room that seemed to stretch the whole length of the shop. Carnaby was hurrying around, lighting candles and large torches, casting all manner of strange shadows. The walls were bare brick, roughly laid, and Bobby had the uneasy feeling Carnaby had dug it out himself. It would explain the lack of electricity. Swords, shields, spears and some weird-looking objects that Bobby could not fathom, hung from the walls. Fighting for space amid the vast array of weaponry were bookcases, packed with tomes of all shapes and sizes. Bobby turned full circle, trying to take everything in. It was even cooler than the stuff upstairs.

'What is all this stuff?' asked Ada.

Carnaby brushed a thick collection of cobwebs from a large candle on his desk, then lit it.

'Souvenirs, let's say, from my time at the ESD. I confess, I never thought I'd end up back down here.'

He glanced up then and made a panicky noise as Nikki picked up a small clay pot.

'NO! Ah! Ahem. Please put the Medusa Requiem down, young lady. It does have tendency to turn the people it doesn't like to stone.'

Nikki set the pot back on the shelf, ever so gently, and then edged away from it.

'Okay, brainbox. If Langley's got that chamber thingy open already, why hasn't he done the breach thing?'

'That, I do not know,' admitted Carnaby.

DJ stuck his tongue out at the others. 'See! You ain't the only one who can ask smart questions.'

'How do we stop him?' asked Bobby.

'The Salus Key can be used to reseal the breach. It's why Langley was so desperate to get it from you.'

'Not the only reason,' said Ada firmly.

Ada told Carnaby about the orb Langley had pulled from inside the puzzle box.

'So that's why he waited. He needed this orb to keep him safe as he crosses,' said Carnaby, sounding impressed. 'Our Mr Langley is full of surprises. Of course, it will still damn the rest of the world, but I don't suppose he cares much.'

'And even if we could stop him—'

'Which we can't.'

Ada shot DJ an angry look. 'I was going to say, we still have no idea where the Apocalypse Chamber actually is, or how much time we have before Langley attempts to cross over.'

Carnaby nodded wearily. 'If Langley does break through the barrier, it will most likely result in the destruction of London and expose the world to a supernatural incursion of biblical proportions.'

No one spoke for a while, each of them trying to comprehend the full extent of Carnaby's words.

'So that includes the school right?' asked DJ, breaking the silent stalemate.

Ada backhanded him across his arm. 'Dummy of course it does!'

'You said the supernatural?' said Bobby. 'Like…ghosts, you mean?'

'Ghosts, vampires, erogians, werewolves, harpies, demons and so forth. Yes,' said Carnaby, as though he were listing his groceries for the week.

To Bobby, it was a shopping list of his worst nightmares, with the sole exception of giant spiders. He decided not to ask Carnaby if there were such a thing, just in case he said yes.

Carnaby pulled a massive bag of fun-sized Mars Bars off the shelf behind him, placing it on his desk. Dust puffed up from the packet, and Ada dreaded to think how much they were out of date. The boys eyed the packet hungrily.

Next, he took a piece of chalk and drew a straight line down the middle of the desk. He cleared his throat then tapped the space on the left side of the chalk line. 'This is us, in the mortal realm, and this…' he tapped the other side, '…is the supernatural realm. Think of this realm as the dumping ground for all the terrifying entities and weird energies pulled from the infinite worlds that exist beyond it.'

Carnaby rested the chalk on the white line. 'Between them lies a barrier. It prevents the supernatural realm from breaking into our world and vice-versa.'

'Who made the barrier?' asked Bobby.

Carnaby pointed the chalk at Bobby. 'Good question, but nobody really knows. Aten, Jehovah, Vishnu, Zeus, Cronos – take your pick of deities or treat it as a natural phenomenon. All we know is that it has always been there.'

Carnaby smudged a tiny section of the chalk line away, then he plucked a Mars Bar from the bag.

He slid the solitary chocolate bar through the gap in the chalk line to the other side of the desk.

'That chocolate bar represents the current flow of supernatural energy from the barrier since the breach, understand?'

Everyone nodded.

'The Faceless Scholars managed to contain the breach within the Apocalypse Chamber, but the barrier was nevertheless weakened. Think of it like glass. Once damaged, the cracks will only widen under pressure. Since that first breach, more entities and bursts of supernatural energy have slipped through the cracks, and we've dealt with them. Everyone still with me?'

Everyone nodded again.

Carnaby emptied the bag of Mars Bars onto the right-hand side of the table.

'Now…this is what will happen if Langley succeeds.'

Using his left forearm Carnaby shoved the whole pile of Mars Bars across the table, obliterating the chalk line, in the process.

Everyone stood there aghast, looking at the table.

'That's a *lot* of Mars Bars,' said DJ.

23

The Price of Boredom

Tony was in a blackness so deep it he thought some giant beast had swallowed him whole. He thought of Jonah being swallowed by the whale in the Bible story. His eyesight eventually adjusted to the gloom and he started to make out the jagged outlines of his prison. When Tony moved, there was a weird jangling sound. He shook his arm and realised what was wrong. There was a metal band clasped shut around his right wrist. A manacle, attached to a thick chain. Tony ran a finger along the chain until it stopped against the wall, where it was fixed to a ring and a metal plate.

Tony tried to slip the manacle off his wrist, but he could not make his hand small enough; he only succeeded in scraping his skin. It caught for a moment on his knuckles and he cried out in pain. He had to slide it back over his wrist to relieve his torment. Next, he tried gripping the chain in both hands. He leant back, put his feet against the wall, and pulled with all his might. Nothing. Tony sank down against the wall, shivering with cold and despair. The panic took him, and he started screaming for help.

'Won't do you any good,' a man sighed. He had an American accent. 'I have been trying to escape for a lot longer than you, son, and I'm still stuck down here. What's your name?'

'Tony Tadsby.'

'Pleased to make your acquaintance. How old are you Tony?'

'Twelve. But I'll be thirteen next April.'

There was a sympathetic groan from the darkness.

'Who are you?' asked Tony.

'The name's Nathan. Nathan Ash.'

Tony gasped. 'Agent Ash! Me and my friends – well I think they are my friends – we've been looking for you. Ada has the puzzle box you gave her. The Salus Key. She figured out most of it. And we found your tapes and everything.'

'Ada Amaya,' whispered Nathan. 'She's every bit as impressive as her file suggests—'

'File? What file?'

Light flooded the chamber, causing them both to cry out in pain. Tony threw himself back to the wall and covered his eyes. He drew his knees up to his chest, trying to make himself smaller. It was instinctive. Protective. Bertram Langley stepped into the cell, carrying a small silver tray.

'Welcome back to the land of the living, boy.'

Langley crossed the room, knelt and extended the tray to Tony. On the tray were some sandwiches and a can of Coke.

'My dad's gonna know something's up when I don't come home.'

'Yes, yes I know all about Father Tadsby. My more pressing concern is…' Langley pointed to the sandwiches, '…whether you'd prefer chicken, ham or cheese.'

Tony's stomach rumbled at the sight of the food, but he did not move.

'I am not a monster, boy. Eat.'

'If kidnapping children is not the act of a monster, Langley, I don't know what is!'

Langley's mocking laughter rang out.

'It was not I who decided to get children involved in this, Nathan. You are responsible for this little mess.'

Tony took the chicken sandwich, finishing it in four quick mouthfuls. He was still chewing as he cracked the Coke open.

'Thank you,' he spluttered between mouthfuls.

'Nice to see some manners still exist, even in this shabby corner of London,' observed Langley. 'Though you really shouldn't talk with your mouth full.' He slipped the tray under his arm and walked back to the entrance.

'Let the boy go, Langley' pleaded Ash. 'He's no threat to you.'

'Ah, Ash – ever the moral arbiter. Do you remember that morning, when we opened the chamber and saw the sealed breach? My wonder at seeing it for the very first time was matched only by your own.'

Ash did not reply, so Langley continued.

'There was a light in your eyes that had not been there before. You told me that you understood—finally, truly understood my vision. And then what did you do? You stole my key, fled the chamber like a filthy rat, and you pressed my most valuable work, the thing I have scoured this earth for centuries to find, into the hands of a child!'

'Safer in her hands than yours, Langley! I stand by my actions. Ada may be a child, but you are unstable. A mad man, seeking to play God.'

Langley sighed. 'What I am is a man whose birthright and genius has allowed him to walk this earth for over three centuries. A man who has buried more loved ones than you can possibly count. I have seen things that would choke the sanity from you in a single breath; wielded power over nations and counselled kings; I have started wars and led great and terrible armies into battle—and I have done all of this, not for my own glory, but for the betterment of mankind.'

'Oh? And what about the Scholars?' asked Ash. 'Was what you did to them for the betterment of mankind?'

'What I did to them was justice!' snapped Langley. 'Without my research those fools would never have found the barrier, much less breached it. And having cracked open eternity, what did they do? They could not conceive how to profit by it, so they forced me to seal it away once more, as though such power could be contained or dismissed. No. They earned their ends.'

'And what about the rest of us? You know the devastation your plan will cause.?' Agent Ash gestured around him, his chains rattling. 'It's why I came here with you in the first place. To help you see sense. Let's get the Salus key back, you and I, then together we can deal with the breach and destroy the chamber. You cannot sacrifice us all on a hope. Help me to end this madness before it's too late.'

'By Heaven, your ego is as vast as your ignorance! What help can you give to a man who has written with William Shakespeare, spied with Harriet Tubman, debated Karl Marx, learnt the sword from General Dumas and explored the cosmos with Galileo? I am the spine of human history sir. Spare me your false nobility, Nathan. When we first met, all you cared about was finding the chamber for your masters and turning it into a weapon.'

'All that changed when I entered the chamber,' said Ash. 'No one should have that kind of power. Not you. Not me. Especially not the ESD.'

Ash pointed at Tony. 'Think of this boy and his friends. Don't they deserve the same chance to lead a full life like you?'

Langley crossed the room then crouched in front of Tony, peering down at him with a sneer.

'When I was this boy's age I was studying the stars and performing scientific experiments, seeking to understand the very nature of existence. What has he accomplished? Where is his contribution to this world, besides being another mouth to feed?'

At that moment, Tony did not know what was worse – the fact that Langley was calling him worthless or that he desperately wanted another sandwich.

'You were different Langley; you were a child genius. It's why the Faceless Scholars recruited you in the first place.'

'And those same scholars, men who I respected, men who I was proud to call friends, imprisoned me for the crime of wanting to know more. But in that prison cell, alone and forgotten by the world, destiny still found me. As I worked on the Salus Key, its growing link to the breach somehow changed me, gave me abilities. I discovered that I could not die' Langley waved his hand in a dramatic flourish. 'Very soon, under the gaze of the Hunter's Moon, I will leave this world. I shall pierce the barrier, pass through that hellish null-space beyond, and I shall be renewed. What better destiny for an immortal than to become an explorer, discovering infinite worlds, shaping them for the betterment of all life until the stars grow cold and dim?'

'But don't you see?' Ash cried. 'Once you unseal the breach fully this world will be devastated as well as the worlds beyond. Every piercing weakens the whole.'

'I'm confident that I can seal the breach behind me and I have several lifetimes of research to support that confidence.'

'And what if you're wrong? What if you can't reseal the breach?'

Langley looked away, tapping his chin as though Ash's question had never ever occurred to him.

'No experiment is without risk Ash,' he replied. 'So I will make you a promise. If this world falls I will work tirelessly to improve my device until I am able to travel without incident, no matter how many lifetimes and worlds I must sacrifice to do so.'

'You really are insane,' said Ash.

'You have to understand, Nathan, whilst you believe all human life is equally important, I know that it is not. In my blood I carry centuries of knowledge and culture. The rest of you are simply autumn leaves, caught in the wind of my stride.'

Langley placed a finger under Tony's chin and raised it until their eyes met.

'Are you scared, Tony?'

Tony nodded.

'Don't be. It is fate you are here,' said Langley, with a reassuring smile. 'You see, I know all about you. All of your life you have been an outsider.'

'You don't know anything about me!'

'Oh but I do, Tony. I was you once. I was the easy target because I was the youngest scholar. I was the best of them and yet I was treated with disdain, my theories dismissed at every turn. They hated me because they knew I would surpass them one day, blow their dusty ideas into oblivion.' Langley held his arms out. 'And here I stand, proof of their failure. And all because they could not understand one simple truth.'

'That science and magic are two sides of the same coin,' said Ash.

'It is good to see you have read some of my work, Agent Ash. You are not quite the dullard I took you for.'

'I've read enough to know you weren't always like this.'

Langley turned back to Tony, his warm smile returning. He laid a hand on the boy's shoulder.

'You shall be my herald, Tony. You will bear witness to my power, and perhaps share in it. Would you like that?'

Tony shook his head. 'I just want to go home.'

'Well we can't have everything, can we?' said Langley, standing up to leave. 'Well,' he laughed. 'I suppose *I* can. As of tomorrow night, I will have everything I've ever dreamed of.'

'And what about the rest of us?' Agent Ash called after him.

'Autumn leaves are legion, Nathan. It doesn't matter if some blow away, there will always be more. You really must learn to think on a larger scale.'

With that, Langley left, locking the door behind him. Darkness returned and with it, the sense of helplessness.

A great sigh came from the other side of the cell. 'Sorry I got you into this mess, Tony,' said Agent Ash. 'I confess, I panicked. I gave one of the world's most powerful artefacts to an eleven year old girl, and in doing so, I've damned the world.'

'She's twelve,' Tony spat. 'And her name's Ada. And she's the smartest girl I've ever met. And it's not just her. Nikki's the toughest person ever, and Bobby? He's a pain in the bum, but he's ten times braver than anyone. We're going to get out of this. Somehow. If anyone can find us, they can.'

24

A Lesson in Evil

Why did you give me that stupid box?

The question blew Ada further adrift on a sea of worry. She remembered how scared she had felt walking home from Carnaby's shop. She'd half expected to find Langley lurking round every corner, behind every opened door. She had barely slept that night and now slouched her way through the busy corridors of St Icilda's to class, thoroughly exhausted. But no matter how scared she felt, it must be worse for Tony. Why had he stepped in front of her?

Bobby and DJ entered the classroom looking just as tired and depressed. If anything, Bobby looked worse than she did. He sat down and stared at the empty chair beside him. After a moment Nikki got up from her seat, came over and sat next to Ada. For a while neither of them spoke. Eventually Nikki leaned in.

'We're going to find him you know?'

Ada turned to her, a tear in her eye.

'I was supposed to protect him...' Nikki's voice faltered. '...I swore to protect you all but I failed. I won't fail again. We're going to find Tony and stop Langley.'

'Promise?' Ada croaked.

'A knight never lies.'

Ada could not help but smile. Looking at the determination on Nikki's face, it was difficult to doubt her.

She smiled to herself. *I'm friends with an actual knight.*

Mr Wattling came into the room, his arms full of exercise books. He said his good mornings and took the register without much fuss. Ada thought it was weird. He acknowledged Tony's absence without any snarky comments.

'Liam, would you hand these out?' he asked.

After grumbling that someone else should do it Liam Patterson, went to the front of the class and took the exercise books from Mr Wattling.

'Gibson. Amaya. Come to the front, please.'

The request sent a hushed gasp rippling through the classroom.

'Silence, class. If I were you lot, I would be more worried about the lengthy discussion we will be having shortly about Monday's homework assignment. Abysmal.'

The oooohs turned into a collective groan as Ada followed Bobby up to Wattling's desk

'You are both to report to Room 10B,' said Mr Wattling. 'Off you go.'

'What for sir?' asked Bobby.

'The sooner you go, the sooner you'll find out, won't you?'

Bobby and Ada left without another word.

'You reckon this is about Tony?' asked Ada, once they were safe in the corridor.

'I hope not,' Bobby sighed. 'I've already had to lie to Auntie Carol about tonight so we can go back to Carnaby's.'

'Anything from your mum?' asked Ada.

'Nah, I think she's really gone this time. 'The pair of them continued in silence until when they reached Room 10B. They pressed their faces against the frosted glass, trying to see inside.

'I count two people,' said Ada.

'None of those shapes look like Auntie, so that's good at least.'
Ada knocked twice on the door. 'Could be your dad, though.'

Bobby muttered something rude.

'Come in.'

Ada recognised Mr Creasey's voice straight away. They walked in tentatively, and things went from bad to disastrous. The other man was Bertram Langley.

'Wipe those guilty looks off your faces,' snapped Creasey. 'You're not in trouble. DS Hoplin here has some questions for you.'

Ada and Bobby sat down shakily, facing the two terrifying men.

'Where's that policewoman gone?' asked Bobby.

'No one said you could talk, Gibson!' boomed Creasey.

Hoplin – or rather Bertram Langley – gave Ada and Bobby a warm smile. It was astonishing how natural it looked. How could anyone be so evil, yet look so nice?

'That's alright headmaster. I'm afraid Detective Inspector Penthrope had a little spill in her office yesterday, Bobby. The poor woman does not remember a thing about how it happened, love her. She's at home resting and has placed me in charge of the case in her absence.'

Ada and Bobby shared a worried look.

'Right now I'm more interested in discovering the whereabouts of your young friend,' he referred to a pocket book. 'Tony Tadsby.'

'You what?' asked Bobby.

'One of my officers had a telephone call from Tony's father this morning,' Langley continued. 'It appears Tony never came home from school yesterday.'

Langley leant forward, putting his elbows on the desk.

'Now, I have learnt that Tony had been bullied at his last school. It was the reason his parents bought him to St Icilda's. For a fresh start. However, it is my understanding that he was bullied on his very first day of school here, is that true?'

Bobby sat there, arms crossed, his face a twisted ball of anger.

'Detective Sergeant Hoplin, asked you a question, Gibson. I suggest you answer him,' warned Creasey.

'Sir—' Ada began, but a scowl from Creasey silenced her.

'We're waiting Mr Gibson.'

'Some kids gave him some grief but—'

'I see,' mused Langley, his face showing fake concern. 'And I believe there was some sort of…altercation on the field yesterday? At least, that's what some of the other pupils have said.'

Bobby was furious now, but embarrassed as well. He couldn't look at either adult for fear of saying the wrong thing.

'It supports the theory I suggested to Tony's parents.' He looked over to the Head. 'That the combination of worries – starting at a new school and the bullying he encountered – was just too much for Tony. He's probably just run off to a friend's house and will turn up in his own time.'

'You would say that, wouldn't you!' muttered Bobby.

'What was that Gibson?' Creasey snapped.

'Nothing, sir.'

Langley smiled. 'I'm sure young Tony is fine, but there is the slim possibility he is in trouble. What you say or do not say here, or to anyone else, could make all the difference to him.'

Bobby leapt to his feet and pointed at Langley. 'You *know* where he is!'

'That's enough, Gibson!' snapped Creasey.

'But he's lying, sir! He knows exactly where Tony is, because he's—'

'Yes, Mr Gibson? What am I?' sneered Langley. His eyes cut like cold steel.

Ada grabbed Bobby's arm and yanked him back into his chair.

'Bobby's really sorry, sir,' she blurted. 'He's just worried about Tony; we both are.'

'That is no excuse for rudeness, Miss Amaya. You owe DS Hoplin an apology, Gibson.'

Bobby chewed his lip then mumbled his way through an apology.

'I don't believe he heard you, Mr Gibson,' said Creasey. 'Try again.'

'Sorry DS Hoplin,' said Bobby.

'That's alright Bobby. I'd be worried about my friend too, if I were in your shoes.' Langley smiled lazily. 'But I'll tell you what I told Tony's father on his fifth call to the station: Tony will likely turn up unharmed, feeling very sorry about all the worry he's caused – but I cannot ensure that happens if I keep being harassed.'

He got up and walked around the table, blocking Creasey's view for a moment. As he did so, his smile was replaced with a cruel sneer. For an instant Ada saw Langley's eyes turn from blue to silver, and his fingertips crackled.

'Do we understand each other?' The crackle vanished, his eyes reverted to normal, and he held out a hand.

Bobby looked everywhere but the hand, huffing his disdain, but Ada reached across and shook it. She thought about the promise she'd made to Tony.

'Yes, Detective Sergeant. I understand you perfectly now. Thank you,' she said. 'And sorry again for any trouble we've caused.'

'No need for apologies,' said Langley breezily, walking back to his chair. 'I look forward to reuniting you with your classmate.'

Creasey slapped a hand on the table. 'Right. Back to class.'

As soon as they hit the corridors, Bobby rounded on Ada. 'Why'd you stop me? I could have told Creasey all about—'

'All about what? The evil immortal that's pretending to be a policeman?' asked Ada. 'The magic box he's been chasing? Or perhaps you mean the secret agent who gave it to me for safekeeping? Use your brain, Bobson. I taught you better than that.'

'Dunno know why Langley wanted to see us in the first place. It doesn't make sense. He's the one who's got Tony, after all.'

'You need to see the clues between the clues.' Ada tapped Bobby's forehead. 'Now think. What was Langley *really* telling us?'

Bobby rubbed his chin and thought hard for a bit. Ada smiled. Bobby always made that face when he was thinking. It made him look like he was desperate for the loo.

'He's saying that if we leave him alone Tony's gonna be alright,' Bobby said at last.

'Yes,' said Ada. 'He's trying to scare us off.'

'What he said about Tony being fine—did you believe him?'

'Not one word. Tony is in terrible danger.'

'So, we are gonna get in his way?'

'Damn straight we are!' said Ada.

The rest of the day passed swiftly for Ada, with her mind focused on a single question: where had Langley taken Tony? She barely spoke during morning lessons, and paid little attention to the teachers. At lunch she just picked at her food, barking at anyone daring to start a conversation with her.

It was during science that Ada had a breakthrough.

'Does anyone know why tomorrow is so important for us scientists?' Mr Roebrush asked.

'It's my birthday!' shouted Kenny Brokhurst.

The class erupted into a mixture of laughter and calls for The Bumps led by Liam Patterson.

Ada rested her cheek against her right hand and sighed heavily. She'd never understood the tradition. It seemed less like a celebration and more like assault.

'No Brokhurst, I'm afraid not. But happy birthday for tomorrow,' said Mr Roebrush, moving over to the blackboard. He picked up a piece of orange chalk, drew a large circle on the blackboard and coloured it in. He stepped back, smiled at his handiwork then turned to the class.

'Can anyone tell me what that is?'

A few hands shot up.

'A football?'

'No Liam.'

'An Orange?'

'No Shamri.'

'It looks like an orange. I've got one in my bag. Are you sure, sir?'

'I am very sure, Shamri.'

'It's a spaceship, right sir?' shouted another boy.

Mr Roebrush placed two fingers against his forehead and rubbed it gently. The migraine was coming, he could feel it. Ada understood; it was frustrating being surrounded by stupid people. They were just so slow.

Ada raised her hand. 'It's the sun isn't it, sir?'

'At last! A sensible answer.'

Ada grinned, despite her glum mood.

'But you're wrong. Well, mostly wrong.'

The smile vanished. She sat forward, steepling her fingers. 'Explain yourself sir.'

Roebrush tapped his piece of chalk against the drawing. 'This is actually the moon.'

'Nah. The moon's silver, sir,' someone shouted. 'Everyone knows that.'

'Ah but it won't be tomorrow,' said Mr Roebrush with a theatrical wink. 'But we can talk about why after you've had a chance to see it. It will be a wonder if we get clear enough skies, but you never know.'

This was classic Mr Roebrush. He loved giving kids little 'tests' to see if they were paying attention At some random point over the next week he had no doubt planned a quiz all about this topic. Ada chewed on that for a while. They had to stop Langley first, or there would *be* no next week.

Roebrush picked up the board rubber and wiped the image from the blackboard.

'Right then, back to the ever-growing world of plants. You get it? Ever-growing?'

Ada loved science, but she had to admit that plants put that love to the test. It was hard to get excited about them and she started to feel her brain go numb. In fact was not until near the end of the lesson, when Mr Roebrush had dragged Shamri to explain the mechanisms of photosynthesis, that the gears of Ada intellect began to turn once more.

'That's almost right,' said Mr Roebrush, tapping the board. 'Photosynthesis is actually the process in which plants take in water, carbon dioxide and light energy for conversion into energy-rich organic compounds.'

Why do I suddenly care about Photosynthesis? thought Ada. *And how can the moon be like the sun?*

Ada's hand shot across to Charlotte Cross's desk beside hers. She snatched a coloured pencil and, ignoring Charlotte's complaints, she quickly drew the orangey moon. Then she sat back in her chair, full of triumph, pencil clamped between her teeth.

'Please can I have my pencil back?' Ada took the pencil from her mouth, wiped it on her sleeve, and handed it back to Charlotte.

'This pencil may have just helped to save the world.'

'That's…nice?' said Charlotte.

Charlotte's table companion started twirling a finger by the side of his head then made a few cuckoo noises. Ada didn't care. Everything was starting to make sense at last.

25

The Hunter's Moon

Ada had been a tornado for the rest of science, furiously writing in her casebook. She'd even stayed behind to quiz Mr Roebrush. After school, on the way to Carnaby's shop, Bobby had tried talking to her, but all she would say was, 'It's the key, Bobson. The answer to everything.'

Before Carnaby had fully opened the shop door, Ada slipped through the gap and stalked towards the back room.

'Why come on in,' Carnaby called after her.

'She's always like this when she's figured something out,' whispered Bobby, stepping past Carnaby.

DJ and Nikki barrelled in, each bagsying the sofa.

Carnaby peered out to see if they were being observed, then he closed the door and locked it. 'I've made the tea and picked up some Jaffa Cakes; I know Miss Amaya has a penchant for them.'

'No time for Jaffa Cakes!' Ada shouted. 'We have work to do.' She threw open the trapdoor and disappeared down the stairs.

Nikki pushed past the shocked boys.

'Did she just say no to Jaffa Cakes?' asked DJ.

Bobby nodded, watching Nikki descend through the trap door.

'Flipping great,' groaned DJ. 'She's gone full Sherlock hasn't she?' Then he shouted 'Oi, Nikki! I called the sofa first!' and ran off after them.

'Any news on Tony, yet?' Carnaby asked.

Bobby told Carnaby about the second meeting with Langley, his dark warnings and false promises as they headed downstairs.

Carnaby clapped a massive hand on Bobby's shoulder. 'By Heaven, you did well to keep your nerve. Both of you. The man is a monster!'

'Well, duh. Course he's a monster,' said DJ, snatching a Jaffa Cake. 'He's got those dodgy eyes, hooded goons, and he's trying to blow up the world.'

Carnaby settled into an armchair, sipping his mug of tea. Ada was pacing, fizzing with energy.

'So, my young detective. I take it you have questions?'

Ada swung on her heels, marched up to Carnaby and thrust the puzzle box towards him.

'We know this pulls energy from the moon, correct? Like plants for photosynthesis, right?'

'Indeed it does. You see—'

Ada waved away Carnaby's words, pacing back to the centre of the room.

'Would it be…more somehow, if it was powered by a Hunter's Moon?'

Carnaby almost dropped his mug.

'This afternoon, in Double Science, Mr Roebrush said the moon was going to change colour tonight. It made no sense to me until I drew it, and then I remembered that a total lunar eclipse could do that. Light refraction or something. He told us about them last year.'

'Can't believe you remember anything that bloke says.'

Bobby punched DJ on the arm and told him to shut up.

'I asked Mr Roebrush about them after class, and he told me this type of lunar eclipse is sometimes called a Blood Moon.'

'The inscription!' said Bobby, flying to his feet. 'Step within the moon's crimson shade to seal our fate. It's talking about a Blood Moon. Nice one A!'

Ada accepted the compliment with a smile.

Carnaby slapped his forehead. 'Of course. How could I be so stupid?'

'Practise?' mumbled DJ through half a Jaffa Cake.

Carnaby gave him a warning look then addressed them all. 'Throughout history the Blood or Hunter's Moon has long been regarded as a powerful source of elemental energy. The Scholars must have used the energy from a Blood Moon to help them contain the breach.'

Ada nodded. 'So Langley is going to use another Blood Moon to—'

'Kick open the breach and make a hole in the barrier,' Bobby finished.

'It's why he's not tried to open the breach yet, even though he has his little travel orb,' said Ada. 'He's been waiting for the Blood Moon.'

'By heaven yes, that would do it,' said Carnaby, setting down his mug. 'He would need to harness then focus the lunar energy along a ley line into the Apocalypse Chamber and the breach... and I believe I know how.'

Carnaby got up and strode to a much larger table on the far side of the room, covered with papers. The others joined him as he excavated a large map.

Carnaby swept everything else aside, laid the map down and peered at it intently. Eventually, he pointed to a spot on the map.

'Here is the graveyard where Ada met Agent Ash and Langley.'

'And Tony.'

'Indeed.' Drawing a pencil from behind his ear, Carnaby drew a large X on the map. He placed his index finger on the X, slid it a few inches diagonally across the map and stopped.

'Here is the Baxter Estate where you found the symbols and faced Langley once again.' He drew another X on the map.

'Still trying to forget that one,' said DJ.

'I'm sure,' agreed Carnaby. He drew a line between the X's. 'Now I can't be sure as that region has never been mapped, but it is possible these locations could sit on the same ley line.

'So what?' asked Bobby.

'If so Langley will use this ley line to channel the energy given off by the Blood Moon into the breach within the Apocalypse Chamber which I believe is somewhere under that graveyard.'

'Great. Couldn't be under a sweet shop or an arcade?' complained DJ, folding his arms. 'It has to be under a bleeding graveyard!'

Carnaby retrieved a large brown leather book from the pile on the floor.

He dropped the pair of glasses from his forehead to his nose, and started turning pages.

'Something stuck in my mind when you told me how you faced Langley on that roof. If he had already used the location spell days earlier – when Nikki saw him – then why had he returned?'

'He said we were interfering with his work,' said Bobby, thinking back to the confrontation.

'Who said?' asked Carnaby.

'Langley did,' said Ada, the words tumbling from her mouth as she began to see the events more clearly. 'He wasn't expecting to find us up there, so what was he doing?'

Carnaby smiled. He had stopped on a page covered in symbols. Bobby peered closer.

'They look like those drawings up on the estate roof.'

'Quite correct, Mr Gibson. The symbols you found were not only to find the chamber, but formed part of a larger ritual to harness energy, in this case lunar energy,' Carnaby told him.

'Steal the moon to light the beacon,' whispered Ada, placing her hands on the map.

'The tower block is the beacon isn't it? So when we saw him, he was finishing the spell, making it ready for the Blood Moon.'

'Very good Miss Amaya, that was my conclusion also. Whatever structure the Faceless Scholars used to harness the Blood Moon's energy originally, has long since gone. Langley had to improvise. He was lucky. The tower block suits his needs perfectly.'

'Luck had nothing to do with it,' said Ada running over to her satchel. She fished out her notebook and bought it back to the table.

'There is nothing more deceptive than an obvious fact,' said Ada.

They stared blankly at her.

Ada let out a frustrated sigh then asked, 'Remember the Keep Out signs all over the estate?'

More blank stares, but Nikki nodded.

'Aeterus Incorporated. It's the name of company who own the estate. It was on those signs.' Ada turned to Nikki. 'The builders said the new owners were a nightmare… Do you remember why?'

The corners of Nikki's mouth twisted up in a grin, shifting her lollipop from one side to the other. She nodded in understanding.

'You wanna share with us thickos?' asked DJ.

'The new company. They were always having a go at the builders if they hadn't followed their instructions exactly.'

'And? Their new boss is a nightmare, so what?' said DJ bemused.

'So what if their new boss is an immortal scholar who wanted a new tower built so he could use it for a ceremony? He said it himself – he's had years building up money and contacts, making things happen behind the scenes.'

'You reckon Langley owns the estate?' asked Bobby.

'I'd bet my life on it. Know what Aeterus means? It's Latin for Eternal. I got Henry to translate it for me.'

'When did you…?' Bobby broke off and laughed. He'd known her for years, but Ada could still surprise him.

She smiled. 'Apart, the facts are meaningless. Bring them together, and we have a pattern.'

Carnaby clucked his tongue in admiration. 'You are a strange and wonderful child.'

'Very strange, according to my mother,' agreed Ada. 'She says it's my finest quality.'

'And a very commendable one but Langley built the Salus Key whilst imprisoned by the scholars, surely he would already know where they carried out the original ceremony and where the chamber was?'

Ada flipped forward a few pages in her notebook then read aloud. 'Bertram will never help us. We cannot risk bringing him here. One of the scholars said that in my vision. They probably kept him far away from the chamber because they didn't trust him.'

Carnaby clasped his hands behind his back. 'So when the Faceless Scholar relics were discovered under the estate, Langley realised the Scholars used this location to channel the power of the Blood Moon into the Apocalypse Chamber when they originally created the breach.'

Ada nodded. 'Of course he would have still needed to find the Salus Key and chamber itself but that's where Agent Ash came in.'

'Yes, that's what I was going to say' said Carnaby, frowning.

Bobby patted him on the back. 'Don't worry mate, you'll get used to her.'

'What do we do now?' asked DJ, raising a hand.

'We rescue Tony, stop Langley and save the world,' said Nikki.

DJ chuckled. 'Yeah, good one.'

Nikki continued sucking the lollipop, entirely serious.

DJ threw up his arms. 'This is crazy, even for us! No way we can do this on our own. We need help.'

'And where do you suggest we find this help?' asked Ada. 'Everyone thinks Langley is a police detective and the Blood Moon is happening tomorrow night.'

'What about that ESD?' suggested DJ.

'The scary secret agent blokes? Yeah good luck with that one,' said Bobby, frowning. 'They're dodgy as.'

'Bobby is right,' said Carnaby. 'The ESD want the chamber for themselves. We are on our own, my friends.'

They all stared at Carnaby.

'What? Is there chocolate on my face?' Carnaby began running his hands over it, checking his fingers for smears.

'You're an adult,' said Bobby. 'You're supposed to be telling us what to do. Or telling us we're too young to be doing all this.'

Carnaby gave booming laugh. 'I fought my first werewolf at your age, then a few years later I helped to recover one of the Fragments of Fate. Age is no barrier, trust me. You have far more power than you know.'

'What's that then, cos I'm pretty sure I can't fly,' DJ snarked.

'Adults underestimate you, dear boy, and that is a very great power indeed.'

Carnaby pointed at the notebook in Ada's hands. 'Am I right in assuming that you recorded the vision you had when you touched the Salus Key?'

Ada frowned at Carnaby so hard Bobby thought the shopkeeper might turn to stone.

'I will take that as a yes,' said Carnaby, holding out a hand. 'Do you mind if I take a look at those notes?'

Ada clutched the book tighter.

'You have my word I will only look at that one section.'

'Let me see your hands,' demanded Ada.

Carnaby held out his hands, palms facing up. He then turned them over upon Ada's instruction. The was some evidence of Jaffa Cakes, which he took time to clean off with his handkerchief.

'I guess they're clean enough,' she said at last.

Ada flipped to the relevant page, took a deep breath and handed the book over.

Everyone waited in silence while Carnaby read.

'Impressive penmanship Miss Amaya.'

'Well?' asked Ada. Her foot had not stopped tapping.

'I believe what you saw was a series of memories, stored within the Salus Key to help find the chamber. Whose, I could not say. Perhaps the Scholars did this to aid someone in sealing the chamber, should it ever be opened.' Carnaby placed the book on the table, jabbing a finger at the small drawing Ada had made. It depicted two cobras in a sideways figure eight, swallowing their own tails. 'This symbol that you saw carved on the giant stone doors – it is the crest of the Faceless Scholars.'

Ada slapped her forehead and swore.

'Idiot! How did I not see it before? It's the same as the one on the Aeterus signs at the estates.'

'Ada,' said Carnaby with a flash of enthusiasm. 'You encountered Agent Ash in the graveyard, fleeing with the key. I do not believe that is a coincidence. It is my suspicion that there is an entrance to the underground tunnels containing the chamber somewhere within the graveyard, through which he was chased. Given what you saw in your vision, my guess would be a mausoleum.'

'How are we going to find it?' asked Bobby. 'That graveyard is even bigger than DJ's feet.'

DJ gave Bobby a shove, but he was chuckling as he did so.

'Leave that to me,' said Carnaby.

'What about Langley?' asked Nikki.

'You've seen the effect salt has on supernatural creatures,' replied Carnaby. 'If I can trap Langley within a ring of salt, it might strip him of his powers and hold him while I deal with any damage to the breach.'

'What's the bad news?' asked Nikki.

'Very astute,' said Carnaby. 'Langley needs the Blood Moon to open the barrier and we need it to give the key enough power to reseal the breach. We cannot make the attempt until tomorrow night.'

'Why can't we go in now?' asked Bobby.

'Because ever since the Apocalypse Chamber has been opened whatever power is keeping the breach sealed will be weakening,' explained Carnaby. 'Think of it like having a sealed food container in the fridge but you leave the fridge door wide open. The food is still sealed away but is starting to go off because the cold from the fridge is escaping.'

DJ blew out a tired sigh 'Knew I should've bunked off this week.'

26

How to Pack for the
End of the World

The following day flew by for Ada, aside from the dreaded PE. She understood the need for physical education, especially as part of her goal to become the world's greatest detective, but it did not mean she had to enjoy it. Still, it provided a good excuse to leave her satchel at home and bring in her rucksack. She'd need the extra space later.

Once school was over Ada met the others by the school gates. Together they headed for Carnaby's once more.

Ada turned. 'Come on DJ, keep up!'

DJ was sweating horribly. His blazer was wrapped around his waist and he gripped the straps of his rucksack for dear life. They were biting deep into his shoulders with the weight.

'Easy for you to say,' he grunted. 'You're not the one carrying four bleeding bags of salt in your rucksack. They're massive!'

'You sure Mrs Clemisky didn't see you?' asked Ada.

DJ shook his head.

'You want me carry to some mate?' Bobby offered.

'Nah it's cool. I'm the weapons guy, ain't I?'

'Did you get the conker shells?' asked Ada.

DJ patted his rucksack. 'Yep and soaked them in loads of salt and oil last night, just like you said. They better work because that's my whole stash for the big fight next week.'

'They'll work,' said Ada.

They have to work, she told herself. Tony and world were counting on them to.

'We all know this is stupid, right?' muttered DJ. 'Taking on an immortal nutter with some conker shells and salt?'

'And Carnaby. And Nikki,' said Ada. 'They ain't nothing.'

Ada stopped dead in her tracks and the others ploughed into her.

Ahead of them, the scholarly giant was being led from his shop by four men. One walked ahead while another marched behind a seething Carnaby. The remaining two men, each gripping one of Carnaby's fearsome arms, marched on either side of him.

'Hide!' Ada snapped, darting with Nikki behind a large parked decorator's van.

Bobby and DJ slipped into the alcove of a closed bakery.

Ada peered out from her hiding place. She recognised the two men who were gripping Carnaby: Agents Orlando and Gans. The agents all stood there for a minute, peering up and down the street.

What are you waiting for? Ada wondered.

Carnaby threw himself from side to side, trying to wriggle free. 'This is madness!' he bellowed, struggling against the two men. 'You have no idea what is at stake!'

'Which is why you're coming for a little ride to tell us all about it,' said Agent Orlando.

'I don't have time for this,' he croaked. 'Langley is still out there!'

'You know as well as I that the ESD keep extensive files on any immortal activity. Bertram Langley is not in any of them,' Agent Gans snapped. 'This is just more lies.'

Ada did not know what was worse; that the agents had captured Carnaby or that Langley was not the only immortal running around.

A large black van pulled up alongside Carnaby's shop, a green car pulling in behind it. The van's back doors were flung open to reveal two more grey-suited men inside.

At that moment Carnaby stared down the street, saw Ada and smiled.

'What about my shop?' Carnaby roared at his captors. 'Everything we need is in it! Don't waste our resources. There's a back door to every solution.'

Then he winked at Ada.

Ada winked back.

Agent Orlando pushed Carnaby toward the back of the van. 'Don't worry Carnaby, you can go back to your pitiful shop once you tell us where the Salus Key is.'

The two men reached out from the van and pulled Carnaby in, bundling him to a seated position. Agent Orlando slammed the rear doors shut then banged the side twice, to signal the driver. The van sped off down the street. Once it was out of sight Orlando, Gans and the remaining agents got into the green car. Soon they were out of sight, following the same route as the van.

Ada waited a minute or two, just to be on the safe side. Satisfied the agents were not coming back, she led the others past the shop and round to the alley at the back. If she had understood Carnaby right... *Yes!*

Although it looked closed at first glance, the fire exit had been held ajar with a pebble.

'Here goes nothing,' she whispered wedging her fingers inside.

The door opened with a melodramatic creak.

Once everyone was inside Ada kicked the pebble and closed the door.

'Blimey!' said DJ, taking in the sight.

The room and the shop beyond looked like they had been hit by a tornado. Shelves had been emptied, the items scattered across the floor, some in shattered pieces.

'They were looking for the key,' said Bobby.

Ada nodded, and picked her way through the carnage to the large grey rug. Together, they rolled back the rug to reveal the trap door.

Bobby grabbed hold of the brass ring and pulled up the trap door.

'Hang on!' Ada ran back to her rucksack. She unzipped it, took out four torches and set them on the table. She could not stop the smug smile when she saw the shocked expressions from the others. Even Nikki seemed impressed.

'Shamri?' she asked.

'Yeah,' Ada replied. 'I promised to help her with her drama lessons. She wants to be in the next school play.'

DJ picked up a torch. 'I'm in her drama class. A cardboard box would stand a better chance.'

'I didn't say it was going to be easy,' said Ada, stiffly. She switched on her own torch.

Their torch beams sliced through the gloom, skipping over all the strange objects as they descended the stairs. Without Carnaby here, the space felt far scarier. A sudden rattling made Ada leap into the air and scream.

DJ stuck a match, its faint orange flow illuminating his mischievous smile. He raced around the room then, lighting any candles he found. Soon there were enough lit to allow them to turn off their torches.

They all gathered around the table. DJ lifted four large tubs of salt out of his rucksack, setting them down on the table.

'I guess we won't be needing these anymore then,' he sighed. 'Mind you, the kebab shop's not far. I could murder a bag of chips.'

Ada ignored him. She was busy studying a new map Carnaby had been working on. Bobby came round beside her and peered down at it. Across the centre of the map was written the words 'Floodgate Cemetery'.

'He was looking for the Mausoleum,' said Ada at last.

'Who cares?' said DJ. 'There's nothing we can do now.'

'Did he find it?' asked Nikki.

Ada tapped a section of the map where someone had drawn a bright red X. 'I'm guessing so.'

'Where's that?' asked Bobby

'It's near where I first met Agent Ash,' explained Ada. 'Look. Here's the graveyard wall and the road we came out on. We can go back in the same way.'

'Cool,' said Bobby.

Ada rolled up the map and stuffed it into her rucksack. Nikki wandered off to explore the rest of the room. Bobby grabbed two tubs of salt from the table. He dropped one into his satchel and handed the other to Ada, who did the same. Then Bobby held his hand out to DJ. 'Pass me some of those conker shells, mate.'

'You're kidding me. You still want to go?' DJ stared at them in horror. 'Come off it. It was different when we had Carnaby backing us up, but now it's just the four of us?'

'Look mate,' said Bobby. 'Even if we went to the police – the real police – they ain't gonna believe us. And you know that ESD lot will just take the key off us. They don't believe Carnaby. For all we know they could be working with Langley. We gotta do this on our own.'

'How?'

'I dunno yet but either way we're going to find Tony and stop Langley.'

'Right!' said Ada.

Bobby put an arm around DJ. 'It'll be fine, mate. Seriously.'

264 · BARRY NUGENT

DJ's expression was not of someone who thought things were going to be fine.

Nikki came back to the table carrying a large plastic tub filled with water. There was a long, thin tube running from the bottom round to a plastic pipe with a handle and a green nozzle at the end.

'What's that?' asked Bobby.

Nikki aimed the nozzle at DJ, squeezed the handle and a jet of water squirted him in the face. DJ spluttered and coughed. 'It's salty!'

'Cool, right? It's one those garden sprayer things. I've seen 'em used at the park. Reckon Carnaby had plans for this. I do, anyway,' said Nikki, joyfully. 'This is going to be awesome!'

It was the happiest Ada had ever seen Nikki, as she squirted him again.

'I hate my life, and I hate you all,' grumped DJ.

27

Chips and Catastrophe

Tony wiped the tears from his eyes and the dried snot from under his nose. He refused to be scared anymore, no matter what happened. Mum and Dad were out there somewhere, looking for him, and so were Ada and the others. Somebody would find him.

'And they ain't gonna find me crying when they do,' he swore.

'Nothing wrong with tears, Tony,' said the agent gently. 'I've shed a few myself here, in the dark. But it's not over yet.'

The cell door opened to the sound of mocking laughter.

'How marvellous. Such optimism!'

Tony lifted his head and saw Langley, leant against the door frame.

'Even if you found the strength to free yourself, where would you go? What would you do?'

'What are you doing here Langley?'

'You know I don't really know,' admitted Langley. 'Perhaps I came for one last conversation with the man who made all this possible.'

'Help will come,' Ash snarled, slumping back against the wall.

Langley crouched down before him and peered into his eyes.

'No, Nathan. It really won't. I have had time to study what the scholars have built down here. I have reactivated the traps you and I disabled when we first found these catacombs,' explained Langley. 'Should the ESD or Tony's little friends find their way into the catacombs they will never reach these cells alive.'

Ash seized Langley's forearm. 'You cared once. You wanted to help mankind. Don't damn us all for a dream!'

Langley pulled his arm free, rose and straightened his sleeve. 'You know I should thank you. I had begun to fear that even my intellect was insufficient to solve the problem of Man. But then you found the Salus Key, and led me to the Apocalypse Chamber. It was then I knew what my destiny was and the price I would have to pay for it.'

Langley swallowed hard and looked away, but Tony saw the sadness in his eyes.

'It told me who I was.'

'And who is that, Langley?' asked Ash. 'God?'

'I am the only sane, only real person in this world or any other. I am the only one strong enough to lead not just this world but a multiverse of worlds. I am the only man that counts. All others age and die, their hopes crumbled to dust, but I go on forever.'

'I'll say you do,' muttered Ash.

'Said the flea to the giant…' Langley rose.

Pulling the cell door shut Langley locked it and then strode away without another word.

'Come on Ada,' whispered Tony. 'Come on.'

***

Bobby tried to ignore the delicious smell coming from his left. Once again he regretted not getting anything from the kebab shop.

'Sure you don't want one mate?' asked DJ, holding out a paper cone chock-full of chips.

'They're proper tasty!'

'Always thinking with your stomach,' moaned Ada.

DJ gave an unrepentant shrug and tossed a soggy chip into his mouth.

Nikki reached into the cone, plucking out a few chips as a passerby stared in fascination at the large garden sprayer strapped to her back.

DJ was outraged. 'Oi! Did I ask you?' He put a hand over the cone as Nikki devoured her spoils.

The four of them turned the corner leading into the darkened graveyard.

The world could end at any moment and you make us stop at the kebab shop so you can stuff your face,' said Ada.

DJ pointed a drooping chip at her. 'Listen, if we are gonna save the world tonight, I'm doing it on a full stomach, right? Besides a little more ammo doesn't hurt.'

DJ set his bag down and opened it.

Bobby took one look inside the bag, threw his hands up and stomped away. 'He's only gone and nicked the salt from the Kebab shop.'

'What? I'll take it back tomorrow.' DJ turned on the flashlight, shined it under his chin, casting his face in an ominous hue. 'If there is a tomorrow.'

'Not funny mate,' said Bobby.

'Not even a little?'

That was it for Ada. She stepped in slapping the bag of chips out of DJ's hands.

'What the hell is wrong with you Dibney?' she screamed, kicking the bag into street. 'Tony could be dead for all we know and you're laughing and stuffing your face like it's all a big joke!'

'I'm here aren't I?' shouted back DJ. 'Not my fault what happened to Smiley.'

Ada shoved him away with both hands. He tripped over his feet and tumbled to the pavement. Ada stood over him, her face now twisted with rage, jabbing a finger at him.

'No it's not your fault but you've taken none of this seriously since the start. If you don't want to be here then just sod off! We don't need you!'

No one spoke as Ada turned and walked on. She had dared to voice their big, unsaid, fear about Tony.

DJ mumbled something under his breath.

Ada stopped. 'What?'

'I SAID I'M FLIPPING SCARED OK!'

DJ pushed himself onto his elbows. He was shaking. Bobby saw tears brimming in his friend's eyes. He held out a hand but DJ slapped it away.

'I tried to tell you. You asked me what was up but I couldn't do it then, not with Tony hanging about. After that you never asked me again.'

Bobby remembered the conversation they had while listening to Ash's tape. Everything made sense now. DJ was right, he had just forgotten about it. His friend had been in trouble all this time and he had done nothing to help him.

'I've been scared everyday since Norfolk,' DJ said quietly. The tears were rolling now. 'And I thought things would be normal this year and maybe the nightmares would stop but then all this happened. So you're right I don't wanna be here.'

Ada turned back to DJ, her angry expression giving way to a guilt ridden one. 'I...I didn't know DJ.'

'Yeah well you two were busy running around being detectives weren't you?' said DJ, forcing a weak smile through his tears.

'Sorry mate,' said Bobby, holding out his hand again.

This time DJ took it, allowing himself to be pulled up.

'So why did you stick around?' asked Bobby. 'Why did you help us?'

DJ sighed. His shoulders sagged as though he were buckling under the weight of his answer.

'You're my best mates you doughnut…what else was I gonna do?'

Ada and Bobby stared at DJ for a long while, no one speaking. Finally, Ada looked over at the crushed paper bag in the street. 'Sorry about your chips.'

DJ shrugged. 'When we get Tony back you can buy a kebab to make up for it.'

'Look DJ,' began Ada, moving closer. 'You don't have to come. We can—'

'Tony's one of us now right?' DJ said, looking at Ada.

'Right,' said Ada.

DJ flicked his gaze to Bobby. 'Right?'

'Right.'

DJ took a deep shuddering breath, wiping away his tears. When he spoke there was no laughter in the words

'Well I ain't leaving my mate behind so I'm going.'

'Look' said Nikki, pointing up.

They all looked. The night sky was clear, and the moon had never looked larger. There was a reddish tinge at the moon's left side.

'The Blood Moon,' said Bobby 'It's starting.'

Nikki slipped off the garden sprayer then braced herself against the graveyard wall.

'Come on, let's get a shift on.'

She interlocked her fingers, bent her legs and nodded to Bobby.

With the help of the leg-up, Bobby grabbed the top of the wall and managed to haul himself over. He dropped down, lost his footing and fell headfirst into a pile of wet leaves.

'You ok, Bobson?' Ada whispered from the other of the wall.

Bobby coughed, spitting out a mouthful of leaves. 'It smells, it's dark, and I think I've ripped my jacket.'

Ada was next over the wall.

'Look at this. Auntie Carol is going to kill me,' Bobby muttered, showing her the torn sleeve.

'She'll be the least of your worries if we mess up tonight,' Ada pointed out.

'Oi you two, stop gabbing and help, yeah?'

DJ was perched atop the wall, one leg hanging down either side. He was holding the garden sprayer, which was making sloshing noises as he struggled to keep it upright. Bobby and Ada held their hands up and DJ passed the sprayer to them. He then turned and bent back towards the other side of the fence where only Nikki remained.

'Up you come,' said DJ.

What followed was a lot of grunting until finally Bobby saw one of Nikki's hands grip the top of the wall, while DJ held the other, in both of his. Nikki's head appeared and seconds later both her and DJ were on the other side. After nodding her thanks, Nikki retrieved the garden sprayer. Ada drew out the map she had taken from Carnaby's shop, while DJ strapped the sprayer onto Nikki's back. Nikki showed her gratitude by spraying him again.

'Leave off!' he spluttered.

'Just testing it. Cheers,' she replied, laughing. A sharp shush from Ada silenced the pair.

'Where to?' asked Bobby as he rubbed warmth into his hands.

Ada turned on her torch and focused it on the map.

Bobby's eyes followed the beam as she swept it around in front of her. It skipped across and between the gravestones, shining in the night like keys on a piano. Some were grand and ornate, others just slabs of stones, the inscriptions worn with age.

'We go there look, then go left towards the centre of the graveyard and look for—'

'Shh!' Nikki slapped her hand over Ada's torch. Tiny slivers of light shone between her fingers. Then Bobby saw what had spooked her. Two torch beams – industrial strength – were slicing towards them from around a corner.

Ada switched the torch off and the four of them scattered behind gravestones.

A few seconds later a gruff voice said, 'You're losing it, Ron.'

'I'm telling you Geoff, I heard voices over here. Could be more of them vandals.'

'It's bleeding freezing out here. Let's go back to the hut.'

Bobby held his breath as the guards came closer.

'I saw lights out here,' protested Ron.

'The only thing out here is corpses, mate and they ain't got nothing to say,' Geoff grumbled.

A harsh beam settled on the large cracked gravestone hiding Ada.

'Let's just have a check over there, then we can head back,' said Ron.

'Listen Scooby Doo I've got a bacon sarnie and a cuppa getting cold. Stay here if you want, but I'm heading back.'

After some grumbling, the twin torch beams retreated, the security guards' voices growing fainter. Eventually all Bobby could hear was the wind, whipping up the leaves among the gravestones.

Ada switched on her torch but kept her hand cupped over it, reducing the beam to a faint glow over the map. The others huddled in around her.

'Where to, then?' whispered Bobby.

Ada looked up from the map and pointed toward the middle of the graveyard. There, nestled between the trees and gravestones, silhouetted against the reddening moon, was a large marble building. Two statues sat on either side of its doors.

Nikki gave a low whistle.

''Cause that's not scary,' said DJ.

'Time to go,' said Ada, switching off her light.

They followed her through the darkened cemetery. Without the torch, their movement was slow and cautious. Bobby tried to banish the image of tripping and falling into an open grave. This was only his second visit to a graveyard, but the first time had been much worse.

'Mum?' he whispered. 'Mum?'

But she was still gone.

The only reply he got was from Ada.

'We're here.'

Ahead of them were the large doors of the mausoleum.

'Are we sure this is the right place?' asked Bobby.

Ada flicked on her torch, revealing two giant cobras carved into the stone doors, seemingly staring out at them. The doors from her vision! The two cobras were entwined forming a figure eight symbol.

'Pretty sure,' said Ada, taking puzzle box out from her satchel. 'Nikki – we all clear?'

Nikki disappeared down the left side of the mausoleum. A minute later she returned from the right and gave a thumbs up.

Bobby stepped up to the door alongside Ada. Together they placed their hands against the door and pushed. Nothing. The door didn't budge an inch. Nikki and DJ joined them and, with two to a door, they tried again.

Finally, their strength and patience spent, they backed away, gasping.

'Well …that…was… a bit rubbish,' puffed DJ, rubbing his shoulder.

'There are no handles. I just assumed it would open,' said Ada.

'What now?' asked Nikki

'You can let me think for a start,' Ada snapped.

She was sorry even as she spoke. Nikki slumped against one of the statues, glaring, but biting her tongue.

'No pressure, but I think we need to get a move on' said DJ, pointing up at the sky.

The last of clouds drifted away, exposing the Blood Moon.

'That's weird,' said DJ, pointing at the statue by Nikki. 'It's Salus.'

Ada took out her casebook. 'Are you sure?'

DJ stepped up to look closer. It depicted a woman seated on a throne. She had one hand outstretched, holding a small dish.

'Pretty sure. The librarian showed me pictures of statues like this one,' said DJ. He patted the stone snake that was wrapped around the statue's right arm. The snake's head was looking toward the plate, as though it were waiting to be fed.

Ada shone her torch onto her casebook as she read the poem. 'Steal the Moon to light the beacon. Pay the goddess to open the gate. Step within the moon's crimson shade to seal our fate.'

Closing the notebook, Ada moved to stand in front the statue then, slipping her book back into her rucksack, she drew out the Salus Key.

Bobby moved alongside her. 'What are you doing?'

Ada placed the key onto the plate. 'Paying the Goddess.'

The sound of grinding stone filled the air, and everyone backed away from the statue. They watched in amazement as the head of the stone snake twisted to face the door, and the Salus Key began to glow. A needle-sharp beam of ethereal light shot from the Salus Key into the snake, wrapped around the statue's other arm. It then leapt from the snake to strike the doors, illuminating shapes and symbols as it went. With a great whoosh, both mausoleum doors swung open, revealing an opening cloaked in darkness.

Bobby flicked on his torch, aiming it through the doorway. The passageway beyond was lined with moss, dried mud and, as a final scary cherry on top, spider webs - lots and lots of spider webs. Bobby shivered, shuffled back a few steps then began brushing himself down as though the sight alone was enough to unleash a horde of eight-legged nightmares across his body.

DJ patted Bobby on the back. 'Spiders, eh? Proper nasty. You go first, yeah?'

'Oi! What the hell do you think you kids are doing?'

They all turned. Ron and Mike were sprinting towards them, waving their arms and shouting. Without thinking, Bobby snatched the Salus Key from the dish. Instantly the doors began to swing shut.

'GO!' he screamed, plunging into the darkness before his fears could stop him. He felt the weight of the others behind him as the doors slammed shut, the only light coming now from their torches. Shouts and banging could be heard from the other side of the doors, but there was no way Ron and Geoff were getting in.

'Nice one,' said DJ, his voice echoing loudly. 'But hang on… We're trapped in here now. How the hell are we going to get out again?'

Bobby did not answer. He was too busy thinking about all the spiders around him in the darkness.

28

Flaming Idiots

To Ada's right, Bobby was gripping his torch in both hands, swinging it left and right as though he were battling horrific creatures that only he could see. Ada knew Bobby well enough to know what he was seeing.

'You know the statistical probability that we will see arachnids at this time of year is really very slim,' she whispered.

'You're just saying that to stop me freaking out,' said Bobby.

'Of course I am,' said Ada. Then she grabbed his forearm. 'But you still led us in here and saved us from those men, Bobby. Your mum would be very proud of you.'

Bobby gave Ada a half smile then drew in a deep breath. He stopped scanning the ceiling and aimed his beam straight down the gloomy passage.

'Come on then,' he ordered, moving forward.

Ada grinned and followed. She might be the smartest person in any room but Bobby Gibson was the bravest.

The passage was wide enough for three people to walk abreast of each other, but Bobby insisted everyone stay behind him. After the business with the snake and the statue, he guessed there'd be more than met the eye down here. Bobby crept along the passageway, his torchlight scanning the dusty floor and the craggy walls with every step. He stopped by a small stone cobra head that was jutting out from the wall.

'Get a shift on mate,' DJ called, from the rear. 'I wanna get out of here before Christmas.'

'We gotta go slow mate, there could be traps,' replied Bobby, gently running a hand over the cobra.

'So, you're an expert on traps now?'

'I'm an expert on playing D&D.'

'Right because this is just like Dungeons and Dragons,' said DJ, shoving his way past Bobby. 'This is nothing—'

CLICK.

Bobby grabbed DJ by the back of his shirt and yanked him backwards, just as spikes erupted from the floor. The razor-sharp spikes embedded themselves in the ceiling with a terrifying crunch.

DJ sagged against Bobby, covering his mouth. 'I think I'm gonna puke.'

'How did you know?' asked Ada, watching the spikes retract into the floor.

Bobby shone a light on the floor ahead. Ada's eyes narrowed. There was no sign of where the spikes had come from but several of the stones were raised. Even as they watched, the stone DJ had trodden on slid back into place.

'Step where I step,' ordered Bobby, straightening his school satchel.

DJ nodded, silent for once.

Bobby picked his way gingerly between the raised stones, his torch fixed to the floor ahead, the others following like lambs.

Once they were on the other side, Bobby blew out his cheeks and tapped his chest. 'Like I said, mate. D&D. And you thought it was kids' stuff…'

The tunnel ended in some curved stone steps leading down into the darkness. Bobby crouched at the staircase edge, sweeping his torch across the first step. Scooping up a handful of dirt, he studied it, then let it run through his fingers.

'Looks good,' announced Bobby, rubbing the remaining dirt from his hands. Nikki and Ada exchanged looks. *Boys!*

Down and down the staircase took them until it led out into another long, much wider tunnel. On either side, several wooden doors were set into the walls. Ada, Bobby, DJ and Nikki stood in a line, their torch beams criss-crossing the passage.

DJ pointed to one of the doors. 'In them D&D games what would you find behind a door like that?'

'Treasure or monsters,' said Nikki. 'Normally monsters.'

'You play D&D?' asked Bobby, surprised and delighted.

Nikki shrugged. 'With my cousins, yeah. Doesn't everyone?'

'If they're a saddo, they do!'

Nikki turned and DJ, realising his mistake, backed away.

Nikki raised the nozzle of her garden sprayer. 'Call me saddo again. I dare you.'

'Nikki?' a voice called out from the gloom.

'Tony!' shouted Ada, running forward. 'It's Tony!'

Ada ran up to the door, grabbing the bars to pull herself up. She shone her torch inside and glimpsed Tony before dropping back to the floor. With several tries, she saw Tony and a man chained to the wall. Each shielded their eyes as the light struck their faces, but they looked uninjured. Relief flooded through Ada.

'Don't worry Tony, we're going to get you out,' she promised, lowering her torch. 'DJ? How are you with locks?'

'Dunno but I'll give it a go,'

DJ took two small metal rods from his pockets and inserted them into the lock. After a few minutes of probing, pushing and turning the thin rods in the lock there was a loud click. DJ stood in triumph.

'Ta-da!' he said, pushing the door open.

Ada ran over to Tony and threw her arms around him. Then she broke away, embarrassed.

'Are you...ok?' she asked, stiffly.

Tony tried to speak but there was just a strangled gasp where his voice should be. He swallowed hard and tried again. He turned to the other prisoner.

'I'm not...I'm not dreaming am I?

'No. They found us,' he replied, relief throbbing in his voice. Agent Ash squinted up at Ada. 'Tony said you would come for us, but I didn't believe it. How on earth did you manage it?'

'It's a long story, and one we don't have time for,' she said. 'We know all about Bertram Langley and the Apocalypse Chamber. What we don't know is how to stop him.'

'Do you still have the box?'

Ada pulled the Salus Key out and handed it to Ash.

'How'd Langley get in here without that?' asked Nikki pointing to the key.

'He didn't need it to get in, once we found the entrance he was able to force the doors open with the power of his mind. He just needed the key for what was inside it, unlike us,' said Ash, turning to Ada. 'Did you have the visions?'

Ada nodded.

'All we need to do is place the Salus Key inside the correct alcove once we're inside the Apocalypse Chamber, to repair any damage to the breach. That's the hope,' said Ash.

'How do we find the chamber from here?' asked Ada.

'Get me out of here and I'll take you.'

'What about Langley?' asked Tony.

'We've got salt,' said Bobby, scratching his head 'Carnaby said we can trap him with salt but he's gonna see us coming a mile off.'

Ash's eyes lit up. 'Ah, there we're in luck. With the amount of power Langley will be channelling through his body he'll need to call upon every ounce of concentration and will-power he has. We could stick a fork in him and he wouldn't notice.'

Ash rattled his manacled wrists at DJ. 'In case you haven't noticed, we're in a bit of a rush here.'

'Can't you do it?' Nikki asked. 'You're the secret agent'

'You'd think so. But I'm afraid most of my work has been in historical research. This is my first field assignment.'

'So you don't know how to pick a lock?' asked Nikki.

Ash shook his head.

'Useless,' muttered Nikki.

'You can make a cuckoo clock that fires darts but you can't pick a look?' asked Bobby.

'Actually, a friend knocked that up for me,' replied Ash. 'Tony told me about your encounter with it…sorry.'

Ada wondered if all secret agents were as rubbish as Agent Ash.

DJ cracked his knuckles then inserted his metal rods into the lock of one of Ash's manacles. 'I can do this; I can do this.'

'Agent Ash, how close are we to the Apocalypse Chamber?' asked Ada.

'Why do you…? No! No, I'm coming with you.'

'We can't wait,' Ada told him. 'The Blood Moon is rising. We have to go now.'

Ash bowed his head. 'This is all my fault.'

'Then help us put it right,' said Ada. 'How do we get to the chamber?'

Ash straightened, drew in a breath, and tapped Ada's rucksack. 'You got anything to draw on in there?'

Ada fished out her casebook and a pencil. Flipping to an empty page, she handed them both to Ash.

'It's a bit of a maze beyond this corridor, but it's not far to the chamber,' he explained as he drew.

'More traps?' asked Bobby.

'Yes,' said Agent Ash. 'But listen, just get out the way you came and call the police. This is no place for children.' Ada leaned in, angrily. 'We wouldn't be here in the first place if you hadn't thought – 'I know let's give this stupidly powerful, world ending artefact to one of my pupils."

She snatched her casebook from Ash and handed it to Bobby.

'Once DJ gets the manacles off, you get him and Tony out of here. I'm guessing you can get them past the blocked way we just came through?'

Ash nodded.

'What? No way I'm—'

'I mean it DJ. Don't follow us.'

DJ held Ada's gaze for what seemed like forever, then returned to his work on the manacles.

'Let's go,' said Ada.

As the three of them turned to leave Tony reached up, grabbing Bobby's arm. 'Thanks Bobby. Thanks for coming after me. And sorry for saying that stuff about your mum; it was out of order.'

'So was I,' said Bobby, awkwardly. 'It's cool. Thanks for saving Ada back at school. That took guts.'

Tony smiled broadly at that, then screamed as Bobby slapped the back of his neck. The sound echoed painfully throughout the chamber.

'What'd you do that for?' Tony whined, rubbing the back of his neck.

'For what you said about Mum,' said Bobby cheerfully. 'You got four more coming.'

Bobby winked then he, Ada and Nikki left the cell.

Eventually they reached an intersection where the passageway split into two. Ada consulted Agent Ash's map. She waved her torch toward the right passageway and, after Bobby had given the area a trap-free thumbs up, they set off again. They repeated this process several times, carefully avoiding a tripwire and a set of suspicious-looking holes, until finally they reached another set of steps.

Bobby lowered his left foot onto the first step. Nothing. He continued down the steps pausing to check each one gently.

'In the last campaign I played, there were some stairs like this,' Bobby explained as they walked. 'They turned into a slide and we ended up in a pit of giant rats.'

Ada forced a smile but inside she was praying. She was terrified of rats.

They reached the bottom of the stairs safely and entered a room not much bigger than the school's science lab. The room was empty apart from a single thick marble pillar, which almost touched the room's high ceiling. Four stone cobras coiled around the pillar, each head pointing toward a corner of the room. Though worn with age, the cobras held a chillingly life-like quality.

Ada shivered. *What is it with these people and snakes?*

'It's a bloody dead end,' announced Bobby, shining his torch beam around the walls.

Ada jabbed a finger on her open casebook. 'It can't be. Look. According to Agent Ash's map, there should be another passage that way.'

'Check the walls,' ordered Bobby. 'There might be a hidden switch or something.'

As Bobby and Ada began to search they failed to notice Nikki creep toward the pillar. It was only when she reached for it that Bobby saw her.

'Nikki, don't!'

But Bobby's warning came too late. As soon as Nikki touched the pillar, a deep rumbling followed. It made Bobby think of a stomach, eager to be fed.

'Sorry!' Nikki cried. 'I don't know why I did that.'

She began to back away from the column as stone began to grind on stone. 'It was like…like it was calling to me.'

'Out!' ordered Bobby.

As the three of them spun to leave, a huge slab of stone slid from the ceiling and slammed down across the door with a thunderous boom. They ran to the slab, trying to shift it without success.

'Flipping great,' panted Bobby.

'Wait. What *is* that?' asked Ada.

The grinding sound was still happening and louder now, as though something were burrowing up from beneath their feet. Ada spun her torch across the floor, trying to locate the source.

'Look!' shouted Nikki.

Ada aimed her torch, capturing the impossible within its bright beam. The eyes of the cobras were now glittering with a menacing purplish hue as their mouths opened as one.

'Time to leave?' Nikki suggested.

'Oh you reckon?' snapped Bobby.

A hideous hissing sound emerged from stony throats.

'It's getting brighter,' Ada observed.

'What is?' asked Bobby.

'The blue light,' she said, pointing at the shimmering glow now pulsing within the mouths of the cobras.

The next thing Ada knew, she was face-planting on cold stone. Bobby had leapt, scooping an arm around both her and Nikki, throwing them all to the floor. A split-second later a column of fire erupted from the mouth of each cobra, the closest jet of flame rolling over the heads of the three children.

It felt like there was a swarm of bees buzzing inside Ada's head. She heard Bobby say something, but his voice sounded weird, distorted somehow. She touched her forehead and when her hand came away, she saw spots of blood on her fingertips.

'The cobras…' coughed Nikki, sweat streaming down her face.

Ada swallowed the fear choking her and looked up. There were four jets of flame being spat across the ceiling from the mouths of the cobras. But that was not what chilled her to the bone, despite the heat.

The pillar of rotating flame spitting cobras was getting lower as it retracted into the floor.

Within a heartbeat the room had become a giant oven, and they were the dish of the day.

29

The Apocalypse Chamber

Bobby breathed in a lungful of hot air, then immediately burst into a coughing fit. He gripped his chest as the heat washed over him. The room was growing hotter as the pillar inched down, bringing the four spinning jets of flames with it. Ada and Nikki lay on either side of him, their faces soaked in sweat and tears, their twisted expressions of terror matching his own. Shaking, Bobby risked a glance into the inferno above them. Flames crackled and spat as they billowed over Bobby's head, jets of white-hot destruction.

Mum, help us please.

But Mum wasn't here. He was on his own.

Come on! There's a way out of every trap, he told himself. *You've just got to figure it out.*

Bobby's mind flew back to the two campaigns he had played over the summer: The Tower of Telos and Catacombs of the Venturian Vampire. Both campaigns contained traps and his character – Nexor, the Obsidian Elf – had always got their party through all of them. The dice rolls were part of it, of course, but Bobby's brain was good at figuring out this kind of problem. He scanned the room, searching for a clue. All traps were built differently, but all of them could be stopped or reset. He just needed to figure out how it was done here. Fast! Lowering his eyes to the floor, he saw a small, easy to miss indentation cut into one of the paving slabs.

That must be it, thought Bobby. *If I was the dungeon master it's where I would hide a reset switch.*

He began to crawl towards it. The heat was almost unbearable now, the stone floor beneath him growing hotter and hotter. Upon reaching the indentation Bobby slid his hand into it, hoping the inside wasn't filled with spiders. Ada was screaming something but he couldn't hear her over the roar of the flames. His fingers wrapped around what felt like a lever.

'Please work, please work' he whispered, pulling the lever.

There was a great whoosh as the flames were sucked back into the cobras, like dirt up a hoover. A section of wall at the far end of the room rose to reveal the hidden passageway, flooding the room with a rush of cold musty air. Bobby slumped onto his back, feeling like he could sleep for a month. Nexor the dwarf would have been proud.

'You two ok?' he asked, sitting up.

Nikki drew in several shuddering breaths, then gave a weak thumbs up.

'How did you know it would do that?'

Bobby grinned. 'Elementary, ain't it?'

Ada shot him a look. 'I expect a full explanation for my notes when we get out of here, Bobson.'

Yeah, she's ok.

At the end of the secret passage they entered another room with bare stone walls, a metal grate for a floor and a single exit.

Bobby aimed his flashlight at Nikki. 'Don't. Touch. Anything.'

Nikki raised a hand. 'Knight's honour.'

'You what?' asked Bobby.

Nikki set off again without answering. Bobby followed, all the while keeping his eyes open for any sign of danger.

Ada wrapped her arms around herself. 'It's freezing in here.'

Bobby breathed out and watched a wisp of grey smoke drift from his mouth. It was joined by countless streams of smoke that were curling up through the floor grate. In the centre of each stream, a pair of glowing lights formed. More cobras? No! The smoke began to take on a more human form.

'The master commands that none shall pass!' boomed one of the smoke creatures. 'As he commands so shall we obey!'

Bobby turned, taking in their numbers until he was back-to-back with Ada and Nikki. They were quickly surrounded.

'Perhaps we can go through them?' suggested Ada. They're just smoke, right?

Bobby took a two pence piece from his pocket and threw it at one of the creatures. The instant the coins hit the creature there was a fizzing sound and what was left of the coins scattered across the floor as a fine copper power.

'Okay, let's…not do that,' said Ada.

The smoke creatures drifted closer. Nikki stepped forward and raised the nozzle of the garden sprayer.

'Nikki don't!' shouted Bobby. 'Get back!'

'No. I won't fail again.'

She aimed the nozzle of the garden sprayer toward the nearest creature and pressed the trigger.

A fountain of saltwater shot out, and the smoke monster hissed, dissolving the instant the water struck it. Nikki spun on her heels blasting away, laughing until the room was empty. She felt incredible.

Until more tendrils of smoke began to emerge, seeping up from the floor like grasping fingers. It was then she realised how much lighter the container was on her back now.

'We can't keep them away for long,' she said.

Through the smoke creatures Bobby could see a stone slab had begun sliding downwards at the end of the room, sealing their fate.

'Go!' Nikki roared, spaying a path clear to the door.

'But—'

'Now!'

Bobby and Ada ran for it, diving through the door as it descended.

Bobby reached a hand back and shouted, 'Nikki! Come on!'

But she was still in the centre of the room, trapped and surrounded. For each one Nikki hit with water several more drifted to life, rising around her.

'A knight protects her friends.' she said grimly. 'It's been an honour.'

Bobby locked eyes with Nikki and the stone slab slammed shut, sealing the chamber with a deafening finality.

Ada started banging against the slab screaming Nikki's name over and over. Bobby scanned the passage, searching every inch of it, desperately hoping he could find a way to lift the slab but there was nothing. Eventually he admitted defeat, slumping back against the slab, his ears filled with Ada still calling out Nikki's name. Before long she too slumped beside him.

Bobby did not know how long they sat there staring into the gloom

'Come on,' he said at last. 'We can't stay here forever.'

'We can't leave her Bobby, not like this,' said Ada.

'She's tougher than all of us put together, she'll be ok.'

She must be ok, he thought.

The image in Bobby's mind of the two pence piece blasted to dust was calling him a liar.

'She still had plenty of saltwater in that thing,' pointed out Ada. 'And if we stop Langley we stop those things too, right?'

'Right,' agreed Bobby. 'So, let's go stop him.'

With one last look at the slab they set off in single file, with Bobby leading the way towards the faint crimson glow emanating from the end of the passage. As they neared the glow, Bobby placed a finger to his lips. Ada nodded. Together they crept into the room.

Bobby shivered, and not just from the damp air. Trapped behind large crystalline panels embedded in the rocky ceiling of the cavern high above their heads, a whirlpool of crackling crimson energy provided the unnatural light for the chamber.

'The Apocalypse Chamber,' Ada said in a hushed tone. 'It's spectacular.'

Strange inscriptions and images were carved into the flagstones beneath their feet, forming a pattern of intrigue across the floor. The walls of the chamber were honeycombed from floor to ceiling with small box-shaped alcoves. Bobby shuddered. Along with the unnatural humming from the energy, it was as though they were walking into a giant beehive.

At the heart of the chamber, happily floating high in the air, was an enormous metallic sphere.

'This is the place I saw in my dream,' whispered Ada, pointing at the sphere. 'But that wasn't there. It must be what happened when they used the Salus Key to contain the breach.'

Before Bobby could reply, a crimson lightning bolt shot down from the crystal panels. It rippled across the sphere's surface before disappearing with a menacing hiss.

'Step within the moon's crimson shade to seal our fate,' said Ada, studying the ceiling, high above them. 'Those panels must have been built to collect the blood moon's lunar energy. Fascinating.'

Bobby was too terrified to be fascinated. He tugged at Ada's sleeve then pointed across the room.

Bertram Langley was sat cross legged on a hexagonal platform located directly below the sphere. The platform, encircled by a wide chasm, could only be reached by a narrow stone bridge.

Langley sat facing them, eyes firmly shut. A dozen flickering candles rotated slowly above his head. Langley's mouth was moving but Bobby and Ada were too far away to hear what he was say-ing. In his hands he held the crimson orb.

Another lightning bolt lashed against the sphere but this time the thin tendrils of multi-coloured light streamed from it. The cave shook as the escaping energy rushed into the cavern, like steam from a boiling kettle. The children closed their eyes against the glare, but it was so bright Bobby could see the patterns through his eyelids. The effect lasted for a few seconds, then the sphere was solid once more.

'What now?' asked Bobby, trying to blink away the tiny white spots body-popping before his eyes.

Ada pointed at a section of alcoves high on the left wall of the chamber. 'There. Right in the middle, that's where I have to go….ah.'

'Ah?'

'In the vision I saw a staircase leading all away up to where I need to go.'

All Bobby could see were the ruins of part of a staircase, the rest lay in pieces scattered along the bottom of the wall.

'Guessing over the centuries it rotted away,' suggested Ada, pointing far above the last set of steps. 'Doesn't matter. That's where I have to put the Salus Key.'

Bobby craned his neck for a better view. 'So how you going to get up there?'

'I can use what's left of the stairs to get some of the way. After that we'll have to climb,' said Ada, taking Bobby's arm. 'Come on.'

Bobby shrugged her off, turning back to Langley. 'You go, I need to sort him out.'

'I know what Ash said but maybe we should just leave him,' suggested Ada, anxiously.

'No way,' said Bobby. 'If he spots us, we're done.'

Ada did her best impression of a confident smile, then let go of Bobby's arm 'Be careful, Bobson.'

'You too.'

30

Where are You Off to Bobby Gibson?

Bobby faced the stone bridge. He looked over at Ada, who was making her way gingerly up the rickety staircase. It wobbled with each step she took. Bobby guessed it was seriously sturdy back in the day but now it looked like it had been built with matchsticks.

Mum? Mum are you there?

But just like before there was nothing.

Bobby took a deep breath then stepped onto the tiny bridge. As he walked forward, blasts of cold air swirled up from the pit below. It felt as though far below in the darkness, some hideous creature lurked, waiting for him to fall.

Another burst of crimson lightning struck the sphere when Bobby was halfway across. This time, several tiny cracks snaked along the sphere's metallic surface releasing yet more tendrils. Was this what Carnaby meant when he spoke of things escaping from the void beyond the barrier? Were they too late already? Bobby stumbled as the tendrils shrieked over his head, but he managed to scramble across to the platform. When he checked on Ada she had left the staircase and was climbing up the wall, nearing the alcove where she would need to place the Salus Key.

Bobby edged towards Langley. The immortal's eyes were closed but he could hear him whispering to himself.

Ever so slowly, Bobby knelt then pulled the tub of salt from his rucksack. Cradling the tub in both hands, he crept backwards, walking around Langley, and all the while the salt poured out in a steady stream.

Bobby gave Langley a sidelong glance as he circled him, but the immortal did not move. Ash had been right.

Bobby imagined the massive party they were going to throw at Buckingham Palace when this was all over. The Queen would order a massive banner draped across the palace gates that read: SIR BOBBY GIBSON - THE BOY WHO SAVED ENGLAND. He would get a sword and a medal that would look ten times better than Errol's rubbish prefect badge. Of course, Ada and the others would get medals too, only theirs would be smaller - a lot smaller, probably.

'Mr Gibson. I thought we had an understanding, you and I.'

The voice shattered Bobby's victory scene. Bertram Langley raised his head. The immortal's eyes were silver, with tiny white sparks dancing across them.

Bobby dropped the tub of salt mid pour.

'And Miss Amaya,' said Langley, gazing across the chamber to the climbing figure of Ada. 'Proving to be as formidable as ever. Such a shame we'll never see what she might have become.'

Bobby screamed a warning but his words could not outrun the power that leapt from Langley's hands.

Ada shrieked as the lightning enveloped her arm, ripping the Salus Key from her grasp. Bobby watched horrified as Ada plummeted, screaming, down the cavern wall. Her fall came to a heartstopping halt when she grabbed the edges of two alcoves. She clung on, her legs dangling as she desperately fought to find solid footing. Bobby ran for the bridge. Sod saving the world, right now all he could think of was saving Ada.

He started to run then pitched forward as searing pain shot though his right leg. He rolled on the ground and saw with shock a jagged bolt of green lightning encircling his leg. Langley closed his fist and the lightning vanished, leaving scorch marks. Clutching his injured leg, Bobby pulled himself up.

'When will you learn boy? I am eternal do you hear me? ETERNAL! I am the flame that burns through the past, present and future of this world. Of *every* world!' Langley scowled at Bobby as though he was something foul on his shoes. 'You, boy, are nothing but ash.'

With that, Langley opened his hand, lifted the flat palm to his lips and blew. A sudden gale catapulted Bobby from his feet, hurling him into the chasm. Bobby fell into the darkness, arms outstretched. He grabbed an outcrop of rock, his arms screaming from the physical jolt and the effort of clinging on. Overhead, Langley continued calling down crimson lightning. With each landed strike, he roared in fury and triumph.

Darkness surrounded Bobby, his heart pounded like a runaway train. He squeezed his eyes shut, holding back the tears as he clutched cold stone. He wanted to move his hands to get a firmer grip but he was terrified. The slightest move might dislodge him.

'I can't do it,' Bobby said, through gritted teeth. 'I can't hold on.'

At that moment something brushed against Bobby's cheek, something familiar. Bobby opened his eyes. The tears he had held back flowed freely, but now they were tears of relief. A face hovered a few inches from his own, with a smile Bobby thought he would see never again.

'Mum,' he breathed.

Her translucent form floated beside him like an angel. He wanted to hug her so badly. She would catch him, wouldn't she?

Where are you off to, Bobby?

The question sparked a thousand memories. All of them ending with Mum telling him he could do anything he put his mind to.

Bobby gripped the stone with a strength he did not know he had.

'I'm...off...'

He found a foothold. Using it for leverage, he reached up to grab a tiny ledge above him.

'...to save...'

Despite the painful complaints from his tired muscles and injured leg, Bobby continued to climb.

'...the world!'

And don't let anyone ever tell you different.

With one last effort, Bobby hauled himself up onto solid ground. He rolled onto his back, sucking in as much air as his lungs would allow.

Langley had his back to Bobby now, facing the sphere, his hands raised toward it. It was covered in a spiderweb of tiny fractures, shining a kaleidoscope of colours from within.

Bobby's eyes found Ada, still clinging to the alcove wall. Ada grinned at him, happy to see him in once piece. Her expression then became serious and she started pointing furiously. Bobby rolled onto his side. A few feet from him, he saw what Ada was pointing at - the Salus Key.

Bobby nodded his understanding. He rose, scooped up the puzzle box and hobbled as fast as he could to the bridge. Langley was too busy doing his best villainous laugh whilst calling down more lightning strikes on the sphere, to notice what was going on behind his back.

Bobby reached the other side of the bridge, still unnoticed. He scrambled up the staircase to the alcove wall then threw the Salus Key up to Ada. She caught it in one hand, slamming it into the alcove beside her head. The box vibrated faster and faster within the alcove until it was a blur. Ada scrambled down the wall as fast as she could, leaping to the staircase landing.

No sooner had Ada hit the ground, a deafening explosion roared out from the Salus Key into the chamber, transforming into a giant spinning column of wind. Lightning flowed out from the column across the chamber, enveloping the sphere, seeking out and sealing any cracks along its surface. Bobby and Ada raced back down the staircase as it began to be torn apart by the ferocious wind.

'No!' screamed Langley, clutching the orb and pointing at the breach. 'This is mine! My calling! MY BIRTHRIGHT!'

He raised his arms higher, screaming his chants now; but against the power of the activated Salus Key he was powerless, a leaf in a hurricane. Sections of the chamber were torn from their foundations and sucked into the swirling maelstrom as the column of wind suddenly reserved its direction. At last the orb Langley held was wrenched from his grip and he was forced to watch it tumble into the maelstrom.

Bobby and Ada flattened themselves against the floor, their clothes flapping like flags.

'YOU!' Langley bellowed at them.

The immortal strode across the bridge, unaffected by the fierce wind. The ring of candles, the salt and several sections of stone swept past him to be swallowed, by the Salus Key. He dragged Ada to her feet.

'Always there, nipping at my heels,' he spat, his face twisted with anger. 'Too stupid, too *ignorant* to realise that I am the champion sent to save you all.'

Bobby tried to free Ada, grabbing at Langley's arm, but he backhanded him across the jaw. Langley dropped Ada and closed on Bobby.

'Do you really think I've endured centuries of pain and loss to have my birthright stolen by someone like you? I am history incarnate! I am destiny's champion!'

'And I... am a knight ...of North London.'

The voice came from behind Langley. Nikki! Standing on the bridge. Langley staggered back, sparks and steam flying from his body as he was hit with the hammer of salt water. He screamed in pain and outrage, but then something seized him. He seemed to stretch backwards, impossibly long before he was pulled screaming into the whirlwind of crackling energy. In an instant, the funnel snapped back into the Salus Key like it was attached to a rubber band. The box dropped out of the wall, hit the floor and rolled to Ada's feet.

Bobby turned around, stunned to see his friend still alive. Nikki leant against one side of the doorway, brandishing the garden sprayer.

'You're ok?' said Ada, managing a smile as Agent Ash moved to her side. 'I thought...I...'

'Yeah, I thought I was a goner too until they showed up.'

Nikki gestured to Agent Ash, DJ and Tony.

'Once I got the manacles off, Ash was able to reset the traps so we could follow,' explained DJ, easing the now empty garden sprayer off Nikki's back. 'It's all clear now.'

Ash helped Ada up then checked on Bobby, who told him to stop fussing over his leg.

DJ picked up the Salus Key. It looked no different than it had before.

Tony stared at it 'Is it over? Is he...?'

'Dead?' Ash shook his head. 'My guess is when Ada used the Salus Key, Langley was still connected to it.'

'So... where is he?' asked Tony, nervously.

Ash placed a hand on his shoulder, gave him a reassuring smile then tapped the cube. 'He's in there. Trapped like a genie in a bottle.'

DJ started shaking the puzzle box, like it was a snow globe. 'He's in this? How's he even fit in there?'

Ada grabbed the cube from DJ. 'How about you don't shake the artefact containing the immortal madman, eh?'

DJ frowned. 'Fair enough - but we still won right?'

A deep rumbling sounded above their heads. Looking up, they saw giant jagged cracks racing across the ceiling.

Nikki thumped DJ's arm as dust and pebbles started to fall. 'You had to go and say it didn't you?'

The ceiling groaned. Two massive chunks of stone broke away from the ceiling, crashing onto the bridge. There was an ear-tearing screech then the bridge crumbled, sections of it spinning down into the gloom.

'Langley's ritual weakened the foundations. The whole place is collapsing!' yelled Ash. 'Follow me!'

Ash sprinted from the chamber, followed by DJ, Tony and Nikki.

'Mum,' breathed Bobby.

Instead of leaving he ran to edge of the chasm. He stood staring into the abyss as forks of crimson lightning shot down into it.

'Mum!' Bobby called. 'Mum!'

Bobby felt someone grab his arm, turning he saw a terrified Ada.

'Bobson we need to go, or we'll be flattened.'

Bobby shoved Ada away. 'No! I saw her! She saved me and now she gotta come with us!'

'Bobby?'

This time when Bobby heard his mum's voice it was not in his head. He turned and froze. Mum was standing there, just she used to when he came down for breakfast or when he got home from school. She was still wearing her carer's uniform from the old-people's home where she worked. Bobby ran to her, but instead of running into her arms, he ran straight through her.

Bobby turned back, dropping his arms in misery.

'I have to go Bobby, and so do you. It's time to say goodbye.'

'No!' shouted Bobby. 'I won't leave you. Not ever!'

One of the crystal panels fell, shattering against the ground.

Ada grabbed Bobby's arm again, tugging harder this time. 'Bobby – we have to go.'

'Can't you see her?' asked Bobby, unmoving. 'She's right there. Mum's right there!'

'Darling Bobby, you have to go. You can do this. Just...say goodbye.'

'NO!' screamed Bobby.

'You need to brave Bobby. You need to run and don't look back.'

His mum began to fade.

'Don't go, Mum! Please don't go!'

'Goodbye, my beautiful boy.'

Bobby stood there, staring at the empty space. Tears rolling down his cheeks.

Ada moved beside him. 'If you say your mum was there, Bobby I believe you—I really do, but I don't think she wants you to stay here.'

Bobby took one last look at the space where Mum had stood then half hobbled, half ran along with Ada. They reached the entrance to find the others had come back for them.

Seeing Bobby hobbling towards them DJ raced forward. He lifted Bobby's arm over his shoulder then put his arm around him. Tony moved to Bobby's other side, mirroring DJ's actions.

'Come on mate, we got you,' said DJ.

Agent Ash ordered everyone to stay behind him. Together, they ran back through the underground passages and chambers. The three boys were moving slower than the others but neither Tony nor DJ would leave Bobby's side. Tumbling pillars and flying debris threatened to crush them at every step. As they sped down a passageway Ada tripped and fell. Nikki hauled her to her feet but was gone before she could voice her thanks. When they reached the steps leading out of the mausoleum, Bobby heard Ash give a hoot of relief.

Thankfully, the mausoleum doors were already opening as they ran toward them. They piled out into the night air, a booming thunderclap and a thick cloud of dust spewing out behind them.

Bobby blinked away the dust from his eyes and found himself blinded once again, this time by the headlights from several police vans. Stood in a semi-circle in front of the vans were several policemen and women. Beside them were Ron and Geoff, the security guards. Everyone was holding flashlights and wearing expressions that ranged from shock to disbelief. In the centre, Bobby spotted DI Penthrope standing there, hands on hips. Lucas Carnaby stepped in front of her, his hand extended to Ada.

Ada stared at him, covered in dust, and lost for words.

'Managed to escape my captors when they stopped for petrol. Took me a while on foot but I came straight here to help,' explained Carnaby. He then whispered. 'Langley?'

'Gone for good I hope,' said Agent Ash, rubbing his wrists. 'Is it really you Carnaby?'

Carnaby patted Ash's arm. 'In the flesh dear boy,'

DI Penthrope, nudged Carnaby to one side. 'I still don't know what you're doing here but that's enough out of you, sir.'

'How did you find us?' asked Agent Ash.

'I got a tip off about some trouble at this mausoleum. We got here to find two security guards waiting outside. They told us they saw some kids breaking in and then you lot come out,' explained Penthrope.

'Hmm, some good Samaritan whoever made that call,' said Carnaby, winking at Ada.

'Do you have anything to say for yourselves?' asked Penthrope.

'Well—'

'Oh I have a great many questions for you Mr Rillington – or is it Mr Ash? – but right now I want to hear from this lot.'

Penthrope stepped closer, flipping out a notebook. 'So come on, then. You lot were so chatty in my office. One of you must have something to say about all this?'

Nikki rose. She was covered head to toe in sludge, leaves, tiny pieces of crystal. She looked more monster than schoolgirl.

She eyed Penthrope and the policemen, pulled a clump of soggy leaves from her hair, then smiled hopefully.

'Any of you lot got a lollipop?'

31

Punishments and Promises

The headmaster's office was large, the bottom half of the walls lined with dark brown oak panelling. The top half was painted white. There was not a speck of dirt nor any kind of blemish to be seen. The faint smell of disinfectant clung to the air and made the children's noses wrinkle.

Ada, Bobby, Tony, DJ and Nikki all waited in silence while Creasey opened the file in front of him and raised his pen. If there was one thing he knew how to do, it was torturing children.

'So, would anyone like to say anything before I call your parents?' Creasey asked.

Parents! Bobby shot Ada a worried look. After their adventures at the graveyard the weirdest thing had happened. DI Penthrope had asked them whether they had told their parents where they were going. Then, when they admitted they had not, she saw to it the boys were dropped off outside DJ's house and girls outside Nikki's house. This was done so they could keep the stories they had told their parents intact. DJ had got his mum to ring Tony's parents after telling her Tony had just turned up on their doorstep safe and sound. Tony's mum and dad had driven straight round to pick him up. Penthrope had made them swear not to tell anyone anything about what had happened. Ada had no problem with that. Between Norfolk and the debacle with 'DS Hoplin', it was hard to see how they'd trust adults with this stuff again.

'Nothing to say, I see,' Creasey mused. 'Well let me help you find your voices.'

He turned his piercing stare on DJ.

'Earlier today, Mr Jennings here was seen replacing the boxes of salt you stole from the home economics lab.'

Ada cut DJ a side-eye. DJ gave a slight shrug. She knew she should have got Bobby to put the salt back—Dibney was about as subtle as a tap-dancing elephant.

'I also have it on good authority that the four of you were outside the school during lunch break, which is, as you know, entirely forbidden.'

The image of Sid Horrun's sneering face slithered into Bobby's mind.

'Not to mention the sources who told me you were all detained by the police. Trespassing on the Baxter Estate? Vandalising the graveyard?'

Ada opened her mouth but she only managed to get 'We never—' out before a sharp look from Creasey silenced her.

Creasey closed the folder then sat back into his armchair. His face was so red, Ada worried for his health. Was this what happened when someone burst a blood vessel?

'In all my time as a headmaster I have never seen a list of crimes this bizarre levelled against one of my pupils, let alone five of them. And as for *you*.'

Creasey's chair squeaked as he spun to face Tony, who was doing his best to shrink from sight.

'For you Mr Tadsby, it appears congratulations are in order.'

'Um…Thank you sir?'

'You are about to set a school record. I've never had to expel a pupil in their very first week before.'

Tony dropped his head, his eyes fixed on the brown, spotless rug.

Creasey leant forward, his hands placed over the folder as if he were protecting it.

'Because have no doubt, if I do not get a serious, full and justifiable explanation for your activities, I will be instructing all of your parents to find new schools for you.'

Ada heard Bobby gulp. She knew expulsion would be the least of his worries when Dad and Auntie Carol found out.

'So, I'll ask again. Is there anything you would like to tell me?'

'We didn't steal anything sir,' said Ada. 'We only borrowed the salt and—'

'I AM NOT INTERESTED IN SALT!' thundered Creasey. 'I want to know what you were doing out of school and how you managed it. I want to know why you broke into a half-finished council estate and whether you caused a bloody *explosion* in a graveyard.'

'Sir, you wouldn't believe us if we told you,' said Tony.

'You'd better hope that I *do* Tadsby, because that's the only thing that can save you now.'

Tony opened his mouth but, after a slight shake of the head from Ada, he closed it once more.

'You and your new friends need to understand that no one is coming to your aid. This is the real world Mr Tadsby and in the real world there are consequences to your actions.'

At that moment, the door opened and Agents Orlando and Gans strolled into the room.

Creasey rose, slamming his palms down on his desk.

'How dare you?'

'Very easily actually,' replied Agent Gans.

Ada noticed Gans was carrying a silver briefcase. He also had a brown folder tucked under his arm.

Agent Orlando closed the office door. 'Please sit down, head-master.'

Creasey remained standing, belligerently.

Orlando dipped into the inside pocket of his jacket and took out a small leather wallet. He flipped it open and showed it to the headmaster. Ada could not see what was inside, but it was enough to suck the rage from Creasey's face.

'Good,' said Orlando, putting the wallet away. 'We understand each other.'

Agent Gans came round to Creasey's side of the desk and leaned in.

'So, if you would like to keep your job I would do as Agent Orlando suggests, and *sit* down.'

Creasey glared at Agent Gans, who simply smiled. Then he obeyed.

'Much better,' said Agent Orlando. 'Now, we are here today to discuss the future of these five children.'

'They have no future at this school. I am about to expel them. What business is that of the US government?'

Agent Gans perched himself on the edge of Creasey's desk, set-ting the silver briefcase beside him. 'The reason is classified, but the fact is irrefutable. You will not be expelling these children.'

Ada wondered if steam could literally burst from Creasey's nos-trils and ears, like in the cartoons.

'Even if you *are* who you say you are, you can't just come in here and bark orders at me,' Creasey growled. 'This is my school. You have no authority—'

Agent Orlando silenced Creasey with a wave of his hand. 'You can be replaced, Headmaster – it's surprisingly simple – so I'm go-ing to give you a choice…'

He took the folder from under his arm and slid it onto the desk.

'Inside that folder you will find copies of sworn testimonies to the effect that these children played an instrumental part in locating your missing teacher, Mr Rillington. So you see, Mr Creasey, these children are to be praised, not punished. Of course we understand there have been some minor infractions of the—'

'Minor infractions!' roared Creasey. 'They left the school grounds, stole school property, and God knows what they did to that mausoleum!'

Agent Gans rolled his neck from side to side, like he was limbering up for a boxing match.

'Did you see them leave the grounds yourself?' he asked.

'Well I…no. But—'

'Ah, perhaps then you received an official report from a Truancy Officer regarding these children?'

'No, but I was informed by—'

Agent Orlando spoke right on over him. 'So you don't have any actual proof, is that correct?' asked Agent Orlando.

'Not as such, but Sidney Horrun is one of my most trusted prefects. His father is—'

'A prefect that several children have reported for bullying, reports that you have chosen to ignore – possibly because of who his father is?'

'How dare you? There's no—'

'Proof?' Agent Orlando interjected, a mischievous gleam in his eye. 'Thank you Headmaster. You have made my point beautifully. Now of course, taking school property without permission is a serious offence, though I understand all the items were returned. Yes?'

Creasey ground his teeth and nodded.

'I think a two week detention should just about cover it. What do you think, Gans?'

'I think that sounds like a very fine compromise, Orlando.'

At that point Creasey's anger burst through, launching him to his feet.

'Get out! I will not stand for this! How dare you swan in here and tell me how to do my job? I have been the Head of this school for more than twenty years, and I will *not* be given orders by a couple of smarmy yanks in my own office!'

Agent Orlando tutted gently, then produced a small white envelope from his pocket. He held it out.

'What's this?' Creasey demanded.

'The consequences of your actions…should you find our terms unacceptable.'

Creasey snatched the letter, tore it open and read its contents. His shoulders sagged and the colour drained from his cheeks. He looked so pale now, Ada thought he might pass out.

Creasey read the letter twice then sat without a word, his hands shaking. His voice, when he finally found it, seemed small. Broken.

'You can't do all this. You do not have the authority. You would need the backing of the school governors.'

'Would you care to test that theory, Headmaster?' asked Agent Gans.

Ada almost felt sorry for the crumpled headmaster. None of this made sense to her. Why were Orlando and Gans helping them? There was no reason she could think of. After all Langley was gone and the Apocalypse Chamber was buried.

Agent Gans extended a hand. 'Two weeks detention, then. And nothing in their school records relating to the events of the last week. Agreed?'

'Agreed,' said Creasey with a sigh.

As the two men shook hands, the answer that had been eluding Ada came to her. There was something the agents wanted in return. Of course there was.

'One more thing,' said Agent Orlando. 'For this to be fully official we would request the children return an item they have in their possession.'

Ada shared a worried glance with Bobby then gripped her satchel.

'The Salus Key, if you please Miss Amaya,' said Agent Orlando.

'I lost it in the cemetery,' said Ada.

'Please don't waste our time by lying, Miss Amaya.'

Bobby stepped in front of Ada, fists clenched, jaw set. 'She said she ain't got it.'

'That's enough, Gibson,' snapped Creasey. 'Get back in line!'

Bobby did not move.

Orlando smiled and held out his hand. 'You played a fine game young lady, but this is checkmate. Give me the Salus Key or face your own consequences. As will your friends.'

Agent Orlando took a pocket watch from his waistcoat pocket, flipping open the lid. 'You have thirty seconds to decide.'

Ada looked over at the others. One by one, they all nodded.

Ada stepped around Bobby, opened her satchel and lifted out the Salus Key. The agents' faces lit up like it was Christmas.

'It's beautiful,' Gans purred.

'I wouldn't try opening it,' advised Ada.

'Not to worry. We've already read an extensive report on its…contents,' said Agent Orlando.

Ada guessed said report would have come from Agent Ash.

'Where are you taking it?' demanded Bobby.

Agent Orlando stepped forward, his gloved hand closing around the Salus Key. 'To a far safer place.'

But when he tried to pull it away Ada held on to it, her eyes meeting his. 'This is not over.'

Orlando's mouth stretched into a thin smile. 'I would expect nothing less.'

Agent Orlando pulled again and this time Ada released her grip. Agent Gans opened the silver briefcase and Orlando eased the puzzle box into the case's plush velvet interior.

'Our business here is concluded,' announced Agent Orlando.

Agent Gans closed the briefcase, flipped down the clasps and left the room without a word.

Creasey held out the letter but Agent Orlando pushed it back. 'You keep that. It'll be a reminder for you, in case you start to change your mind later.'

Agent Orlando turned to Ada. He bent down, his face splitting into a wide grin

'Consider your continued presence in this school your reward for stopping Langley,' he whispered. 'You're welcome.'

With another smile to Ada, Agent Orlando walked from the room. The office was silent for a long time. Creasey just sat there, staring at the letter in his hand. When at last he did speak, it was low and menacing.

'You will all report to Mrs McAlister after school to begin your detentions, now get out of my sight.'

The five of them spun as one and dashed for the door. As Ada's hand touched the doorknob the headmaster's grim voice sounded behind them.

'Do not think for a second you have got away with this. All you have done is put yourselves on my radar. I may not be able to expel you, but I can still make your lives miserable. You put so much as a toe out of place and no force on earth will be able to save you.'

Ada stomped down the stairs, incensed, leaving the others behind.

'I guess it could've been worse,' offered Tony, shrugging.

'How?' Ada howled, rounding on him. 'We've just given the Salus Key to the ESD! Who knows what they're going to do with it!'

'Ada's right,' said Bobby. 'We saved the world and what do we get? Two flipping weeks of detention. Nah mate, that's bang out of order.'

'Did you see the look on Creasey's face though?' said DJ, his laughter carrying down the stairs ahead of them. 'Was almost worth it to see that!'

Out of nowhere Nikki too began to laugh, and soon everyone, even Ada cracked a slight smile.

'I thought Creasey was going to wet himself,' said Bobby, wiping tears of laughter from his eyes as they reached the bottom of the steps.

'Feeling pleased with yourselves, are you?'

Detective Inspector Penthrope was waiting for them at the bottom of the stairs, arms folded. She did not look happy—not one bit. It was a look Ada was getting used to today.

'It seems you lot have some very influential friends.'

'What are you talking about?' asked Ada.

'What I'm talking about, Miss Amaya, is that your activities have been classified by the Home Office under the Official Secrets Act, and as such I am to take no further action against any of you.'

'What's an Official Secrets Act when it's at home?' asked Bobby.

'It's the legislation that handles the protection of state secrets and stuff when it relates to national security.'

Everyone stared at DJ.

'What?' he asked, all innocence. 'I never broke it.'

Penthrope crouched so she was eye level with all of them. 'According to my superiors, you are off-limits, but you see... I'm a little like you lot. I like breaking rules. So from now on, you five are going to be my pet project and sooner or later I will find out what happened. I promise.'

Penthrope marched off with straight shoulders and a determined stride, but then she stopped, turned around and tossed something small to Nikki. The girl let out a gasp of delight and brandished it with wonder. 'Cola flavoured with vanilla twist!'

'So what?' asked DJ.

'It's my favourite,' Nikki mumbled, shoving the lollipop in her mouth. 'How did she know?'

Penthrope pointed two fingers at her eyes then one at the children. *I'm watching you…* She strode away, her heels clicking noisily against the polished floor. As she pushed through the doors she shouted, 'Oh, and I've arranged a little surprise for you at the school gates.'

'Well now I'm scared,' said DJ. 'What surprise?'

After they had given DI Penthrope a big enough head start, the five of them walked out through the double doors. They were welcomed by a warm breeze, courtesy of the setting sun. There were still a few kids milling around outside, but for the most part it was empty.

Bobby broke the silence as they rounded the building and followed the fence to the exit.

'So, we have Creasey, those even creepier agents, Psycho Sid and the police on our case now. Great… Bloody great. Anyone else wanna have a go at us?'

Nikki sighed and gestured towards the school gates. 'Just them.'

Bobby groaned. It seemed the entire school had gathered on the other side. The cause of the crowd was nosiness, thanks to the fleet of police cars. A group of adults were being shepherded out of them and towards the school. Penthrope smiled and waved from the sidelines.

Ada spotted her mum at once. Joining her, vying for most angry parent on the planet, were Bobby's dad and Auntie Carol.

'Hey look, it's my mum and dad,' shouted DJ, waving energetically.

His parents just stood there, oozing bitterness and disappointment. His sister popped laughingly out from behind them, miming strangulation. *Oh dear...*

Tony pointed at a tall, angry man who was wearing a stylish black suit and arguing with one of the policemen. 'Who's that?'

'My stepdad,' said Nikki.

Bobby looked Nikki's stepdad up and down then whistled. 'He looks made of money.'

Nikki fell silent, her expression blank. Shoving his way between the dapper man and the copper was a storm cloud in vicar's clothing, bellowing and pointing at the children through the gate. Tony gulped.

'Seeing as I'm going to be dead meat anyway, I just want to know one thing,' said Tony

'Go for it Smiley,' said Bobby.

'Are you lot ever going to tell me what happened in Norfolk?'

Ada narrowed her eyes and took a deep breath. As she released it, she studied her mother intently, trying to read her body language. Mum's arms were folded twenty percent tighter than normal, her lips were pursed and her cheeks were drawn in so tight it looked like she was sucking the world's sourest lemon. Taking this into all into account, Ada made several predictions about her fate.

No friends, no TV and I won't be allowed in the consulting room for... hm... approximately two and a half weeks. Ada guessed. *A harsh but fair punishment.*

Mum looked ready to reduce Ada to ash and bone with a blast of heat vision. Ada adjusted her calculations.

Four weeks. Perhaps five.

Epilogue

The Knights of North London

'FREEDOM!' shrieked DJ, pumping both hands in the air. 'I swear if I have to clean the home economics lab or write one more essay, I'll lose it.'

Bobby grinned. It was the last day of their two week detention, which for him meant the lifting of the ban Dad had placed on him from seeing his friends outside of school.

'Freedom?' Tony snorted. 'Speak for yourself, mate; it's a nightmare at home. Mum is watching me like a hawk plus I have to help Dad in the church after school every day.'

Ada scowled. 'I'm still banned from the consulting room for another three weeks, and I have to help Henry clean the shop. He's my *boss*. It's a nightmare!'

Bobby was sure he had it the worst. The minute he got home from school each day Auntie Carol was waiting with a list of rubbish jobs for him to do, before *and* after dinner. The jobs would take him right up to bedtime. He had to waste his weekends doing all his homework – it was so unfair! For his brother Errol, it was the best two weeks of his life. He spent most of it living like a king because Bobby had to do all *his* chores as well as his own.

Dad was supposed to be proud of him. Bobby had helped stop an evil man, he had saved the world—but he couldn't tell anybody. So all he got were angry silences and disappointment. He wouldn't have minded that from Auntie Carol, but she kept reminding him how much he had messed up and how lucky he had been. *You wouldn't have been able to sit down for a month if it was me,* she'd say, or worse, *Your mother will be turning in her grave.* That one hurt more than he could ever say. He had not seen or heard Mum in the two weeks since the Apocalypse Chamber. However, despite Mum's silence, a lot of other things had happened in those two weeks.

A special assembly had been held during the first week, where Mr Rillington thanked everyone for their support and concern. He explained that he had simply got lost on a fishing trip. He went on to announce that he would be leaving his job at the school immediately to focus on getting better. The assembly marked the first and last time Bobby had seen Ash since they had saved him.

As soon as his speech was finished, Agent Ash was ushered from the stage by three tough looking men in grey suits. ESD agents, the children reckoned privately. As Agent Ash was led past the row where Bobby and the others sat, he mouthed *Thank you* to them. Ada had mouthed back *Why me?* but the agents hustled him towards the exit. Ash managed an apologetic look over his shoulder, then he was gone, along with a lot of unanswered questions.

It did not take long for all talk of Ash's disappearance to fade away. However, everyone was still talking about how Creasey had suspended Sid Horrun for the rest of the first half of term. Bobby was pretty sure Sid blamed him for his suspension. Bobby crossed the street, trying not to think what would happen once Sid came back to school next term. For now, school over, he was properly back with his mates and there was one very important thing they had all been waiting to do.

Ada arrived first at the shop door. She pushed it open and everyone followed her inside.

Lucas had his back to them. He was in the process of placing a delicate glass figurine of a ballerina on one of the shelves.

'Detention over?' the shopkeeper asked, without turning.

'How did you—'

'Know it was you Mr Tadsby?' said Carnaby. 'I could hear Miss Panilides devouring that lollipop halfway up the street.'

'Rude,' said Nikki.

Carnaby twisted the statue so it sat within the shaft of light streaming in from the window. He grinned, then stepped back to admire his work.

'You could get me into a lot of trouble by being here.'

'DI Penthrope talked to you, didn't she?' asked Ada.

'A rather intense woman, even for a Detective Inspector,' said Carnaby. 'She will be watching me, apparently.'

'Yeah, she says that to everyone,' said DJ glumly.

'So why have you risked the wrath of the police, not to mention the school and your parents, to come back here?'

'We want you to teach us,' said Ada.

Carnaby's head flew back with a booming laugh so loud it shook dust from the walls.

When no one moved or said a word Carnaby arched an eyebrow. 'Oh, you're being serious.'

Tony stepped closer, wringing his hands. He looked like he wanted to be anywhere but here. 'I wish we weren't, Mr Carnaby, but we all thought that if weird things are going to keep happening, well… we need to be ready.'

Carnaby walked over to Tony and placed a hand on his shoulder.

'Langley can't hurt you anymore lad,' he said gently. 'He's gone, and that blasted chamber is sealed forever. You're free of him.'

Ada moved beside Tony. 'You said that if any energy escaped from the chamber it could weaken the barrier further, letting even more things through to our world, right?'

'Yes, but—'

'Mr Carnaby, a lot of energy escaped before we closed the breach. An awful lot.'

'Even if it did, this is not a problem for you,' argued Carnaby. 'You did your part.'

'We live here, and so do our families and friends,' said Tony. 'And we know about it now. We can't pretend that we don't.'

'We've talked about it,' said Ada, glancing at DJ. 'This time we're all in this together.'

DJ smiled back at her.

'We want to be ready if something like this happens again,' said Bobby.

'You barely survived last time! The police will be watching you, and it's hardly likely the ESD will forget you either.'

'And I haven't forgotten them,' said Ada firmly. 'I can't. I still don't understand why Agent Ash gave me the Salus Key in the first place. How he knew I would figure it out.'

'Wasn't just you,' muttered Bobby.

'Obviously,' said Ada.

'It was probably cos of that file they've got on you.'

Ada rounded on Tony. 'What file?'

With five pairs of questioning eyes on him, Tony started to shrivel. He backed away. 'Sorry. With everything going on I kinda forgot. We talked quite a lot when we were chained up.'

Bobby followed Tony, grabbing his arms. He repeated Ada's question as calmly as he could.

'When we were down in that dungeon place,' began Tony, 'He said you were every bit as impressive as your ESD file. So they must have been watching you before all this stuff happened. I don't know why. He didn't say and... and I didn't ask. Sorry.'

Ada just stood there, her mouth open.

Almost a minute passed before DJ asked 'You reckon her batteries have run out?'

Ada took a deep breath, then levelled a stare at Tony that could shatter glass. 'You're lucky the police are watching us,' she told him. 'However you and I are going for a long walk after this.'

Bobby wondered if Ada was going to be coming back alone from that long walk.

Ada turned back to Carnaby. 'This is even more reason for you to start training us.'

'YOU'RE TWELVE!' roared Carnaby, his voice desperate now. 'Twelve year olds go to school. They do their homework. They watch too much television and they eat too much chocolate. They do not train to fight the supernatural.'

'Mum says age is just a number,' DJ pointed out, slashing the air like a pirate with a rusty length of metal he had swiped from a nearby shelf. Carnaby snatched it from him.

'And this is a two hundred year old replica of the Sword of Solomon!'

DJ put up his hands. 'Alright, Gramps, keep your hair on.'

Carnaby placed the artefact back on its plinth. 'And if I say no?'

'Then we'll do it anyway,' said Ada, crossing her arms. 'But if you didn't think we could do it, you wouldn't have told us where to find the stuff in your workshop when the ESD grabbed you.'

Carnaby scratched his beard. He stared at the ceiling, as if searching for inspiration in the dusty rafters.

'Very well. If only to keep you from running off on your own and getting yourselves killed.'

Carnaby pointed at DJ. 'In the next room Mr Jennings, you will find a cabinet, inside of which is everything you need for your first lesson.'

DJ scurried to the other room as ordered, while Carnaby headed for the front door.

'There's only load of brooms in here!' called out DJ. 'You gonna teach us to fly 'em?'

'No. Your first lesson will be to clean this shop from top to bottom and then…' Carnaby gave a sly smile as he flipped the open sign on the shop to CLOSED. 'And then, my knights of North London, we shall see what mischief we can cook up between us. Mr Gibson, go and fetch the brown leather book on the table in my workshop. You can't miss it; it's called Monsters, Myth and Legends for the Stout of Heart by Lord Mark Preston.'

Bobby headed into the other room. He rolled back the rug then lifted the trap door. As he descended into the gloom he paused for a moment. He swore he heard something – a whispered question at the back of his mind.

Where are you off to, Bobby?

The End

THE AUTHOR

Barry Nugent wrote his first story at the young age of 11, after seeing Raiders of the Lost Ark, and he has never looked back. He is the co-founder of the podcast called Geek Syndicate which focuses on all aspects of pop culture.

He lives in sunny Northamptonshire (well sometimes it is) with his wife and two cats.

Barrynugent.com

ACKNOWLEDGEMENTS

They say writing is a solitary job but that's not strictly true. As always during my writing, there have been so many people who have helped me along the way.

I want to start by thanking my wife, Sue. She was supportive and inspirational throughout the process always ready with wisdom, comfort, and a large boot, when needed. Cheers love.

Alex Moore did amazing work bringing Ada, Bobby, DJ, Tony and Nikki to life on the covers. Equally, on the art front, Conor Boyle went above and beyond to provide the character art for the limited-edition hardback. Huge thanks to you both.

To my test-readers Dave, Vickster and Cat (yes you were test readers, and you didn't even know it!). Thanks for your honest feedback and support; both were invaluable.

I owe a massive debt to my editor Dion. He was always pushing, always challenging me to go that one step further, and the final manuscript was so much better for it. I hope I did you proud sir and sorry for all those Facebook messages.

To everyone I went to secondary school with, thanks for making my school days among the adventurous of my life. It might not have always been the best of times, but it was never dull. This story was fuelled by that time in my life.

Finally, a special thank you to Davina who posed the question to me: *'Have you ever thought about writing middle grade fiction?'*.

I hope you like my answer.

Lightning Source UK Ltd.
Milton Keynes UK
UKHW011851301021
393115UK00002B/7/J